BENEATH THE CURSED VEIL

WINTER DUET

FAETED SEASONS

AURELIA JANE

KEL CARPENTER

Beneath the Cursed Veil

Aurelia Jane and Kel Carpenter

Published by Raging Hippo LLC

Copyright © 2025, Raging Hippo LLC

Cover by Book Brander Boutique

Chapter Spreaders by Manuela

Photography of Lylith Sammons, courtesy of Cody Sammons

About the Authors

Kel Carpenter and Aurelia Jane are the hilarious team behind the international bestselling book, Reject Me.

They pride themselves in being absolute weirdos, spending hours on the phone coming up with detailed worlds, and laughing about crazy ideas for torturing characters. While they believe they each have the personality of a rabid badger, people still seem to like them okay.

They share a love of coffee, snarky t-shirts, and tacos, and they've made some adorable tiny people with their equally weird husbands. Best friends and work wives, Kel has the audacity to live in Maryland while Aurelia lives in Texas, but they try to see each other as much as possible.

instagram.com/kelandaureliabooks

patreon.com/kelandaureliabooks

"Cards on the table
Mine play out like fools in a fable,
Oh, it was sinking in (Sinking in, oh)
Slow is the quicksand
Poison blood from the wound of the pricked hand
Oh, still I dream of him"

- Taylor Swift, "The Prophecy"

To our past selves, this story is what started your journey as co-authors. It was worth the risk. Keeping taking chances.

CHAPTER 1

MEERA

"Tase him again. He's pissing me off." Sadie kicked the legs of the wooden chair where our thief sat tied up, bound in a magical rope. We were in the back room of my antique shop. It wasn't the most conventional torture chamber, but it would do in a pinch. Most of my inventory was small and lined the shelves along the wall, leaving the center space empty with plenty of room to cajole our *guest*.

Something told me the half-fae wouldn't enjoy his stay. Not that he had anyone to blame but himself. It's not like someone forced him to bet in the underground fighting rings my family ran. He'd definitely pay up, one way or another.

I walked by, chewing my thumb nail absentmindedly. "It's not a taser," I mumbled around my nibbling.

"Tomato, to-mah-to," my sister said, shrugging her slender shoulder. "It's still funny to watch."

I sighed, pressing the metal prongs of the stun gun against his bare rib cage, not bothering to look toward the man. He jerked violently, trying to angle his body away as if that would help him at all. When I released it, Jenkins began breathing in and out in rough gasps.

I had to give it to him. He lasted longer than I expected. With his slight build and unmarred skin, I didn't expect much of a pain tolerance. Sure, he was half-fae, but those traits didn't seem particularly dominant in this guy. His ears were rounded. He didn't have persuasion—otherwise he would have used it. Not to mention the most obvious of traits: his ability to lie. High fae couldn't do that, but halflings—like me—*sometimes* could. Which is what landed him in this predicament. The stupid fuck bet money I was beginning to think he didn't have. Otherwise, why else would he hold out for two hours under Sadie's ministrations?

He could be a masochist, not that there would be any sexual gratification at the end of this.

Or he was just greedy and hoping we would give up, something he should have known better than to assume.

Alas, his reasons didn't particularly matter to me.

Normally, I welcomed the surprise. It kept life interesting when people didn't always act the way I expected.

However, in this case, I was growing a bit impatient. I'd just gotten to the good part in my latest romance novel. The hero had kidnapped the heroine and was slowly winning her over. I gave it no more than two chapters before they boned. Three tops.

Instead of living vicariously through fictional characters, I was playing the good cop to Sadie's bad. Mostly. I still held the stun gun.

"We've been at this for a while. Wouldn't it just be easier for me to persuade him?" Even as I said it, I knew my sister wouldn't go for that option. Sadie didn't care whether something was easy or not. While the most straightforward method appealed to me, she preferred more sensational techniques when dealing with hustlers and thieves.

"That's too nice. I have a reputation to maintain, and Jenkins here" —she motioned to the shirtless asshole between us — "doesn't deserve to be let off with a slap on the wrist. After all, this isn't the first time you've tried to stiff me, isn't it?"

Jenkins groaned, blood and drool trailing from the corner of his mouth. Sadie had already done a number on him before having me bring out the stun gun. It was a game we played often. Sisterly bonding and all that shit.

Smoothing over her long red hair, she gathered it high on her head, wrapping a tie around it, displaying her pointed fae ears. Tilting her head to the side, Sadie cracked her neck. Blood decorated her brass knuckles, droplets sprinkled on her right arm as she crouched in front of him, bringing them face to face. "Where's my money?"

"How many times do I have to say I already paid you? Crazy bitch."

I sighed. "C'mon, man. The longer you hold out, the more she's going to drag this out, which means I have to be here too. She's going to get it out of you in the end. So just tell her what she needs to know, and we can both be on our way." I made a little shooing motion, which was a piss poor attempt at motivation.

"Why are you even here?" Jenkins glared at me incredulously. Big mistake. I might be the good cop here, but I wasn't going to save his ass.

"Moral support," I answered him flatly.

Sadie punched him in the face. The sound of cartilage crunching echoed as his head snapped back and he let out a loud groan. My sister's speed caught me off guard as well.

There was a reason she was a top-tier fighter. You just never knew when her right hook was coming.

Turning to me, Sadie started talking like she hadn't just broken his nose. "Hey, didn't you say something about a date later?" She blew a strand of hair off her face, letting Jenkins sit and bleed for a while. "Please tell me I didn't imagine that. It's been like six months since you dated that poon. What was his name again? Donald? Deacon?"

"Darren."

Sadie snapped her fingers. "That's right. He worked in accounting and liked to fuck in missionary. Yawn. I told you when you started dating him, it was a waste of time. I went on a date with his brother, and they were entirely too much alike." She stuck out her tongue, making a "yuck" sound.

I pinched the bridge of my nose. "Can we not do this right now?" I pointedly looked over her shoulder at Jenkins, whose glare wasn't nearly as effective as he thought it was with his face having been pulverized.

"What?" She looked back at him. "Have you decided to talk?"

Silence greeted us, but despite his non-compliance, I sensed we were nearing the end of this little session.

For one, Jenkins was breathing like he'd ran a marathon.

For another, his muscles were twitching. Shock was setting in.

Some might think we were fucking off, but this was just part of the process.

While the immediate hits hurt, there was an ache they left behind the longer he went without medical attention, and that was the real torture. The pause in his assault served as a moment to let him feel the damage, and with any luck, come to the right decision.

If he didn't . . . let's just say I wouldn't want to be him when we called our big brothers in. Sadie might have a love of violence, but she was no murderer. The same couldn't be said for all of our family.

Sadie shrugged, turning back to me. "As I was saying, hot date tonight?"

I barked a laugh. "Ah, no. I'm meeting someone at the shop later." I glanced at my watch. "A buyer."

Sadie scoffed. "Lame."

"You're lame," I muttered, not having a better come back at all. She gave me a deadpanned look, letting me know she thought it was weak too. "For your information, I had a date last week."

Her eyes lit up. "Really? You didn't say anything. With who?"

"Axton Reyes." He was a regular at her gym who was trying to get in on the fights. While his skills weren't bad, he lacked the drive, and it showed. My sister had dismissed the idea of training him a while back, which meant my brothers had no idea he existed.

That was important, given their ability to pummel anyone who they deemed unworthy of their little sisters' affection. It left most of the guys I might actually be interested in unavailable, leaving me with lackluster options.

Sadie motioned with her hand for me to continue. "It was . . . less than ideal."

"He had to be better than Darren, and you were with that twat for months," Sadie said, crossing her arms and shifting her weight to one side.

"Two. You act like it was more than a fling. Besides," I pulled a package of Twizzlers from my back pocket and pulled one out with my teeth, speaking around it before taking a bite. "His idea of a good time was having his mom cook us dinner." My sister wrinkled her nose and shook her head in disgust.

"I take it back. That might be worse."

"Yeah. Exactly. He also casually stated he thought foreplay was overrated, so count me out. His mom was a good cook, though. Maybe I should date her." Sadie blew out a raspberry and I chuckled. "I don't know, Sade. Dating is the worst. Being alone isn't all that bad. All I need are batteries and a good imagination." Or a romance book. Speaking of . . .

"Still holding out for that 'dream' guy, huh?" She winked at me, waggling her brows. I threw a Twizzler at her, my eyes widening.

"Shut up," I said, laughing. Of course she'd bring up my dream man. I'd told her about him a couple of months ago when I was drunk and stupidly agreed to a game of truth or dare. Thank the gods my brothers had passed out and didn't hear my admission.

I couldn't remember my dreams. Ever. Except *him*. I don't know how long I'd been dreaming of him at this point. Years, maybe? His features changed. Sometimes his teeth were blunt and other times he had fangs. His tipped ears marked him as a fae, but the way his nails shifted into claws suggested something *more*. Maybe Lycan? I didn't know. He was faceless, making it impossible to determine, but his voice was always the same. I'd never heard it before in my life. Of that, I was entirely certain. For a while there, I'd wondered if he was real. It seemed strange to dream of someone I'd never met so frequently, but as time went on, I chalked it up to my unfulfilled sex life and overactive imagination. There was just something about him that was . . . intoxicating.

"You redcap bitches are crazy," Jenkins grunted, interrupting us. We both turned our heads in his direction, pulling me from my musings. I wasn't a redcap like my sister, but I didn't correct his assumption.

Most assumed we were blood related because of our red hair and familial ties. Where Sadie's was a deep, dark color that rivaled that of blood—mine was lighter, more of a copper than a true red. Then there was the skin. Mine was pale and burned if I spent too long in the sun. The rest of my family were varying shades of olive and sepia. Despite frequently staying indoors, Sadie stayed a golden color that reminded me of the Saharan desert. When we visited Greece a few years back for our high school graduation, she'd turned a beautiful chestnut under the Grecian sun.

"Hey, fuck you," I said, jamming the taser into his lower abdomen. We'd stripped him down to his boxers to give me ample surface area. The shit didn't realize how lucky he was that I hadn't shocked his dick yet. "Can't you see I'm having a moment with my sister here? If you're not going to give her the money, the least you could do is keep your trap shut. You're the dipshit that stole from her."

Sadie barked a laugh while his body writhed in pain. "Prick."

"I didn't take anything from you," he said once I let go of the trigger, gulping in air and then spitting a glob of blood onto the floor.

I rolled my eyes and checked my watch again. My sister noticed, raising an eyebrow. "What kind of 'buyer' is this?"

Sighing, I mouthed the answer to her. "Lou."

Sadie's eyes narrowed. "Trusting that creep is a bad idea, Meera. He's tricky."

Pointing my Twizzler at her, I defended myself. "He also pays well."

"Speaking of payment . . ." My sister turned to Jenkins,

grabbing his nipple and twisting painfully. Blood vessels burst under his skin at the sheer strength of her hand. "You placed a bet at my match. With my bookies. At my ring. What's more, this isn't the first time. Nor the first time you've lost. Do you remember what I told you would happen if you ever pulled that stunt again? "

"I fucking paid you," he countered. "I don't know what you want from me." Blood dripped from his face, running in rivulets down his chest. His bottom lip was busted open, and his eye had swelled shut on one side. While those injuries had to hurt, I wagered the shattered cheekbone was worse. I knew what would happen next if he didn't fess up.

Sadie pulled the cash from her back pocket, holding it out in front of me. I smirked, blowing gently over the top. The bills shimmered, the spell on them flickering. Counterfeit. Jenkins paled, somehow managing to shrink in on himself even though he was tied down. "How did you . . ."

"Meera finds things, understand? That's her specialty." He looked at me and I waved, taking another bite of my candy, uninterested in the exchange. "People come from all over, paying for her services. Me included. Of course, I get a family discount, but that's beside the point. See, Meera knows that underground fighting is a dangerous business, and a few of our patrons are sketchy. So I had her find me a way to track and expose spells on money. Can't have little weasels like you stealing from my profits, now can I? How would I feed my family, Jenkins?"

"What did a weasel ever do to you? Poor thing doesn't deserve to be compared to him," I muttered, butting in. She side-eyed me and I shrugged. "I'm just saying."

She shook her head, looking at Jenkins again. "I'm going to make this really simple. Make my money appear in the next two minutes, or I'm going to start cutting things off." She glanced down, insinuating she'd start with his manhood. Would she actually do it? Ehhhhh. Beating the shit out of someone was one thing, but real, true torture? We usually leave that to Cadoc, our second oldest brother. However, threatening a guy's dick typically proved to be their breaking point.

Shocking, I know.

Sadie sighed, holding her hand out to me. "Hammer."

Reaching over to a shelf, I grabbed one and exhaled just as long and loud as she had, but that was all it took.

"Okay, okay!" Jenkins shrieked, nodding his head in quick successions. "I have it. Just give me a phone. I'll get your money."

My sister bent over and patted his cheek gently, then softly pinched his nose as though he were a child. "See? Was that so hard?"

"Well, my part here is done." I waved my hand in a circular motion. "It's been lovely, Jenkins. Say hi to your sister for me. Don't steal from my family again. Better yet, get help for your gambling addiction. You suck at it, and it's going to get you killed. Just my two cents."

"Thanks, sis," Sadie said, giving me a hug. "I'll lock up back here."

I gave her a salute and left the room, closing the heavy wooden door behind me. She'd call Fearghal, our youngest brother who was still older than us by three years, and he'd handle moving Jenkins through the back door to the unmarked van that would take him to a random drop location.

Strolling through the quiet space, I sat behind the counter on my favorite stool and placed a Beatles record on the record player. I set the needle on as it started spinning, turning down the volume so it was more of a soothing background hum. The lights of my store had been dimmed for hours, and the closed sign had been flipped. Not that it was likely someone would stop by, given I hadn't had a buyer in weeks. Human buyers were scarce, but their antiquities weren't my primary focus—just the front I gave to the world for the occasional straggler that wandered through.

No, my real specialty was finding items of magical variety. Rare trinkets, imbued with power. I was more interested in their history and creation, but their usefulness is what usually brought in the cash.

Unfortunately, in the last few months, work had been scarce. While I had quite a few items in my back room, my antiques shop still couldn't pay the bills. Which made my dream, this store, more of a hobby than a business. Something like failure burned in my chest. I knew Sadie would lend me the money, but I would never ask. I didn't want her to know that the business I poured my heart, soul, and savings into was floundering. I'd chosen this line of work for myself because it's what I loved.

The family business was fighting, but it wasn't *me*. While I could hold my own in a fight, I didn't live for it the way Sadie did. I didn't feel that rush in my blood that she described. I attributed it to the fact I was adopted, and not a full redcap. I didn't have the full-blown desire to beat the crap out of things like they did. I was more . . . crafty and suited to undercover type work. I suppose in a way that was a saving grace, because taking those undercover jobs for specific buyers was the only thing keeping me afloat right now. Besides, getting hit sucked. As a fighter, you had to be willing to dish it out *and* take it.

I didn't want to take it. The very idea of being in the

fight ring made me cringe. No, I'd much rather acquire rare knickknacks and read romance books.

When the cuckoo clock started its loud, obnoxious announcement, I wondered for the hundredth time why I kept the damn thing. It was horrible, and the shrieking grated on my nerves. It was no wonder it hadn't sold. The only reason I hadn't gotten rid of it was because it served as an excellent security system, going off anytime someone stepped foot in my shop.

"Well, well, well," I said casually as my 'buyer' came around the corner. "If it isn't Lousy Lou, late as usual."

He smirked, glancing at his watch. "It's good to see you too, Meera, the mighty pain-in-my-ass. See, we can all do nicknames, ya' fiery ginger."

"It's about time you showed up. I was going to close up if you kept me waiting any longer." I slid from my stool and arched my back, letting out a series of pops.

Lou tutted playfully as he stepped into the light, his smile mischievous in nature. His tall, wiry stature was cloaked by a black trench coat that went down past his knees. He wore a matching deerstalker that tucked away his jet-black curls, his beard kissed by droplets of rain. "You weren't," he said, calling out my lie.

I huffed, settling my hands on the curve of my waist, tilting my hips to the side. "That hat looks ridiculous on you. You look like Sherlock Holmes."

"You don't like it? I wore it just for you, lass." He winked, grasping the edge between his index finger and thumb, tipping it just slightly.

Always the charmer. I fought the emotion playing on my lips, biting down on the side of my tongue. As much as I valued my working relationship with Lou, this past job pissed me off and I couldn't give my amusement away by doing something stupid like grinning.

"I highly doubt you do anything for my benefit, Lou." I swallowed, holding my ground as I narrowed my eyes at the leprechaun. "Now, if you don't mind, I'm missing my bed, so let's get this over with so I can go home. Unless you don't have the cash . . ."

Was I tired? Yes. Did I have a book to finish? Also yes. Was I behind on the building's mortgage and needed him to pay me no matter how brazen I acted? *Gods, yes.*

"Relax. I wouldn't show my face around here if I didn't have the money," he said, stepping closer to the counter. Reaching beneath his trench coat, he pulled out a wad of cash. I went to take it, but he pulled it back quickly. "Did you get what I asked for?"

"Would I be here if I didn't?" I rolled my eyes, reaching beneath the counter and pressing my hand onto the scanner of a biometric safe. It looked like any safe you'd buy at a sporting goods store, but this one was enchanted. It didn't just read my palm print. It read my scent. My magic. And most importantly, my intent. That last bit was a special addition I was quite proud of. And it cost me a pretty penny to imbue it in such a way, but when you worked with magical artifacts, the last thing I wanted to do was leave them unsecured. They were just as important as the cash.

I pulled out the pouch, showing him the small leather bag. A grin curled up one side of his face and his emerald green eyes sparkled with mischief as he plunked down the stack of neatly organized bills. I shook it around, slightly smiling in return before I tossed it to him.

I had half a mind to kick him out the door before he could say anything else. Instead, I watched him open the pouch, take out the glass eyeball and hold it up to the light.

He turned it this way and that, twisting his fingers as he looked at it with appraisal.

"Aye, Meera," he said with pride, "You're my favorite bounty hunter. You always pull through for me, darlin'."

Scoffing, I flipped through the money, checking to make sure it was all there. Not that Lou had ever screwed me over, but there was a first time for everything. A huge sense of relief flowed through me when every dollar was accounted for. This was enough to keep me afloat for two more months. "Keep your terms of endearment. Your charm doesn't work on me."

"My charm works on everyone, love. To what extent, well," —he shrugged playfully— "it varies."

He was working an angle. I'd done business with him long enough to know some other offer was coming. "Just say it."

Lou raised his brows innocently. "Whatever do you mean?"

I sighed. "Stop beating around the bush. You're trying to be cute so you can butter me up—"

"You think I'm cute?"

Shooting him a stony glare, I sighed. "I said you were *trying*. Not succeeding. Now speak up or get out."

He tutted. "You're awfully brazen tonight. Some might think I'd done you wrong."

"Getting that eyeball was a nasty job, and this"—I held up the wad of money—"isn't enough to cover how gross it was. I had to crawl through a sewer to get into that guy's house. A sewer, Lou. There isn't enough magic in the world to block that stench. Do you have any idea how bad that was?" I crossed my arms, jutting my hip out. "I should've gotten paid at least twice this. You set me up."

"I did not," he said firmly. "If I knew how to find it, I'd have saved the money and done it myself."

"You would have crawled through a sewer?"

"Eh," he shrugged. "Maybe not. Either way, we both know I can't do your job. That's why I hire you. I'm just the middleman, lass."

As much as I wanted to argue, it was the truth. He was nothing more than a broker. The go-between. Lou got paid to find rare items for wealthy buyers. Only he couldn't actually find them. His expertise wasn't in retrieving things, so much as knowing who to ask to find them. He had contacts all over the realms and knew how to keep his mouth shut. It granted his buyers anonymity and his bounty hunters a small layer of protection. Or so he said. Honestly, I didn't trust him, but I also didn't have a lot of options.

He paid well, and I was desperate.

Hence why I crawled through a fucking sewer and why I wasn't kicking him out right now.

I sighed, not in the mood for games after the past couple of hours interrogating Jenkins. "What do you want?"

"I have another job for you."

"Obviously." I angled my head at the pouch as he tucked it away in his coat's inner pocket. "But if it involves taking a swim through excrement, my answer is no."

I might be desperate, but even I had my limits.

Lou grinned, the cunning glint in his eye making the hairs along my arms rise. "It doesn't."

"You're sure? Because you claim you didn't know about this last one."

"I didn't know, and I am sure. Now, do you want it?"

The record had stopped playing, leaving only a lazy static circling the air. "What's the pay?" Some might ask what the job is first, but in the end, they were all the same. I found whatever thing needed to be found, whether it was a glass eyeball or an enchanted cuckoo clock. Ultimately, the object didn't matter. It's what he was willing to pay that did.

Lou took a step to the side, picking up a pair of antique bone dice that sat in a bowl on the shop counter. He rolled the hand-carved trinkets as I waited for him to answer. The dice clattered against the counter, producing snake eyes. Lou looked up at me slyly. "More than any other job I've given you."

I bit my bottom lip, moving the dice aside so I could think without him distracting me. "Give me a number."

"A hundred grand. Cash." Lou leaned his hip against the checkout, watching in amusement as I choked.

"A *hundred* grand?" I knew he wouldn't joke about this. Leprechauns were serious about money. Especially Lou.

Even if I ended up in the sewer again, this would be worth it. With a hundred grand, I could almost pay off my mortgage. A year or two and I'd own the building outright. My shop. My apartment. Keeping up with maintenance and utilities after that would be a breeze. And most importantly, it would buy me time to figure out a long-term solution to my money problems that didn't involve doing shady jobs for Lou or mooching off my sister.

I licked across the bottom of my tiny-fanged teeth.

"You sure this gig is real?" I asked, suspicion filling me.

Lou straightened up at the accusation, placing a hand over his heart. "I swear on my mum's grave. It's as real as I am."

For a mythical creature in a mundane world, that answer wasn't as reassuring as I hoped it would be. To be honest, maybe it was just how light-headed I felt by the amount. That number was . . . unthinkable. There was no doubt the price tag came with a healthy dose of danger. Why else would someone pay that much?

He pulled a sealed wax envelope from his coat pocket. Once I broke the wax, the hunt would begin. An agreement bound by magic.

I could turn down the job, up until then. But once I knew the objective, there was no turning back. The job had to be completed in the specified time frame. If I tried to delay, I'd be compelled to start. If I tried to tell someone what I was after, I'd be rendered mute.

And if I tried to break the contract?

It wasn't even an option.

When Lou approached me the first time, I'd almost turned him down. But the leprechaun had a knack for sniffing out desperation. When the job turned out to be easy, I took another. Then another. And another.

Each time, I was wary. And yet, I never turned them down.

The money was the primary reason, but a small part of me also enjoyed the thrill. The challenge. I could find anything, and I do mean *anything*. I'd tested the bounds of my gift thoroughly, but even if the object weren't in this realm—I could still track it.

That part was easy and gave me a sense of peace because I wouldn't be left unable to complete the contract out of inability.

It was the pursuit that gave me satisfaction. Following that thread and facing whatever risks lie in my way.

In a mundane world, I craved the experience for something . . . new. Uncommon. A glitch in the matrix that was my life.

Some called it wanderlust, but it wasn't simply the

desire to see new places. I wanted to experience *everything* life had to offer.

Even danger.

"Well?" Lou prompted. "What'll it be, lass?"

After a long moment of silence, I finally said, "I'm in. What do I need to find?"

Reaching across the counter, I took the envelope from him. My stomach twisted. The feeling of dread coiled tight. I hadn't experienced the feeling so viscerally since my first job all those years ago.

I ignored it and cracked the seal. The magical agreement snapped into place as I stared at my assignment.

He couldn't be serious.

This had to be a joke.

Except magic didn't lie, and I knew it was too late to turn back now.

There was a glint in Lou's eyes as he smiled wickedly. "For that price, it's not *what* you need to find, but *who*."

CHAPTER 2
MEERA

"I swear, by the demons in every hell . . ." I muttered to myself, touching up my foundation with a powder brush while checking my appearance in the mirror. "Why? Why did you take that envelope, Meera?"

"Money," Sadie said flatly, picking her nails with a small dagger while I fumbled with my earrings. She lay sprawled on my bed while I sat at my vanity getting ready. "When was the last time you were even in Faerie?"

Faerie. That was where my current bounty hunt would send me. The kingdom beyond the veil. A world where fae didn't have to pretend. Magic wasn't hidden. It would be freeing if it wasn't a hellish frozen wasteland. My parents had told me when I was young that the land there was cursed. It hadn't always been that way, but as things got worse, fae migrated to the human world. It was harder for us in the sense we had to disguise our true nature and try to make it in a world that was never meant for us, but food was easier to come by. Eternal winter didn't exactly lend toward a plethora of crops, which plunged the realm into a famine many years ago. Starvation was what brought my family earth-side, and it was enough for me to stay. The times that I had crossed through had been so few and far between, it took a minute to think of the last time I was there.

"About three years ago," I finally said, recalling my previous visit. "I was hunting for . . ." The magical gag prevented me from saying anything. I swallowed down the pause and moved on. "It was another contract, now that I think about it."

She knew exactly who gave me the contract. Sadie pieced it together without effort years ago. I think that was the only reason I could ever say anything around her.

"Faerie is cold as shit, but it's better than a sewer," she mused. I met her gaze in the mirror as I gave her an annoyed glare. She just shrugged. "Either way—you could have saved yourself the trip if you'd asked me for the money instead of working with that deceitful snake."

She didn't even know half of it.

Sadie assumed I was after an object. I'd never hunted a person. Hell, I wasn't even sure it was possible until I tried to engage my ability and saw the thin gold line I always did.

If she knew what I was actually up to . . . Lou would be running for his life. There was no way I would have taken the job if I knew it'd be a kidnapping. Something Lou had to be aware of, which is why he waited for me to open the envelope to say anything. Bastard.

I was never taking a job from him again. It didn't matter how desperate I was. Stealing objects was one thing. Sure, it was wrong, but it wasn't the same level of wrong.

My stomach pitched, nausea building at the prospect of what I had to do. I swallowed down the bile rising in my throat, focusing on my sister. "Would you have asked me if the situations were reversed?" I asked.

Sadie twisted her lips. "Maybe."

"Liar."

"Fine. Probably not."

"Exactly," I said as I pinned strands of my ginger hair into a low chignon. "You're just as stubborn as me." Or stupid. Which one would be decided later.

"I prefer *determined*." She smirked at me, grabbing a pin and tucking it in my hair. "So this mysterious bounty is going to be at a fae ball," she mused.

"I never said that." I literally couldn't. While I could name where I was going in a vague sense, like the realm, I couldn't give any specifics that would lead back to the assignment.

"You're dressed to the nines and going to Faerie, so there's only one place you'd be headed tonight, and instead of trying to blend in with the help, you're trying to blend in with the upper echelon of fae society. Interesting . . ."

My sister's observational skills were almost as good as her fighting. It's part of the reason I got ready with her. If I went missing from this, she at least had worked out enough on her own to have a vague idea of what happened. It was my poor attempt at a backup plan.

Realistically, if I got caught, I was a dead woman.

"You know I can't confirm or deny."

"I know, I know," she said, backing away and holding her hands up. "Lou must pay a pretty penny for such thorough contracts. Maybe I should ask him who he uses next time. Would save me a lot of trouble if we used a similar contract for everyone that placed bets at the rings."

"You'd miss beating the shit out of people."

"True." She shrugged, dismissing the thought before heading to the front door of my apartment. Sadie picked up her gym bag that she'd left by the end table where I kept my phone and keys, calling out to me as she exited. "I'll see you tonight at the fight?"

"You know it," I answered, wiping my finger under my eyeliner once, making sure the smudge I'd made was cleared up. "Might be a bit late, but I'll be there."

When Sadie was gone, I focused on my appearance, adjusting the pleated, floor-length gown. My hand pressed against my upper thigh, shifting the hidden slit in the dress to cover the glint of silver. A dagger lay strapped to my leg, concealed beneath the thick, luxurious fabric. All I needed was my fur-lined cloak and I would fit right in once I crossed the threshold of the portal.

I stared at my reflection, feeling a combination of guilt and foreboding doom. Guilt because I was going to be responsible for the kidnapping and possible torture or death of another fae, and doom, well, that one was obvious.

I sighed and pointed a stern finger at my reflection, wagging it with frustration. "You are better than this, Meera Wylde. If you don't lock the door the next time Lou comes around, he's a dead leprechaun, and it'll be all your fault."

Of every living creature to ever exist, my bounty just had to be fae royalty.

CHAPTER 3
VARECK

"You look like a twat," Corvo said. My familiar tilted his head in amusement as he watched me from his perch. The Maine coon sat regally; his chest puffed out. The silver of his mane framed his black face, giving him an ethereal quality. If only he weren't such a prick.

"Thanks. You're so helpful." I deadpanned.

"I try."

Try to get on my nerves, maybe.

"Don't you have something better to do?" I grumbled, trying to adjust the collar of my dress shirt. "A box to sit in? Or a mouse to hunt?"

"Hunt? Please, that's why I have you, Can Opener. Why would I expend the energy when I can sit here and judge you instead?" His black and white tail flicked behind him. "Besides, what's better than watching you fumble with buttons so you can attract a lady friend?"

"Lady friend? That's the best you can do?"

"Fine. The imaginary female that you think is real." I rolled my eyes, used to his antics. "And people say I'm mad."

Not for the first time, I questioned myself. What he said was true in a sense, if delivered in the most sarcastic way possible.

I'd been dreaming of a fae woman for years. In the beginning I'd thought she was just that—a dream. But then it continued to happen.

In all my life, I'd never experienced anything like it. Which meant someone was playing with my head—or she was real. Given I'd seen every healer from here to Belfast and they'd all claimed I wasn't under some sort of enchantment, that led me to believe the latter.

She was real. She had to be.

So why haven't you found her? a little voice in my head whispered. It was one of the many questions that bothered me. Despite hiring detectives and even a few unsavory sleuths to search the realms, they'd all yielded nothing. Finding this woman was like trying to catch smoke.

Not that they had a lot to go on. I didn't have a picture of her, let alone a name.

Corvo turned his judgmental gaze toward the door, alerting me to the presence on the other side. "You have company. Think they brought dinner with them?"

"You already had dinner."

"Not second dinner."

A single knock rapped the door before the handle turned. There was only one person in the castle that would enter without waiting for a response.

"Your Majesty," a warm voice greeted, the two who followed behind her lingered in the hallway, heads bowed. Kaia, my personal guard and best friend, entered the room before gesturing to one of the two behind her. A man carrying a pillow with my crown. "Your guests have begun to arrive."

"Yes, right. Set it on the armchair." I motioned to the empty chair in the corner of my room. The guard dipped his head, avoiding eye contact as he slipped past me to do just that. Kaia watched him, tilting her head toward the door a moment later. He followed her silent command.

"You're excused," she said without looking at them. Her foot nudged the bottom of the door, closing it quietly. Wicked amusement danced in her purple eyes.

"Arguing with the house pet, again?" she teased, winking at Corvo. Her ebony braids were pulled into a high ponytail, highlighting her pointed ears. She was already dressed in the formal blue tunic and pants, leather armor strapped above it. Twin steel blades crossed her back in their holster, while a variety of knives decorated her hips. The ensemble was complete with a gold emblem that adorned her chest, displaying her status as commander of the royal army.

Corvo narrowed his golden eyes at her, flicking his tail in annoyance. "I am not a house pet. I am a god—"

"Yeah, yeah, we know," I said, waving my hand at him in a mocking gesture.

Corvo's tail flicked in displeasure. "I'll remember that next time you need a favor."

"Need I remind you that you just referred to me as Can Opener?"

Kaia snorted while Corvo and I held a staring contest.

It ended when the cat rolled his eyes. "Whatever. I'm going to the kitchen. Call me if someone dies. Actually, don't. I'm taking the night off. You peasants can fend for yourselves."

With his little tantrum over, Corvo turned and lifted his tail—showing me his asshole. The smug fucker glanced over his shoulder to make sure I got the point, then disappeared in a blink.

Fucking cat.

"Never a dull moment with you two," Kaia snickered, then frowned as she looked at my dress uniform. "Your riband is crooked."

"I know," I said, throwing my hands up. "I've been fumbling around with the aiguillette. I can't get either of them right."

"You're hopeless," she said, shaking her head with a suppressed smile.

"Remind me why I'm doing this again?" I asked as she straightened the sash across my chest.

"Because you can't go door-to-door looking for a woman you don't know. It's creepy," she said, patting my chest and scrunching her nose at me.

"Right . . ." Some might argue hiring people to search for her was also disturbing. At least Kaia had. It's not like I was paying them to peep through blinds. I just wanted to meet her, if for nothing else than to figure out why we had this connection.

Was it something I'd done? Was it her doing?

I twisted my lips, frustrated by my lack of answers. My expression must have given me away. Kaia sighed, her lips pulling up into an empathetic smile as her eyes softened with concern.

"I'm worried about you, Vareck."

I swallowed any annoyance because logically I knew her worry was warranted. If the situations were reversed, I'd feel the same. "I'm fine."

Kaia scoffed. "That's exactly what someone who wasn't 'fine' would say."

I didn't respond. She was right, as usual, but what was there to say?

I ruled a failing kingdom that was perpetually on the brink of starvation. My court of sycophants both hated and revered me. My father was the cause of this endless winter, but I was the only one who could end it. I was fairly certain that was the only reason I still breathed. Someone would have tried to assassinate me by now simply out of rage—and succeeded—if not for the prophecy that stayed their hands.

"Please don't shut me out," Kaia continued.

This time I couldn't hold in the sigh. "I'm not trying to, but we've had this conversation. I might not be the happiest of kings, but I think it's understandable given the state of *things*."

"Things," she repeated.

"Should I make a list?"

She narrowed her eyes, not amused. "The issues in Faerie aren't the cause of this. That's an excuse. One I've let you use before because I sensed you weren't ready to talk about it."

"Then what's changed?"

"You," she answered simply. "I've known you for a long time. You may feel guilt over the circumstances that led you to being king—but that's never stopped you from trying your damnedest to fix it. The greenhouses. The robust trading system. While your ideas haven't fixed the problem at hand, they've made it a hell of a lot better. Faerie would be a barren wasteland right now if not for you."

"I'm not seeing your point."

Kaia's jaw tightened. "My *point* is that you've always been singularly focused. Driven. Sometime in the last few years . . . that's changed. I don't know how to describe it,

29

but I can see it in you. You're only half present at meetings. You're letting the courts of the high and low fae make decisions on your behalf. We're losing you, Vareck."

"I'm right here," I said softly.

"Physically, yes. But mentally? You're withdrawn. I know it has something to do with your mystery woman. Every time one of the private investigators you sent out turns up with nothing, a little bit more of you slips away." I opened my mouth to refute her, but she silenced me with a hand. "Don't insult our friendship by spouting false truths. What started as a curiosity is slowly turning into an obsession."

I let out a harsh breath, my chest tightening. "I know. I know you're right, but I . . . I can't let this go. You don't understand, Kaia. I dream of her every single night now. I'm *with* someone, and yet I've never met her. In the beginning I could write it off as me needing a reprieve from my role as king, but now" —I paused, running a hand through my unruly hair— "she has to be real. If she's not, then we have a bigger problem at hand."

"You're not crazy," Kaia said sternly.

I half smiled. "Corvo thinks I might be."

"Corvo is a fucking cat who enjoys ribbing you because it's entertaining for him. He's just bored."

"Doesn't mean he's wrong."

"Doesn't mean he's right either," she retorted just as easily. "I get why you're doing this. The search parties. The balls. If you weren't king, you'd be out there looking yourself." I didn't correct her. She knew me well. Kaia tilted her head back to stare at the ceiling as she took a deep breath.

"Do you believe she's real?" I asked quietly. It was a question I'd thought about many times but could never bring myself to voice.

"I don't know," my best friend answered honestly. "For a while I assumed it was the stress of everything. I thought it would go away. Then it didn't. Now . . ." She shook her head, letting her words trail off.

"You know what comes next if I don't find her."

Kaia went stiff. "You are *not* your father."

"His insanity started the same way. Like it or not, we can't deny the facts."

"Deimos was a sociopath. He was mad. There were obvious signs of it well before the massacre or the dreams." Her stern tone left no room for an argument. I shrugged.

"Promise me you won't let it get that far."

"No."

"Kaia—"

"It won't, because we're going to find her."

I laughed bitterly. "I've been trying for years. Even Drayden hasn't found a lead. I'm not sure what else I can do." If Kaia was considered my second-in-command, Drayden was next in line after her. They were the only two I trusted. He was currently searching for my dream girl, and he knew how important she was to me.

"Drayden is due back in a few weeks." Kaia rolled her shoulders and ran her thumb over her bottom lip in thought. "After he gets back, you're going to announce that you'll be taking a tour of the kingdom. It's been over a decade. This will give you a chance to search every major town and fulfill your role as king at the same time."

"And if she's not in this realm?"

She shifted side to side, seeming to consider something. "I've heard rumors . . . of a leprechaun that can find anything. For the right price."

I tilted my head, regarding her. "You think that extends to people?"

Kaia shrugged. "Maybe. Only one way to find out."

"Why haven't you mentioned this before?"

Kaia looked away, not in guilt per se, but definitely discomfort. "Two reasons. The first, I only heard about it six months ago."

"And the second?"

"He's a fugitive you banished from Faerie."

That would be a problem. "Which makes him unlikely to help, assuming he even can."

Kaia nodded in acknowledgement. "It's a last resort option. Let's get through this and schedule your tour, then I'll see if I can hunt this guy down. Okay?" She reached out to grip my bicep, giving me a comforting squeeze.

"If this doesn't work . . ."

"We'll cross that bridge when we come to it and not a second earlier. Now, if you're ready—you have a ball to oversee and a woman to find."

CHAPTER 4
MEERA

Snow crunched beneath my leather dress boots as I approached the palace. The gates were lifted, and the courtyard had been opened for guests to enter. Footmen opened doors to grand carriages. Lords and Ladies exited gracefully, not looking at anyone around them. For a brief moment, I felt so out of place, I wondered if Sadie had been right. Disguising myself as one of the castle servants might have been better, but I also knew it was my nerves talking. I was exactly who I needed to be for the evening. Sexy. Seductive. High class.

Why?

My target was the fucking prince, and he would never give a servant—or a commoner—a second look.

The king's annual masquerade was really the only easy chance I had to get his nephew's attention. Events like this weren't frequent in this realm. Famine and economic struggles tended to be a downer for parties. Go figure.

The entirety of Faerie had been invited this year. The only stipulation was that you had to be at least part fae to enter. The big question on everyone's mind was why the sudden change. Rumor had it that the fae king was working toward a more equal system. He couldn't abolish the millennia old classism that ran deep in our society, but he aimed to minimize it.

It wasn't a bad idea, but a ball couldn't exactly fix the years of inequality. While the vast majority of the populace lived in poverty, the high fae court didn't have to suffer the same, and it showed. While they never had an overabundance of food, their families never went without. The injustice had caused riots in the past. Deaths. The usual. All the things that happened when people were pissed off in the human world happened in the fae realm too.

The reality was, even if those handfuls of high fae families did share in the hardship—it wouldn't change anything. Faerie was cursed. The kingdom couldn't support and feed all its occupants.

I couldn't blame those with more power for doing what little they could to protect their loved ones. That didn't stop me from understanding the contempt everyone else felt for not being as privileged.

It was a shitty situation, no two ways about it.

The guards at the gates at least acknowledged everyone that entered somewhat equally. They were dressed in royal blue tunics and pants, weapons holsters fitted over their clothes. Nothing lavish, which I assumed the king had intended. I smiled demurely as the one on my left appraised me. Half a second later his gaze moved on to the next guest.

So far, so good.

A thin gold line no one else could see led me toward my mark. I couldn't see him, but I sensed his closeness. It wasn't an exact science, my tracking magic. The closer I got to my target, the more restless I felt. It was an itch I couldn't scratch. A trail of goosebumps rose along my skin. My magic drove me onward as if stuck in a compulsion I couldn't fight.

The feeling was familiar, but always unsettling. I was rarely around this many people when on a job. *Better than a sewer,* I reminded myself. In an attempt to blend in, I paused next to one of the glass lilies in the garden leading to the castle. The translucent petals were so fragile. Ice clung to them, turning the glass slightly opaque around the edges. I'd always been enamored by this particular flower. So much so that my mom always got them for my birthday, one for each year that passed.

But like all beautiful things, they weren't meant to last.

Glass lilies were bound to the magic of Faerie. Plucking them from the ground started the countdown and taking them to earth only hastened it. Still, I looked forward to those couple of days a year where they sat on my bedside table.

Someone bumped into me, pulling my attention back to my mission. They muttered an apology in my direction that didn't sound all that sincere. Sadie would have tripped them and smiled. I had to grin and bear it.

Pricks.

Following the rest of the crowd, I headed toward the entrance. I wasn't sure what the castle was made of, but it resembled white marble with streaks of dark blue and flecks of gold that shimmered and pulsed. I'd never seen anything like it on earth.

I was only a few steps past the door when a servant requested my cloak. I twisted my lips trying to hide my annoyance but handed it over regardless. It would be out of place for me to wear one inside, which would draw attention. That was the last thing I needed. Still, it was a pity. My fur-lined cloak was pretty, but once I had the prince, I needed to get the hell out of here. There would be no checking out with the guards or servants while dragging him behind me.

Hundreds of fae gathered in cliques inside the great hall, talking and drinking. Cold, stone walls rose to ceilings that must have been forty feet or more in height. Crystal chandeliers hung above me, glittering as though they were made of ice. Maybe they were. Anything was possible with magic.

People gravitated toward large double doors at the end of the hall. Music filtered out, indicating that it was the ballroom. Unease tightened my chest. I focused on the sensation, forcing my muscles to relax. I had this. Sure, it wasn't an object I was taking. Yes, I had some moral qualms about kidnapping a person. I didn't have much choice in the end. I either completed my job or I was enslaved to Lou. Permanently.

Considering fae were long-lived, death would be kinder.

Besides, I had a plan to make everything right again. I just needed to carry out the contract and then I'd be free of the consequences.

My hands smoothed over the silky onyx and ruby ombre dress, tightly fitted to my form. A black band hugged my waist, emphasizing my curves the flare of my hips.

I reached into my clutch for the last piece of my outfit. Pushing the magical handcuffs aside, I pulled out my mask. Red velvet with faux rubies, and black feathers protruding from the corner. It tied in the back with a satin ribbon, just above the chignon I'd styled low on my neck. With the price of everything else I was wearing, the mask wasn't nearly as exquisite, but I was relying on the cut of my dress to keep the fuckboy prince's attention.

With that in place, I stepped into the main ballroom.

Step one: enter the palace. Check.

Onto step two.

Find the prince.

Grabbing a flute of wine from a passing waiter's tray, I took a small sip. Drinking on the job wasn't usually advised, but in this case, liquid courage was needed.

I followed the gold string toward the food spread. It was modest, compared to the things I'd seen on earth, but an abundance for Faerie. I wondered if that was intentional, to feed the commoners that weren't used to being full.

My heart hurt for them as I took in the thin forms of the surrounding guests. Fae were naturally slender due to a higher metabolism. What that meant in reality is that we not only starved but we also didn't die quickly, prolonging the torture.

I had a good metabolism, but slender I was not. I didn't care. I'd learned to love my curves long ago, and I leaned into the shape of my body. It suited me. As fighters in a realm where we didn't starve, my recap family were built stockier and meatier. I didn't know what I was, and maybe that played a part in my shape. We did well enough in the human realm, and many fae weren't so lucky.

To simultaneously feel saddened yet thankful my parents had moved us away from this place was an experience that would overwhelm me if I let it, but I had to focus on the job at hand.

I couldn't help them. I could barely help myself.

Thus the reason I was here to begin with.

The thread moved, veering off to the side of the ballroom.

I pivoted, listening to the excited chatter circling through the air. Speculation was the name of the game.

"Do you think he's going to announce something important?" one man asked his group, adjusting his simple oak-carved mask. "Would explain why he invited the kingdom."

"Oh, do you think he's going to marry?" a woman in a poofy yellow ballgown stuttered with excitement. "I bet that's what it is."

"It's about time," another answered. "I wonder who the lucky lady is."

"Who says it's a lady?" I piped up with a cocked eyebrow.

Three heads snapped in my direction; their lips parted in surprise.

The woman closest swallowed a rather large gulp of wine then nodded. "That's fair. It's not like the women of the court have had any luck getting the attention of our king these past years. Perhaps someone else has finally caught his eye."

"Could be anyone." I shrugged, moving on from the trio and letting them carry on with their gossip. I probably shouldn't have spoken, but the assumption irked me.

The thread continued to shift, making me weave through a throng of people. Left. Right. Back. Forward. If I didn't know better, I'd think the prince was trying to evade me. The thought snuck in, a sheen of cold sweat breaking out over my skin.

What if he knew?

What if Lou set me up?

No . . . I shook my head. He wouldn't do that. He never has before. What would he have to gain from my arrest and execution? Nothing. Lou looked out for number one, and I was the best bounty hunter he knew. That meant he got paid.

40

My eyes trailed over the crowd, paranoia still eating away at my logical brain.

A stranger stopped, grabbing my hand, making my breath catch. I watched, too stunned to react as a man my height kissed the back of my wrist. He released me and bowed deeply. "My dear, would you honor me in a—"

I didn't hear the rest. The moment he looked down, I vanished into the crowd. Claws worked their way up my throat.

I closed my eyes and breathed deeply. In. Out.

Come on. I scolded myself. *Get your shit under control. If the prince knew you were here to kidnap him, they'd have arrested you at the gates.*

My chin dipped as I nodded to myself.

Pep talk successful.

Another man in a black mask with a long beak stepped up to me. His costume reminded me of a plague doctor. I braced myself for another attempt at flattery. Before he could speak, I raised my glass, downing it and then giving him an awkward thumbs-up. "Great wine," I said quickly. "I need another drink. Here, hold this." I shoved the empty glass into his hands, leaving him stunned as I walked away in search of another waiter. It seemed like this was a two-glass job, after all.

I stopped a woman with a tray, grabbing another flute of wine. As I sipped, a strange feeling crawled up my spine, tickling the hair on my neck, just adding to the discomfort I'd been feeling since my arrival. This was different compared to how my magic made me feel during a hunt.

I froze. The world around me continued to dance and laugh—but someone was watching me.

I forced myself to move, gripping my glass tighter. My gaze swept the room slowly, searching for the source. The ballroom was simple yet luxurious. A large dance floor took up the center, lined with towering pillars supporting a second-floor balcony. The back wall featured stained-glass windows, a mural depicting Faerie's history. Each new king carved out his own section of the story.

And in front of that sat a throne of . . . glass? That couldn't be right. The substance twisted and turned at the base, transitioning to deadly spikes at the top. It wasn't clear, but it wasn't opaque either. Maybe it was a crystal of some sort.

My musings trailed off as I took in the imposing figure sitting front and center. The source of my unease.

King Vareck.

Regal and commanding, he sat at the edge of his chair, hands gripping the armrests tight enough to make his knuckles whiten. His full mouth was parted as he stared at me with an unreadable expression. Piercing icy blue eyes held mine prisoner, his long chestnut brown hair wild beneath his crown. Handsome was an understatement. High fae were often beautiful, but this was something else. Vareck was a god amongst men, which made it all the more terrifying that he noticed me. In a room full of hundreds of fae, his attention was not what I expected. Nor was it welcome. Yet, I couldn't seem to make myself move.

The king's gaze heated to a searing temperature. The intensity of it did things to my body I hadn't prepared myself for. A flush crawled across my skin, rising to my neck. He took my breath away, something that had never once happened in real life—and that alarmed me.

Beside him stood a tall, beautiful woman with umber, brown skin and black braids pulled into a high ponytail. Her royal blue uniform fit her like a second skin, but the golden emblem she wore just about her breast marked her as more than a simple "guard." She touched his shoulder with familiarity as she leaned in close, speaking to him. The king's broad shoulders tensed before a noble walked up the steps, breaking our eye contact.

As though a spell had been broken, I sucked in air, my heart thundering in my chest. I slipped out the door behind me, desperate to get away from whatever had just taken place.

The sound of my boots echoed softly in the empty hall. I needed to get away. Abort the mission. I didn't know what had just happened, but I wanted to get the hell out of Faerie.

This wasn't paranoia anymore. The anxiety coursing through me wasn't unwarranted.

I'd drawn the attention of a predator. A king.

Like any good prey, I should run.

Except I was bound by a magical contract. I owed Lou— or whoever he collaborated with—a prince. Specifically, the crown prince.

I had a bounty to collect, but it was about more than just the money. My very freedom was at stake, and this might be the only chance I had to just waltz into the castle without anyone batting an eye. With my power, I could certainly find Prince Damon anywhere, but getting to him was another thing entirely. While this wasn't my only chance, it was the easiest one by far.

I let out a quiet, but frustrated groan.

Tucking myself into an alcove next to a statue of a fae with large wings, I focused in on my power. It was easy for me to use enough to conjure the thread between us. To go deeper, I had to concentrate. My eyes narrowed, their hazel color shifting and glowing a bright, vibrant green. My vision faded to black around the edges, painting the world in shadows.

Images flashed in my mind as I focused solely on finding him.

Damon's voice was a low, deep rumble as he whispered to a woman about meeting him in another room. His smile was charming, quirked to the side. His hair was as dark as a forest at midnight, eyes almost as brilliantly blue as the king's—I flinched at that detail, almost losing the trail.

Blowing out a shaky breath, I started to walk.

Moving carefully through one of the many doors and hallways, I treaded softly, almost unable to see the lights that danced and flickered from the chandeliers above. Everything was blurred and dark except for my direct path. Sounds were there but muffled.

All of my senses were dulled when I used this power, especially to this extent, but it was what made me so good at retrieving. While the thread was easy enough to follow for an extended length of time, the sight was harder. I saw the path like a map, knowing exactly where I would end up.

If he moved, the sight would follow.

Except it drained my senses.

All magic had limits and mine was no exception.

The more I used it, the longer I would be numb to the world after—which is why I rarely engaged it to begin with. The king's gaze had forced my hand. Something deep within me said I was running out of time.

After a hazardous set of stairs, avoiding three groups of guards, and almost knocking into a statue, I spotted the prince. Letting go of the magic, my eyesight slowly returned to its normal state. Sounds were still warped. My sense of smell was shot. I couldn't feel the chill of the realm, nor the heat of the blood pumping through my veins, but I was aware enough to remain upright.

I smoothed out my dress and adjusted my boobs, pushing them up for effect. My efforts were wasted when I stumbled over an uneven ridge on the floor. Or air. Honestly, I couldn't feel it so either option was equally possible.

I twisted mid-air, my body falling in a way that I wouldn't break anything. I hoped.

Upside? I landed right in front of the prince.

Point to me for getting his attention.

Downside? The undignified sound that came out of me was also unplanned and somewhat embarrassing. The very distinct rip of my dress as it tore from the floor to the top of my thigh didn't help.

"Oh my," a feminine voice tinkled with false sympathy. She looked down at me, blonde curls framing her face. A pale green and yellow dress swished next to my head.

The prince ignored her, squatting at my side to put us almost at eye level. *Wow*. The looks in this family were something else. He didn't take my breath away like the king had, but he was gorgeous, and it was easy to see how a woman could get caught up in his charms.

I cleared my throat. "Apologies, My Prince. I wasn't paying attention."

It wasn't exactly a lie, and Damon gave me a charming smile and offered to help me. "No apologies needed. Are you okay?"

Nausea churned in my gut once more as I took his hand.

I nodded and Damon pulled me up with ease. I placed a hand over my racing heartbeat, drawing attention to the keyhole of my dress where my cleavage was exposed. It worked. His hungry eyes flickered down and back up to mine as I shifted closer, shortening the distance between us.

"Well, if she's fine," the woman said, attempting to wrap her arm through the princes as she tugged him in the opposite direction. "We'll be on our way."

Tinkerbell was going to be a problem.

"Oh," I breathed, then wobbled on my feet, gripping the prince's other arm for balance. I looked into his eyes as innocently as possible. "Perhaps not as well as I thought. Would you stay with me for a moment?"

"Charissa and I were—"

"On our way to somewhere more private," she finished smugly, not hiding the irritation she felt at my presence. "*Alone.*"

"I was going to say headed to my room. It's the next door down." Damon glanced at her in mild surprise at the revealing nature of her statement. I imagined not a lot of noble women openly admitted they were on their way to bed a prince. Damon cleared his throat and returned his attention toward me. "You can recover there," he said, reaching into his pocket and removing a silver key. "Let's get you some water."

My competition pouted her bottom lip obnoxiously, whining as she protested. "But Damon—"

"That's very kind of you," I interrupted before she could sway him. She pinned me with a glare. "If that's alright with you . . .?" If she refused now she'd look even more like a bitch, something she seemed to consider as she let out a huff.

"I don't mind," Charissa said flatly.

Damon either didn't notice her hostility or didn't care as he turned the key into the ebony lock and took us inside.

The bedroom was simple, yet elegant. A king-sized bed

sat front and center with white fur blankets. A light-colored wooden dresser was pushed up against the opposite wall. Across the room a window with cross-hatched iron filigree fogged from the temperature difference, making it impossible to see inside or out. Two armchairs were placed in a seating area with a small table between them. I took one, and Charissa took the other.

Her shrewd gaze narrowed on me whenever the prince wasn't looking. She needed to be out of the equation—and she needed to have no memory of me.

While Damon poured a glass of water from a pitcher sitting on his dresser, I leaned over to Charissa, persuading her in a barely audible whisper. *"Tell him you want to get some wine for us. Return to the party. Forget about me."*

"I want to get more wine," she said abruptly. I pulled back to glance at Damon as he turned around.

"I have wine—" Charissa stepped out while he was still speaking, and the door snicked shut. He stood there, puzzled, and finished his sentence. "Here."

"Strange girl," I said, taking the water goblet and taking a sip.

He shrugged, and I detected a hint of disappointment. "They usually are."

"They?" I asked, setting my drink down and smoothing out the skirts of my gown. I knew exactly what he meant. All the women that came after him, only wanting status and the hopes of becoming his princess. Gag.

"My apologies," he said, shaking his head and pressing his lips into a forced smile. He poured himself a cup of wine and sat in the chair next to me. "I was thinking out loud."

"I'm sorry to have ruined your evening with her," I began, placing my hand on my chest again, drawing his attention as I took a deep breath. There it was again.

Hunger. Desire. I knew what he wanted. At the core of it, he was still called the Wicked Prince for a reason. I traced the keyhole of my dress with my finger, and he watched intently. "Perhaps I can make it up to you."

"Come again?" His brows shot up, and I winked. It only took a moment for a wolfish grin to appear. He appraised me, head to toe. "I can honestly say I wasn't expecting that from you. Takes a lot to surprise me."

I crooked my finger, beckoning him toward me. "Oh, I'm just getting started."

CHAPTER 5

VARECK

"Nobility at its finest." The words were cast from beneath my breath as the music paused. Men, women, and creatures of all kinds broke off from their dances and began to move to their prospective cliques. A clean separation between the noble and the common split down the middle. So swiftly, they parted the floor and went from dancing to drinking and gossiping. The nobles cast sideways glances at the commoners of the kingdom, laughing snidely at whatever disgusting comments they shared at the expense of those less fortunate.

"You're the one who wanted to throw the party," Kaia murmured so only I could hear it. "You know how they are." I glanced sideways at the lead of my royal guard. She stood beside me, the dark blue of her formal armor was a stark contrast to the gowns that filled the room.

I felt eager and restless. I didn't want to be sitting on the throne. I wanted to know if the woman in my dreams was here. It was a small chance, and I knew that, but it didn't stop me from looking. "In hindsight, we should have changed tradition this year and not had a masquerade ball.

It's a sea of masks out there. How can I find her when most faces are hidden?"

"Slight oversight," she agreed stiffly, scanning over the guests again, her deep purple eyes focused as she looked for anything out of place.

"Relax," I said, shifting my weight on the throne. "No one is going to try to start a coup."

"You don't know that."

I huffed. "Some of them may hate me, but no one really wants this job, Kaia. Hell, even I don't."

She softly shushed me, glancing around to make sure no one heard me. It was the truth, and she knew it. I was here because it was my birthright. My father had been a terrible king, a horrendous leader, and an even worse husband and father. I suppose my outspokenness in those facts encouraged the people of Faerie to at least trust that I would get us out of this mess.

While the nobility of Faerie wanted rank, privilege, and wealth, they most certainly did not want the responsibility of a cursed kingdom to rule.

A coup was the last thing on anyone's mind.

Even within a ballroom filled with people, I felt disconnected from it all. My legs were spread out to the corners of the chair, leaning back to rest my cheek in the palm of my hand. I tried not to seem bored as nobles approached and music floated through the background. Apparently I was failing. Kaia nudged me gently, giving me a chastising look, a scolding crease formed between her brows.

"What?"

"Mind your posture," Kaia leaned in, whispering, her voice playfully scolding. I rolled my eyes, swatting away her hand. She considered it a minor success. "And fix your face."

The overwhelming desire to laugh was difficult to ignore, and I covered my mouth with the back of my hand to block the smirk that begged to appear. Only Kaia would speak to me this way . . . and Corvo.

"Lord and Lady Stone approach," she whispered as a high fae couple dropped the masquerade masks they'd held up to their faces. Those accessories always seemed to be a nuisance. I'd rather a mask that tied, but so many nobles wanted to be *seen*, so they often used the type that was handheld. The vanity was obnoxious.

I inclined my head, greeting them by name, which clearly pleased them. Points to Kaia. She had an impeccable memory for names and faces.

"King Vareck, you're looking exceptionally handsome tonight." The woman curtsied, holding the flowing fabric of her gown to the side. Pieces of her bodice shimmered in a unique way I'd never seen before.

"I say, this is the best party I've attended in ages. Wouldn't you agree?" her husband added, bowing slightly in respect.

"We're pleased you could attend," I said, wishing they would go away. "I hear your greenhouses are doing well this year. We owe you many thanks for all you provide to the kingdom."

Faces I may forget at times, but their importance to the kingdom was something I always knew. In a land of perpetual winter, greenhouses were a primary source for growing food. Only half of our livestock could handle the cold—long-haired cattle and draft horses—while the remainder were housed in a similar fashion in order to survive. They needed warmth too, so greenhouses were the solution for both. It was how our kingdom survived. That and trade with the human world.

The Stones' greenhouses were our source of kale, zucchini, lettuce, bell peppers, and a various assortment of other greens. Every year was different as to whether the crop yielded results, and the past year had seen a decent bounty. Much of the kingdom had been pleased to see the return of those items in the markets, though the greenhouses with fruits weren't fairing as well.

So delighted that I had acknowledged them, they jumped into conversation about how production had been. I nodded politely on occasion, but otherwise I found it difficult to focus.

Another tug in my chest pulled my attention, twisting uncomfortably. I gripped the armrest of my throne. I idly searched the crowd, skipping over nobility. It was a lost cause. She wasn't here. I would have seen her by now.

That was when it hit me. A strong note of citrus caused my nostrils to twitch, and my eyes began to search through the crowd. The air was fresh, like a new day in spring. Soft rain could have poured down in the room, clearing the earth of decay and ruin. It was enticing. *Intoxicating.*

My eyes widened, pupils turning into thin slits as I desperately scanned the crowd, and still nothing. My frown deepened, and the scent was lost when I spotted Prince Damon. Of course, my nephew was here to be the life of the party.

Damon tilted his wolf mask up to wink at the two fae he was chatting up. He must have said something amusing because they were soon laughing. The blushing one almost spilled her wine down her pale green and yellow dress. I figured she must have had too much to drink to find him humorous, or she assumed she could gain status by bedding him. Tucking a blonde curl behind her ear, the woman held out her hand to the prince, and he took delight in kissing the back of it. I forced myself to look away as Damon took the other woman on his arm.

"Pissant fuckboy," I huffed, moving to press a finger into my temple.

"I beg your pardon, Your Majesty?" Lord Stone asked, standing near the foot of the stairs by the throne.

I looked down at him, unsure of what to say. He stared at me in question, and I looked to Kaia for help. I could see the mild annoyance in her eyes. A look only I knew. And one that only she could get away with.

Kaia jumped in, saving me. "Your incorrigible brother-in-law, sir. The one you were just telling us about."

"Yes, your wife's brother. He is obviously a fool of the people," I added, thinking about my nephew. "Just because he knows how to charm them, they see him as perfect." Kaia stole a glance toward me but remained silent, the noble's face turning to excitement that I had so readily agreed with him.

She and I both knew the sentiments were held exclusively for Prince Damon. His level of charisma was mildly annoying. He knew how to get what he wanted without being pushed over, all while making someone else think it was their idea when it failed. Twerp.

"Those are my exact thoughts, Your Majesty. It's like you—like you plucked them from my mind. How invigorating!" the noble continued to falsely praise me over nothing. I was slightly thankful that my input was relevant, if only so I didn't have to reply a second time. It wasn't until a few minutes later that Kaia finally took pity on me.

She stepped forward, placing a hand over her chest. "The king must now prepare for his speech."

"Oh, my. Yes. Thank you, Your Majesty." The man stumbled over his words with a bow before he and his wife giddily scurried off. My shoulders dipped in relief, and I continued staring straight ahead, hoping to find the woman I'd spent years searching for.

"Well, you certainly made him the happiest man of the evening," she mused, returning to her position at my side.

"That's what I'm here for," I said dryly.

"C'mon, Vareck," she began, "lighten up."

"If hell melts, perhaps," I quipped. "I would say when it freezes over, but we're already there."

Kaia pressed her lips together, holding back a huff of a laugh.

Another note of citrus took over my senses, tickling my nose and making my chest tighten. "Do you smell that?" I asked, sitting up straighter as I searched the banquet tables and crowds.

"Smell what?"

"Citrus. Lavender."

Kaia turned and looked at me with a hint of concern. "I don't smell either of those. Maybe someone's perfume. Lavender is common enough, but the citrus crop hasn't survived for the past three years."

"I think it's her," I murmured, focusing all my attention on the throng of guests, trying to find something that would confirm it.

"Where?" Kaia stiffened, snapping her head in the direction I had been looking.

"I don't know," I said under my breath. "Just a feeling . . ."

"Vareck, we can't find a feeling. What makes you—"

Kaia said something more, but I could no longer hear. My mind had wandered, replaying aspects of my dreams, whispering promises of hope, if only I could find her.

Just as I thought the prospect of losing my mind was

higher than I'd previously suspected, I saw someone. A lone woman, traversing the crowd as though she was searching for somebody important. A black and red dress hugged the curves of her figure. The ginger color of her hair reminded me of the morning dawn, bringing the warmth of a long, forgotten sun.

Surrounded by people who paid her no attention, she picked up a flute of wine, tipping the liquid back. Her soft, supple lips caressed the glass. Loose waves kissed her cheeks, having long ago freed themselves from the bun pinned on the nape of her neck. A matching mask concealed her face, but as she turned, brilliant hazel eyes locked with mine.

The world around me became foggy. My mind blanked and my mouth turned dry. All I could do was stare. An intense fire simmered in my stomach, heating parts of me that had long been turned to ice. Gripping the arms of the throne, I watched her watching me. A hand on my shoulder shook me from my reverie and my entire body tensed.

"Your Majesty," Kaia said quickly, "Lady Eleanor is here."

I cursed as my sister-in-law stood in front of me, blocking my view, and I stood up quickly, only to find that my mystery woman was no longer there. "Not now, Eleanor."

There was never a time I wanted to listen to my late brother's wife prattle on about the lack of an heir and securing her son's succession, but this moment was especially inconvenient. She spoke, but I couldn't hear her over my own thoughts as they continued to race through my mind.

"Vareck, are you listening—"

"Not now," I barked, causing several guests to turn

toward us. She flinched at the rebuke, but I didn't care. The firmness in my stare was enough for her to pinch her lips and bow her head in respect as she walked away.

"What are you doing, Vareck, you're making a scene," Kaia said through a false smile and clenched teeth.

"Black and red dress," I mumbled, searching for a glimpse of her again, skimming the color of gowns in the crowds.

"Pardon?"

"Her hair . . . like the embers in my hearth . . ." The words were barely audible, only Kaia could hear me. "Her eyes . . . they are like fresh foliage from underneath the snow."

"What in the netherworld are you talking about?" Kaia whispered harshly. "Stop speaking poetry."

I grasped Kaia's shoulders firmly, staring eye to eye. "I found her. She's here."

Her lips parted on a gasp. "Are you sure?"

I nodded. "Cover for me."

She shook her head, scrunching her features in confusion. "Cover for you? What does that even mean? You're the king. I can't 'cover' for you," she whisper-yelled at me while I walked away. "Where are you going?"

"To find her," I said, heading down the steps and toward the main doors while Kaia cursed behind me. It didn't matter. I felt . . . free? Almost lightheaded.

It was her. I knew it; deep in my bones, I knew it. After all these years, I would get the chance to be near her. Nothing would stop me.

A woman with blonde curls bumped into me in the hallway, and I apologized with the intent to move on swiftly before the color of her dress made me pause. Pale green and yellow. The giggling fae that had been all over my nephew earlier. The one he'd left with not long ago.

Creeping dread inched its way over my skin and sunk into my stomach, filling my mind with visions that enraged me.

Here she was, returning to the party, far too soon.

Alone.

Damon was nowhere in sight.

That meant one thing.

Not for the first time, I wondered what would happen if the king of Faerie killed his successor.

Tonight, the kingdom might learn the answer.

CHAPTER 6
MEERA

Prince Damon tasted like wine and bad life choices. I knew the taste all too well.

Basically like every ex-boyfriend ever, except this guy was a damn good kisser. I'd never had to seduce someone. I wasn't even good at flirting. I had quite literally tripped and fallen at the prince's feet. Not exactly a sexy and enticing maneuver. This lifestyle wasn't for me. I was far better off sneaking around and finding artifacts.

Tilting my head to the side, I bit down on Damon's lower lip. I wrapped my arms around his shoulders, clutching my bag in one hand. My fingers fumbled with the opening, trying to get the magical handcuffs out while pushing him toward the bed. Damon let out a low chuckle and moved back to unclasp the collar of his shirt.

"Impatient much?" he said with a grin.

"You could say that." *Impatient to get out of here.*

"Slow it down," he said, grazing his thumb down my cheek before he held my chin and tilted my head up so he could look at me. "We have all night. Let me take care of you."

Said no man I'd ever been with. I could see why women found him so charming. He was still a pig, but if he was looking to give out pleasure and not just receive it, that was an appealing quality.

"Take care of me?" I let him move my body, giving him access to trail his lips up my neck. "That's generous for a no-strings attached one-night stand."

He pulled back, and I tensed, fearing I'd said the wrong thing. My poor attempt at flirting might have just cost me my edge. Right now, he was putty in my hands, and I didn't have to use magic.

"No-strings attached?" he asked. "Not out for a favor or to gain status in the court?"

"Do you sweet talk all the girls this way?" He shrugged playfully, and I fiddled with the collar of his shirt, gripping it tightly as I looked him in the eye. "No favors, and I don't care about status."

"Guess there's a first time for everything," he mused, pulling me against him as his hand moved to my face. His five o'clock shadow brushed my chin, tickling skin as he pressed his lips to mine, then moved down the column of my throat.

"We have all night?" I asked, trying to use my most playful and seductive voice. He hummed the confirmation as he kissed my neck. "If that's the case, how adventurous are you?"

He chuckled against my skin, sending goosebumps over my arms. His husky voice taunted me, and my heart began to race. "What'd you have in mind?"

I took a chance. If I could do this the easy way, I'd be in bed with my book by ten. Pulling the handcuffs from my clutch, I held them up, dangling and swinging them lightly while I raised my brows in question. He smiled wickedly in return.

"I'm all yours," he said, his voice darkening as he backed up a few steps until the back of his legs hit the edge of the bed and he began unbuttoning his shirt further.

"Yes, you are." I followed and leaned in to kiss him, smacking the cuff against his wrist hard, hearing it click as it rounded over and caught the other side.

The bedroom door flew open and cracked against the wall with such an intense urgency, both Damon and I startled. He accidentally bit my bottom lip, and I gasped. My clutch had fallen to the floor. Red lipstick smeared over the prince's lips.

"Uncle?" he said, both pissed off and alarmed.

Uncle . . . Unless he had another uncle I didn't know about, King Vareck was standing in the room with us. *Oh gods, please leave.*

I froze, fearing what would happen if I turned around.

"What are you doing here?" Damon demanded, but the king didn't respond, stepping inside and slamming the door behind him. I kept my back to him, thinking of all the possible outcomes. None of them were good.

I wondered what prison was like in Faerie. What was the punishment for attempted kidnapping of royalty? Did they chop off heads here, or just wait until you turned into a popsicle in the dungeon while they starved you?

"Get out," the king growled, and my entire body went stiff.

I gasped, unable to hide my reaction.

His voice. I'd heard it before . . . My heart began to pound, and I could feel the adrenaline shooting through my veins. Maybe I wouldn't lose my head. I'd die of a heart attack first.

"This is my room, and she's my companion for the evening," Damon argued, "you get out!"

"This isn't your room. You'd never bring a woman to your actual room. This is your fuckboy playroom, and it's in my castle."

What were the odds that 'get out' was aimed at me?

I cleared my throat softly, thinking I could just keep my head down and excuse myself. "Pardon me, Your Majesty. I'll leave you and the prince to . . . um, do whatever it is you need to do." I turned slowly, staring at the floor, hoping that he'd let me pass by.

"He's going. You're staying here," he said firmly. My stomach tied itself in knots. I *definitely* knew that voice. My lips parted, and a lump formed in my throat as I struggled to breathe. Struggled to think.

I may not have recognized his face, but that was because in my dreams, his face—his features—were never clear. Each night I dreamed of him, yet all I could remember when I woke was the heat and desire in his every touch. The way his warmth enveloped me, keeping me safe. More than anything, I vividly remembered the sound of his voice.

I would know it anywhere.

I just never thought he was real.

And I never in a million years thought he was the king of Faerie.

"Oh my god, it's you," I whispered so quietly, I wasn't entirely sure I'd spoken it aloud. Not until he responded.

"You know me, don't you?" he asked, a hint of hope laced in each word. He stepped forward, and my body finally had the good sense to unglue my feet from the floor. I took a step back, holding out a hand for him to stop.

I shook my head, swallowing thickly. The denial was on the tip of my tongue, but I couldn't seem to voice it.

Very convincing.

"You do. I can see it in your eyes." His voice had a raw edge to it, and though it was a little less harsh than when he'd been addressing Damon, it still sent a shiver down my spine. I could feel the weight of his gaze. Persuasion—one of those little parlor tricks all high fae were known for. The same trick I'd used to get rid of Tinkerbell was now being turned against me. "Answer my question."

"Um, of course I know you. You're the king." The words were strained. Not a lie, and yet not the truth. His presence was suffocating. I stepped back, dodging around the side of an armchair, trying to put distance between us.

"That's not what I meant."

I bit my bottom lip, inhaling deeply. Gods, his voice did things to me it shouldn't. Especially not now.

"Well, this is awkward," Damon said with a heavy sigh, taking a step toward the door. "I think I'll just..." He pointed toward the exit with his thumb. "Maybe leave now."

"Stay," I commanded, and Damon numbly sat on the bed.

Vareck groaned in frustration, stepping around Damon. "I want to talk to you."

"Sure," I said, circling around another chair. "We can talk. From a distance."

He held up his hands, but didn't make any move to step away. "Why did you come here?"

"For the ball." I moved away, stepping closer to the bed and positioning myself near the door. "Stay back."

"I'm not going to hurt you." He scrunched his brows. "Why are you acting this way?"

"Because you're freaking me out," I blurted, the pitch of my voice rising.

"I just want to talk to you. I want to know you."

"Yeah, that'll calm her down. Not creepy at all," Damon muttered, and the king shot him a look.

"Stop talking," Vareck told his nephew before returning his attention to me.

"Why are . . ." I paused, trying to catch my breath. His eyes were intense, and for the first time in this little slice of hell, I fully grasped that he didn't know what I was here for, but for an entirely different reason, he was here *for* me. I wasn't sure which was more dangerous. "Why do you want to talk to me?"

"Because I *know* you," he began, shaking his head like he'd said the wrong thing when I flinched back slightly. "What I mean is, I've dreamt about you—that came out wrong." Vareck raked a hand through his thick chestnut hair. "Fuck."

A whooshing sound clouded my hearing as my heart pushed blood through my veins at a high rate of speed. Mouth dry, my balance faltered, and I stumbled.

How could he . . .? If I had dreamed of him . . . and he was dreaming of me . . .

Too many questions. I couldn't breathe. It was as if someone had sucked the oxygen from the room.

"What did you say?" I choked. "That's not possible." I couldn't look away. My heart hammered in my chest, but I tried to stay in control. Shaking my head in disbelief, I blinked rapidly, replaying his words in my head, too shocked to figure out what they could possibly mean.

"I knew it." His eyes widened as he looked at me with realization. Vareck took a step forward.

"Stop*!*" I cried out, not knowing if my magic could work on someone as powerful as him, but to my surprise, it did.

Vareck froze, darkness clouding his gaze.

I let out a stuttered gasp. That just happened. I just used persuasion on the king.

Well. I was going to die. Dream girl or not, I was pretty sure that was a capital offense here.

Damon coughed a laugh, pulling me back to reality. "This night has taken a weird turn, but I have to say, it's a good look on you, Uncle."

My hands shook as I scrambled to Damon, my magic still holding both of them in check. I couldn't believe what was happening.

"Stay. Don't move," I commanded. I used my magic again, my voice trembling, "Good. Good boy... err, man... king. Good king."

I was running on fumes now, my energy rapidly draining. This whole thing was confusing on every level, and I had to get out before it was too late. I'd figure out the rest of it later.

"Get up and follow me." I grabbed Damon by his cuffed wrist, dragging him out of the room. I didn't dare look back. The cold metal clicked as I wrapped it around his other wrist, securing it tight.

"Question, if you don't mind me asking," he said casually as I pulled him behind me.

"I do mind." I tugged on the chain, trying to recall how to get out of this damn palace.

"Still, I think I have the right to ask why you're taking me with you. I mean, sure, we could have had fun. I'm all for tying each other up, cuffing to the bed, and what not, but the mood is gone, don't you think?"

Left, right, staircase, left? Or was it right, right, staircase? I stopped at a corner, peeking around to make sure the hall was empty before I turned to him. "You really are a wanker."

"Maybe, but I'm not the one who's lost," Damon said with a shrug.

"You're right." I shot him an angry glare, pushing more of my magic into the command. "Show me a secret way out."

"You could say please," he teased, but I wasn't in the mood for his jokes.

"Now. Hurry," I barked, shoving him along. I could feel my power waning. Holding him and the king drained more than I could have ever imagined. I couldn't summon the energy to persuade Damon to shut up.

"Yes, ma'am," he replied, almost dragging me along as he took the lead and stopped by a large portrait. He angled his head toward it. "It's a door. I'd open it for you, but I'm sort of tied up at the moment." He waved his fingers in the cuffs, smiling.

Of course I'd be kidnapping the class clown. I groaned, following his instructions and then entered the hidden passage.

"My uncle will probably have your head for this," he mused as we snuck through narrow hallways in the castle. "But then again, he said he'd been dreaming about you. That was weird. Don't you think it was weird?"

"Do you ever stop talking?" I muttered.

"No, not really. It's part of my charm."

"I can see why your uncle doesn't like you," I muttered, though the thought of the king made my thighs clench.

As we neared an exit, I felt the pressure mounting. I glanced back once, the weight of the situation finally threatening to crush me. I was stealing the prince, and I'd just subdued the king of Faerie. This turned out to be a fine evening.

Damon had taken us through a maze of secret hallways

and successfully led us to the outside of the castle, right by the corner gardens. A hedge maze of glass lilies and indigo snow dahlias took us further from the castle. Our path was marked in the fresh snow, but there was nothing I could do about it. I might be part high fae, but I didn't possess an ounce of their elemental abilities. The chilled night air bit my skin, making me shiver and wish for my cloak.

"Take me to the center fountain," I whispered through chattering teeth.

"The portal?" he asked, raising a brow. "Yeah, that makes sense."

"What makes sense?" Though I tried to keep my tone neutral, I failed, and a touch of bitterness leaked through.

He looked me up and down with a crooked smile. "You didn't strike me as someone from around here. For one, you've actually got some curve and an ass; a beautiful one at that. Few women in Faerie do, given the whole starvation problem."

I sighed and pressed my lips into a thin line. He was baiting me, or he was just truly this annoying. Either way, if I didn't respond, he wouldn't get what he wanted, and that was for someone to pay attention to him.

As we exited the gardens, two guards came into view, standing by the main gate. We just had to get past them, and we'd be clear to head to the portal at the fountain. Like a sixth sense, I felt Damon ready to start talking again, but I cut him off. Looping my arm through his, I draped my hands over the chain to block it. "We're going for a walk. You will tell them nothing else."

His jaw clenched as he tried to resist. That's when it happened. My magic flickered, losing almost all the strength I had left . . . and a feral roar sounded from inside the palace. I no longer had a hold over Vareck.

The guards turned, looked at each other in panic, then rushed to the palace doors. My heart was racing. We had minutes, at most, but it felt like seconds. I could hear the shouting and screaming from inside the castle walls.

Damon tutted in disgust. "Oh, fine soldiers, they are. Kaia will have their armor for abandoning the front gate," he said, watching them leave a wide-open exit for us.

"She can have their armor, whoever she is. Just move," I growled, running swiftly on the frosty pathways leading to the center fountain, thanking the stars I had good boots on. He kept pace beside me, not that he had much of a choice anymore.

When I saw the fountain, I felt a rush of relief, even as my adrenaline skyrocketed. I could hear the shouting outside now. Guards would be flooding the city soon.

"Well, here we are, milady." He stopped at the edge of the fountain, dipped his chin, giving a slight bow. "Have a pleasant evening. While I'll admit that watching you persuade the king was truly a highlight in my life, the rest of it has been. . . well, strange. Have fun. Please don't come back."

I twisted my lip and scrunched my nose. "Afraid you're coming with me."

He huffed a playful laugh. "As you so eloquently stated earlier, my uncle doesn't like me. He won't pay a ransom."

"Sorry, princling. This isn't for ransom." For the first time all night, real emotion crossed Damon's face. A mixture of confusion and worry. A pang of guilt rang through me. I had no idea what was going to happen to him, and the thought made my stomach roil. Whoever hired Lou had plans I wasn't privy to. Maybe it involved ransom. Maybe it didn't. The reality hit hard, threatening to consume me.

Damon put in true effort now that he realized my intentions. His will battled mine, fighting for the right to control his body. "Why are you doing this?"

"Because I fucked up." I didn't stop to think, my words slipping out in a rush. Pulling a small vile from my cleavage, I tossed it into the frozen fountain, watching the glass shatter and the liquid spill over it in a shimmering wave. His frown deepened, and I mumbled 'sorry' before tackling him around the waist and throwing our weight toward the fountain.

CHAPTER 7
VARECK

The guards claimed she'd gone through the public portal in the fountain, taking my nephew with her. Despite Kaia's reservations, I followed.

She was the woman in my dreams, of course I had to follow. She had recognized me. For years I'd wondered if she was real. Beyond confirming her existence, the one question that had always been plaguing me was if she had dreamed of me too. Based on her reaction to my admission, the answer was a yes.

The way her body had tensed. Her breathing changed. The shock written all over her features. Yes. There was something there.

How many times had I'd imagined meeting her? Countless, and yet—nothing like this particular series of events had played out in my head. Partially because I thought I'd be far more articulate in my approach and the reality was I'd stumbled through my words like some flustered schoolboy. The other reason was my annoying nephew hadn't been part of the equation.

Seeing them together had thrown me, and all decorum

went out the window. After years of planning how I'd talk to her if we ever met—I couldn't think past the roaring in my head.

Then she ran, and what's more, she took Damon with her.

I'd feel jealous if I thought for a moment it was for her benefit, but the vibe in the room didn't suggest she was interested in him. Her gaze was too cunning, too calculating.

I exited through the portal inside The Witching Hour. It was hidden in a back room where the fae could come and go as they pleased, shielded from the eyes of those that didn't know we existed. It allowed us to travel with ease, not needing potions or cloaking spells, though a small fee was paid to the bar for its use.

It had been a while since my last visit. I generally came on official business, and my arrival was pre-planned and announced ahead of time. Today, I was alone, and I was on the hunt. The thumping of the music vibrated from the main club. The faint trace of my dream girl's aroma reached me, and my heartbeat picked up in speed.

She was here.

Leaving the portal room, I walked through the club swiftly, following hints of her distinct scent. It led to the bar, but as I searched the crowd, I couldn't find her or Damon.

The dark-haired barkeep looked at me in surprise when I approached, inclining her chin. "K-king Vareck. To what do we owe the pleasure?" Her voice wavered slightly. The customers tensed, grabbing the drinks she'd made for them and shuffling away.

"I need to find a woman. Red hair, black and red dress. She came through the portal, likely with Prince Damon . . .

accompanying her." *Accompanying, my ass. Being compelled by her impressive magic is more like it.*

"I'm sorry, my king, but I haven't seen anyone matching that description. They might have left before I started my shift. I've only just arrived."

"Any rooms?" I asked, while I looked around, searching for other doors and hallways.

She pointed to the back of the club, near the stage . "Just our storage closet and inventory rooms. You're welcome to check them."

"I've seen your lady," a patron slurred into his glass. He jutted his thumb toward the exit. "Walked out not three minutes ago. Got into a car."

I tossed a coin to him with my thanks, then rushed outside, but the moment the door closed behind me, the crisp, cold night air lacked familiarity. Her scent, so fresh and bright, slipped away completely.

There was no way she'd left the bar through here. Even with the light misting of rain in the air, some of her scent would still be present.

The drunkard had lied, or perhaps feared me and just wanted me to leave. I was tempted to return to the bar and teach him what happened when people lied to me, but he'd technically done me a favor. She would exit eventually, whether it was the front door, or the back door that led into the alleyway, and I would be right here waiting when she did.

Slipping into the shadows, I stayed in the darkness until my senses were once again filled with the enticing perfume I'd come to recognize as uniquely *her*. I'd know it anywhere, and I'd follow it to the ends of the earth.

CHAPTER 8
MEERA

I pushed through the portal, my fingers reaching for the other side. The vile ensured our arrival would be untraceable, sending us to a location other than the public exit. What would normally be a smooth transition was now a chaotic mess. Darkness welcomed us, followed by pain—the first sign that the prince and I were back in the human world. We crashed into the walls of a utility closet, tripping over buckets, mops, and cleaning chemicals.

A groan escaped my lips, frustration building as I knocked my shoulder against a shelf in the dark space. With a quick flick of my wrist, I yanked the chain hanging from the ceiling.

Exhausted didn't even begin to cover how I felt. My body ached, and I was glad for the brief moment of respite. Damon was sprawled on the floor, covered in dust and debris. A bucket had landed on his head, making me snort in amusement as he lifted it off. The prince didn't see the humor in it like I did. I suppose I could understand. If I'd been kidnapped, I'd be pissed off too.

"I see I'm working with a real professional," Damon complained.

I couldn't help but grin sheepishly and shrug. Yeah, we were both soaked in sweat and clearly out of our element.

"All right, pretty boy," I sighed, tapping into my persuasion again, a wave of mild vertigo hitting me as I fought to stay focused. I was going to crash for a solid day after this much power usage. Maybe longer. "Follow me."

Damon kicked aside a bottle of bleach, dusting off his shoulder with a charming smile. "You think I'm pretty?"

I rolled my eyes. "Desperate much? You know you are, otherwise you wouldn't ask."

A smirk pulled at his full lips. "Pretty enough to let go?"

"Nope, not happenin'." His smirk fell away, expression turning to something almost . . . dark? I wondered if this was the real Damon, beneath the charm and seduction.

"Are you going to elaborate on why you fucked up?" His voice was light, but it felt forced.

I sighed. "Because I took a job I shouldn't have." I rubbed my shoulder, where I had slammed into the shelf earlier. Definitely going to leave a bruise.

"For?"

"Cash."

Damon tsked. "I meant for *who*?"

"Ah," I hummed. "No idea." I steadied myself, focusing on the boom of the bass coming from just outside. I grabbed the door handle, nudging Damon forward.

"You don't know who you're working for?"

"I work with the middleman. No idea who wants you. Got any enemies?"

Damon huffed. "I'm the crown fucking prince. What do you think?"

His sarcasm was unwarranted. As far as kidnappers went, I was a goddamn delight.

Sure, I compelled him to come with me after trapping him in magic-nullifying handcuffs. But it wasn't like I drugged or assaulted him.

Instead I was quietly conversing with my bounty to keep both of us calm.

"Welcome to The Witching Hour."

I opened the door, and thick fog poured in, swirling across the cheap linoleum floor. Glitter covered every surface of the bar, glinting like the herpes of the magical world. The flashing lights from center stage lit up the entire space and in the spotlight were a pair of twin pixies, their long green hair curled in ribbons down to their lower backs as they twirled around poles. The only thing covering their delicate bodies were black thongs and thigh-high boots with a stiletto heel that would put me in the emergency room if I attempted to walk in them.

I pushed my way through the busy crowd, making my way to the back bar as one of the pixies pulled off an aerial move that had wolf whistles and dollar bills following.

"Amelia!" A single woman ran the bar. Anyone else on a busy Friday night would need assistance, but not her. Waving her hands like the conductor of a symphony, bottles swooped toward patrons, filling their empty glasses. The witch moved with a flourish, crossing her wrists in the air as sparks of fire erupted from her hands in a small, contained firework show. Cheers erupted around the bar.

"Amelia!" I called again, raising my hand to get her attention. She turned, and her eyes lit up when she recognized me. She bounced over, lifting her long lacy dress and giving me a smile.

"Meera! Figured I'd see you tonight. Loulou's in the back waiting for you."

I rolled my eyes at the pet name, sighing. "Lou must've charmed you."

"Who's your cute friend?" Amelia purred, glancing Damon up and down. When she saw the cuffs, her smirk widened. "Guess it's all work and no play tonight? Total shame. I'm kind of into the whole handcuff thing."

She flicked her wrist again, and a curtain appeared on the wall that was previously empty, pulling open to reveal a back hallway to The Black Lounge, an exclusive and well-hidden place for those of us with dark secrets.

"Thanks," I tossed over my shoulder, guiding Damon forward. He opened his mouth, probably to ask for help, but seemed to think twice. We passed through a few rooms, each one filled with elite guests talking over wine and enjoying their privacy. Some closed the veils, activating the silencing spell cast over each room, courtesy of Amelia. I ignored them all as we made our way through the dim corridor.

A wet suction noise beneath my leather boots made me pause. My nose scrunched in annoyance that I'd stepped in the remnants of someone's spilled ice wine. The bottle was broken, and the sticky liquid clung to the floor—and now my shoes. "Watch your step," I muttered.

"Thanks," Damon huffed sarcastically. "Because some spilled wine is my biggest problem right now."

"Fair point."

There was a single door ajar at the very end of the hall. Lou's way of saying he was waiting for me. My temper flared again at the sight of the leprechaun, and tension built in my chest.

"Ah, Meera the Mighty!" Lou laughed, flexing his arm as he leaned across the table. "I knew you could do it, lass. No problems, I presume?" He offered up his pipe with a grin, smoke curling from his lips.

I glared at him. "You are the worst leprechaun I've ever met."

"Aye! I'm probably the only one you've met, love. Makes me the best too."

"Consider this my resignation. I quit." My frustration seeped through, but exhaustion was fighting to overtake it. I pushed Damon forward. He stumbled into a chair, sitting down at the table.

"Now, now, lass. Let's not be hasty—"

"I've had one hell of a night because of you."

The man next to Lou raised his hand, but Lou waved him off. Damon shifted uncomfortably, looking between the three of us. "You asked if it would involve crawling through a sewer again, and I answered honestly. Besides, it's not like I coulda told you anything if you didn't open the envelope."

"You could have mentioned it was for a person."

"No, I really couldn't. The terms of the contract bind me as well."

My lips twisted as I crossed my arms over my chest. "I'm still not happy with you."

Lou raised his hands. "You're still in one piece. I wouldn't give you something you couldn't handle. Now have a little faith and relax, would ya?" Lou pulled an envelope from his pocket, sniffing it before winking at me. It held a magical form of payment. Not cash, but the agreement of it, and it smelled just like money.

"That better be all of it or I—"

"Oh, calm your pretty self. You've got too sweet of a face to make threats. Take the charm off him, and the money is yours, transferred to your account as agreed upon. That ought to cover your shop's rent for a while."

I exhaled slowly, letting my magic fade from Damon. He inhaled sharply.

"This... this was seriously over rent money?" he hissed, the envelope sliding across the table. I caught it before it hit the floor and shrugged. Guilt ate at me, but nothing I could say would make this better. I had a plan to fix it, but Damon didn't know that. Mostly because if I told him, I ran the risk of him running his mouth to Lou or the client.

"It's my mortgage. Some of us don't live in a castle," I replied. My words were scathing, but my tone was neutral.

Damon stood, looking dangerous, his eyes glowing with an eerie, powerful light. "I am the prince of Faerie. Release me and I can get you whatever you—"

Before he could finish, Lou slammed a pistol into his head, knocking him out cold.

Lou smiled at me. "Pleasure doing business. I suggest you leave now, lass."

I held the envelope to my chest, my gaze flicking between Lou and the unconscious prince. The deal was done. It was out of my hands.

For now.

Part of me wanted to compel Lou and the mystery man beside him, then take Damon and run.

There were two problems with that plan. One, Damon probably weighed two hundred pounds and was well over six feet tall. I was stronger than a human woman, but not that strong. Two, I'd burned myself out on my magic. If I used anymore, I risked it seriously affecting my physical health. Fae were magical creatures, but without our magic we suffered.

I backed away slowly, casting one last look at the unconscious prince. Silently, I vowed to get him back, then I hightailed it the fuck out of there.

I tossed a handful of bills down, paying for the use of the secret portal. Before it even hit the counter, a drink slid toward me. Amelia gave me a sly grin, raising her own shot glass. "A ginger orange shot for my favorite ginger."

With a weak smile, I raised my glass in return. "Next time bring Sadie with you, but leave those brothers of yours at home. They're still banned after the last fight they caused."

I downed the alcohol, slamming my glass down on the table. "You got it."

"Don't be a stranger," she called after me as I walked out the door.

After what felt like an eternity dealing with this batshit plan, I began my walk home. It wasn't too far from The Witching Hour. Most fae and other magical beings that had left Faerie lived in certain areas, clustered together for comfort and familiarity. My family and I were no different.

It was dark and drizzling, the cloudy sky overhead made the city seem smaller. Depressing too. My dress grew heavier, weighed down by the rain. I crossed my arms over my chest, annoyed that I didn't have my cloak anymore. In a city like this, no one would take a second glance at my unusual attire. They'd likely assume I was a theater actor, or just weird, and that was if they even paid any attention to me.

The streets weren't too busy, and most people kept their heads down to shield their vision from the oncoming storm, but I kept turning to check behind me. My exit from

Faerie hadn't gone unnoticed. No one had followed yet, but it was only a matter of time. Guards would be pouring into the streets soon, searching for Prince Damon. The magical handcuffs may have covered his scent, but without wind or a true storm my own would still linger. The reminder encouraged me to pick up my pace.

When I approached my building, I did another quick glance. The hairs on the back of my neck lifted. I scanned my surroundings, but nothing was there. The few people on the sidewalks bustled by without a glance in my direction. I shook my head, pushing away the paranoia. They hadn't caught up yet, but I knew I was on borrowed time, and I needed to split town. That's all it was. With a shake of my head, I headed inside and ascended the rickety stairs.

I was swaying on my feet by the time I reached the third floor. It took me a couple of tries to get the right key into the lock on my door. When I finally pushed it open and stumbled inside, a sigh of relief escaped me.

I dropped my keys on the counter, my body screaming for rest.

Unfortunately, that wasn't an option right now.

Not only did I draw the attention of several attendees who could identify me, but I met the elusive fae king. Only it wasn't my first time. Or my hundredth. For years I'd been dreaming of him and had no idea.

Then I went and persuaded him so I could escape.

"Fucking leprechaun. Fucking job. Fucking fuckity fuck," I muttered under my breath as I walked to my bedroom. I cast my bed a single longing glance and then turned for my closet. As much as I wanted to sleep, it would have to wait. I couldn't imagine it would take them long to find someone that could track me, and I needed to be long gone when they did.

I opened my phone, scrolling through my top contacts until I found my sister's name and I quickly typed out a message.

Meera [11:39 pm]: I was seen 2night. Packing. Gotta get outta herw.

I hit send, my fingers trembling.

Typos aside, I was sure Sadie would understand and relay the message to our family. They were into enough shady shit that they knew how to go underground when necessary.

Before tonight, they'd never needed to.

Neither had I.

But on the off chance there was someone else with a gift like mine, I had to get the hell out of here before I led them straight to the only people in this world that I loved.

My phone vibrated, and I glanced at the screen without opening the text thread.

Sadie [11:40 pm]: *Are you all right? Is someone following you?*

I wanted to call her and explain, but I didn't have the time. I didn't even have time to change. Leaving as quickly as possible was imperative. Empty duffle bag splayed open, I started throwing clothes inside, not caring whether they matched or not. A couple of pairs of boots. A phone charger. Some protein bars from the kitchen and a pack of Twizzlers. My toiletries, which was simple enough when I opened the little purple bag that Sadie got me for Christmas a few years ago and I swept my arm over the counter until everything was dumped inside. I tossed it in the duffel then took a slow perusal of my room, trying to figure out if there was anything I'd forgotten.

My phone lit up again because I hadn't responded.

With a sigh, I tugged the zipper on my duffel and threw

it over my shoulder. Screw it. If I forgot anything, I could buy a new one with the cash I'd earned tonight.

Ready to go, I paused to text my sister back.

Meera [11:43 pm]: *Probably. I need to get out of here. Go into hiding for a little bit. I'll call you when I get to the safe house, okay? Take care of yourself. Tell mom and dad I'm sorry.*

Before I closed the thread, she texted back.

Sadie [11:43 pm]: *I'll meet you there in a few days. Be careful, okay? I love you. <3*

A small smile flicked across my lips as I shook my head. It pained me to leave like this, but I couldn't risk it. While it was unlikely they could track me tonight, I had no doubt they would eventually catch up to me. With how Vareck acted . . . I chewed my thumbnail nervously. Yeah, they'd show up eventually. I let out a long sigh and quickly texted back, my thumbs swiping over the phone screen.

Meera [11:44 pm]: *Yeah, yeah. Luv u too. Give me th*

Before I could even finish typing, the message was sent early, and my phone slipped from my grasp. Every part of me tensed as a hand clamped over my mouth, strong arms pinning me against a hard body.

My fight instinct kicked in. I moved to stomp on the intruder's foot, then elbowed them in the stomach. Only they didn't move. On the contrary, the more I struggled, the stronger they gripped.

That was when the masculine scent registered.

Snow covered fir trees. The crisp bite of cold. Winter.

I shuddered. *No way.* There was no freakin' way he'd already found me.

My exposed skin from my ripped dress pressed against the ice-cold fabric of his posh clothes. A shiver ran through me. My phone buzzed against the floor with a slew of messages from my sister. I could see them, but I couldn't respond.

Sadie [11:45 pm]: *Meera?*

Sadie [11:45 pm]: *Give you what?*

A deep voice whispered in my ear, his ragged breath sending chills down my spine.

"Hello, Meera, darling."

CHAPTER 9
VARECK

Meera stilled, her skin warm against my palm. I held her tighter, breathing her in. She smelled like blood oranges and vanilla. The same as she did in our dreams.

The ones she tried to deny.

Fury coursed through me when I thought about that.

Her device buzzed against the floor, its light casting eerie shadows. It's how I learned her name, reading the texts as they came in. We didn't have phones in Faerie, but I understood how they worked well enough from my travels to this realm.

"Don't move. I'm going to let you go, but you will not compel me. Understood?" Unfortunately, I had to use my own compulsion to ensure she didn't do anything crazy. The minx had already proven herself powerful and it would be a mistake to underestimate her again. A beat passed, then she nodded.

I released her mouth slowly, instead grabbing her chin and turning her head to the side so she looked at me. Fire burned in her hazel eyes.

"Are you armed?" It wasn't the question I wanted to ask, but it was the one I needed. She'd restrained Damon with a pair of handcuffs that I could only assume were enchanted—otherwise he would have fought back with his own magic. My nephew might be useless in almost every aspect, but self-preservation ran strong with that one. "Answer me."

"Yes," she hissed, clearly not thrilled to be on the other end of compulsion.

"Where?"

Her eyes flicked downward, then met mine again, sparking with defiance.

My free hand slid down her thigh, fingers grazing warm, smooth skin. She stiffened, trying to mask both her fear and desire. I found the dagger strapped to her leg, pulling it free. With a flick of my wrist, I embedded the blade into the wall.

"Anything else? Where's the handcuffs?"

"Gone and no."

"Good. You were impressive earlier. If I could trust you not to run, I wouldn't have to do this. Your persuasion is . . . unusually strong."

"Because that makes it so much better," she muttered, voice dripping with sarcasm.

"You compelled me first," I pointed out.

"Would you have let me go otherwise?"

"Before you kidnapped my nephew, yes. I wanted to talk to you. Not . . . this."

Guilt flashed across her features before she could bury the emotion behind a mask of indifference. "How do you know I kidnapped him?"

"I heard you compel him. Not to mention the small

detail that guards saw you push him through the portal. Your exit wasn't exactly subtle."

Her lips twisted. "I can't tell you where he is, even if you compel me. My job was to snatch the prince and get him to the drop location. Nothing more, nothing less."

My brows drew together. "Do you know who hired you?"

"No." Something flashed behind her eyes, making me wonder if I was missing something.

"You do know that taking the crown prince of Faerie is a crime, correct?" I didn't use persuasion. I didn't need to.

Her lips thinned. "I'm aware."

"But you still did it anyway," I said. "Why?"

Her expression shuddered. "Because I'm a fucking idiot and took a job from a broker that I shouldn't have."

I tilted my head. Her answer wasn't what I expected. None of this was. It was strange to think that I knew her so intimately, and yet not at all.

"Then why did you?" I pushed, needing to know more. To know everything.

She laughed without humor. "I'm broke and desperate. Maybe not in that order."

Her reason for being in Faerie was both understandable and disappointing. Some part of me had hoped that maybe she was there for me. If her shock at seeing me was anything to go by though, Meera had no idea who I was until I barged into that room.

Lost to my own thoughts, I didn't notice her move until it was too late. Jaw locked tight, she pulled away from my loose embrace and sprinted toward the wall perpendicular. Surprise made me slow to react as she grabbed the handle of the dagger and pulled it from the wall.

She flipped it with a flick of her wrist, catching it by the tip.

I cocked an eyebrow. "Do not—"

Too late.

I side-stepped the throw, but the edge of the blade grazed my cheek. The cut stung, but I suspected it was superficial at most. I looked from her to the blade. "Was that necessary?"

She opened her mouth, but nothing came out. Her lips bobbed as she choked. She was trying to persuade me, but my own compulsion kept her from speaking.

She'd broken through my command to not move, but her energy was draining. Meera teetered on her feet.

"I . . . don't . . . feel . . ." Her eyes rolled to the back of her head, lids falling shut. Her knees gave out at the same time that I lunged.

Her limp body fell into me, held up entirely by the arms I wrapped around her waist.

Fuck.

I'd spent years looking for this woman, but I never could have guessed how I'd find her. Indecision warred in me as I debated my choices.

Stay here, wait until she wakes up, and then chance how long it took her to break my persuasion—again.

Or . . . I could bring her home.

The device on the floor buzzed again. A picture of her with another woman, both laughing against a backdrop of blue ocean waves. A world she had seen. One I was taking her from.

The decision snapped into place, like a click of a lock.

Kidnapping the prince was reason enough to bring her back. Everything else . . . I shook my head. It didn't matter.

I picked Meera up, cradling her against my chest while I carried her bride-style. The tension in my body eased when her head lolled against my shoulder, duffel bag swinging with every step away from her apartment.

When I first saw her, I wanted answers.

Now? Something told me I wouldn't stop there.

CHAPTER 10

MEERA

I floated, weightless, wrapped in a warm, blissful embrace. My cheek pressed against something impossibly soft, and I let out a contented sigh. It was perfect—until I shifted, the need to move nagging at my limbs. Bones popped and cracked to the side as my skull rolled against what felt like a doughy cloud. Every muscle ached, as if they'd been stuck in the same position for too long.

My eyes fluttered open, my vision blurry despite my attempts to focus. The ceiling above me was unfamiliar, pale blue with hanging lights. I squinted trying to make out the shapes. They looked like . . . flowers? White flowers with petals that changed from dark blue at the tips to a brilliant white light at the center. They were mesmerizing.

Until I realized what should have been glaringly obvious. My apartment ceiling was the old popcorn stuff that went out of style thirty years ago. I had 'boob lights' as my sister called them—weird half spheres that tapered to the slightest dark point in the middle. That wasn't the only thing that tripped up my senses. This mattress was divine, which meant it definitely wasn't mine. That sucker had springs that creaked if I breathed too heavily.

Panic flickered at the edges of my thoughts. Had I gone to the bar last night?

I struggled to gather the scattered fragments of memory. There was wine. Someone's lips against mine. Music that pulsed through my veins. A rush of energy, something electric beneath my skin. But everything was fractured, floating in and out of reach. The only thing I was sure of—besides the deep ache in my joints—was this odd pressure on my legs, an unfamiliar weight pressing down.

I groaned, the multiple flower lights stabbing into my skull like tiny daggers. This was a hangover. Had to be. And I was definitely dehydrated now. Still, did it matter whose bed this was when it was this comfortable? Maybe I could stay here forever. The pull of sleep was tempting, and I moved to roll onto my side.

"Hey! I was sleeping there," a masculine voice protested.

I shot upright, my head spinning from the sudden movement. Everything lurched, the world tilting sideways as I fought against the vertigo. I squeezed my eyes shut, willing my equilibrium to return.

"Always the moment he walks out. I called it. Told him it would happen," that same voice grumbled.

My breath caught as I turned. He sounded like Ryan Reynolds, but I couldn't be so lucky. He wasn't even a man. A massive cat lounged across my legs, his head tilted slightly, one ear twitching as he studied me. What kind of cat was that big? A Maine Coon, maybe? His black and silvery white fur seemed to ombre from his neck down. His mane was fluffy and white, framing a black feline face with orange-golden eyes.

There was no way. Maybe someone spiked my drink with something. That would explain the voice—

"Fine, I guess I'll just handle everything myself. Like always." He sighed, lifting a paw to his face and licking it with lazy precision.

I froze. The voice was *definitely* the cat.

What the *what*? Where was I? Fucking Wonderland?

I panicked. My gaze darted wildly around the room, taking in the fireplace, the reading nook, the massive bed draped in fur-lined blankets. The wooden posters were intricately carved, familiar in a way I couldn't place, though none of this was truly recognizable.

It was too weird. Too much.

I looked down, my breath catching as images from last night began piecing themselves together. The ball. The chase. The fountain. The prince. I had gone home, started packing, and then... Sadie. I texted my sister. But that message—it had been interrupted by a voice.

Not just any voice. *The* voice. The one I would recognize anywhere.

My hand flew to my lips.

No. *No. He didn't*—

A door slammed, but it wasn't in this room. A quarrel filtered into the room with jarring clarity, and a female voice rose in righteous indignation.

"Vareck! What are you doing? Why is—"

Whatever miniscule hope I still had that this was just a random one-night stand vanished like smoke in the wind.

"Is that any way to greet your king?" another woman said. Her tone was deeper. Less pitchy. Definitely chastising.

There was a short pause.

"Apologies," the first woman said stiffly. "*Your Majesty,* my son is still missing—"

"We're working on it," the second female said. I didn't get the impression she cared for the first woman much. "Guards are sweeping Seattle's Arcane District as we speak." Gods. My family. Were they safe? The Arcane District was my home. It was the supernatural equivalent of Little Italy or Chinatown. Most major cities had a version of it, but the one I lived in was the very first of its kind.

"Working on it? It's been over thirty-six hours!"

I gasped in shock. Holy shit. I was out for that long?

"And you have the abductor in your rooms! Why isn't she in the dungeons?"

Suddenly I understood the disdain. I wasn't one to make snap judgements, but something told me I'd be in a world of pain if the first woman had her way.

"Eleanor," Vareck said, deep voice rumbling. Goosebumps broke over my arms, and it wasn't because I was cold. "I'm handling it."

"But—"

"Are you questioning me?"

A short pause followed. "N-no . . ."

"Kaia, please escort the lady back to her quarters. We can continue this conversation when you return."

"I can walk myself—"

"Of course, my king." A note of amusement touched her tone. "Lady Eleanor."

A loud feminine harrumph sounded before someone stomped away. A few seconds later, the silver door handle turned. My attention snapped back to the predicament I found myself in.

Frantic, I kicked at the blankets, trying to free myself from the tangled mess of fur and fabric. The weight lifted from my legs as I swung one over the side of the bed, but before I could fully escape, my other foot caught on the cover.

I tumbled off the bed with a heavy thud, groaning as I landed in a heap on the floor. My dress had hiked up over my hips, and the blanket still clung stubbornly to one of my legs.

"She is beauty, she is grace," the cat drawled as the door closed. A lock clicked into place, making my heartbeat thrum like a hummingbird's wings.

The memories of last night rushed forward—his words binding me, demanding my compliance. Fear and fury crashed through me in equal measure. I pushed myself upright, scrambling backward until my back hit the wall.

I dug my heel into the carpet and shoved backward, kicking at the tangled blanket in a desperate attempt to free myself. I thrashed, wild and unrelenting, my breath coming in sharp pants—

"Meera?" The soft rumble of his voice made my chin snap up.

Dark brows knit together in concern. He had both hands lifted in a sign of surrender, but I don't know why. He wasn't the one in danger. I noticed a tattoo on one hand with deep red lines that twisted around his wrist and formed a sword in his palm.

Instead of approaching, he knelt at the other end of the bed, putting us near eye level.

"Where . . . where am I?" My voice was hoarse, every note grating.

"Where do you think?" He arched an eyebrow, as if challenging me to answer my own question. I swallowed, but it hurt, my throat was too dry.

"Faerie."

Vareck nodded. "We're at the castle."

"This," I swept my eyes over the room. "This is your bedroom?"

He hesitated for a moment before inclining his chin once more. "It is."

"Why did you bring me here?"

"Why do you think?" he asked in return. I scrunched my nose in annoyance.

"You can't just answer every question I ask with a question."

His full lips twisted, like he was fighting a smile.

"I can't?"

"Ugh!" I threw my head back without thinking. Stone met the back of my head, and I groaned in pain. Something suspiciously like a laugh sounded from the bed. Probably the damn cat.

"Don't do that."

"Do what? Hurt myself? Wasn't trying to," I muttered, rubbing at sore spot.

Vareck shook his head. In amazement? Confusion? Disbelief? Let's be real, it was probably all the above.

"You're not what I expected," he said slowly.

I snorted. "I hope that's a compliment."

His lips pulled up into a grin. "It is."

We stared at one another and the tension pulled taut. Warmth ran through my veins. My breath hitched. Vareck cocked his head, definitely hearing that sound. His pupils dilated, eating up the icy blue.

I cleared my throat, breaking the spell.

"Why did you bring me here?" I asked again, harder this time. I tried to reach for a thread of compulsion but failed miserably when a slight wave of nausea washed through me.

Vareck must have noticed what I was attempting because he lifted a brow once more. Still, he didn't comment on it. "Here being the castle or . . .?"

"Yes."

Vareck sighed, moving to sit on the floor as well. He bent one leg and extended the other. His elbow propped up on his knee. For such a large man he moved silently.

"How much do you remember?"

"You must heal fast, given the cut I gave you didn't scar," I replied. It was true. Where his cheekbone had split, there was only smooth unblemished skin now. Vareck chuckled.

"So you remember enough, then." He inclined his head. "After you threw the dagger you collapsed, leaving me with two choices. Either I stayed in the human world and waited for you to wake, or we returned to Faerie. As you can see, I chose the latter."

I huffed a humorless laugh. "Returned to Faerie? That's a nice way to say kidnapped."

This time both his brows lifted. "You really want to accuse someone of kidnapping right now?"

I pressed my lips together. He had a point.

"Why here specifically?" I said, changing course. "Surely there are enough rooms in the palace that you didn't have to bring me to *yours*." Another laugh sounded from the bed, and it was definitely the cat.

Vareck smirked, ignoring the feline. "That's what's bothering you?"

"I never said it bothered me."

"You didn't need to," he replied. I waited for him to continue, but Vareck seemed content with his non-answer.

"So—" A quiet knock at the door interrupted me.

"Vareck?" I recognized the voice as the second woman from earlier. The one called Kaia.

"Come in," he answered, still speaking in that quietly confident tone.

The door opened and closed once more. Footsteps sounded, then a woman came into view. I eyed her warily, recognizing her instantly. She had been standing beside him at the masquerade.

"Meera, this is Kaia, the commander of the Royal Army."

Neither of us spoke.

A smirk curled up one side of Kaia's full mouth. "Nice to meet you, dream girl."

My eyes flashed to Vareck's, and he looked away, as if embarrassed.

"I wish I could say the same," I replied after a beat. "Are you here to torture me?"

Vareck's head snapped up while Kaia merely snorted.

"No," he insisted.

My eyebrows drew together in confusion. "But the prince . . ."

"Vareck, can I have a word with you?" Kaia said.

He hesitated, his face unreadable when he looked me over. I'm not sure what he found there, but with a heavy sigh he got to his feet. They disappeared from view then exited the room. Muffled voices sounded from the corridor a moment later, letting me know they hadn't truly left.

I slowly got to my feet, intending to listen at the door so I could hear what they were talking about. Instead, my head swam the moment I stood. I rested a hand against the wall to steady myself.

"He won't hurt you."

"Huh?" I turned, remembering the talking cat was still here. His tangerine eyes watched me with interest.

"Vareck. He's got a reputation for being ruthless, but he won't hurt you."

I stumbled away from the wall. "I kidnapped his nephew."

The cat chuckled. "Yeah. Most entertaining thing to happen in a decade if you ask me. Eleanor is in a tiff. Damon will be fine, though. Probably." He didn't sound very concerned. I suppose that was to be expected. He was a cat, after all.

"What makes you so sure he won't hurt me?" I asked, glancing around for a glass of water to soothe my parched throat. No such luck.

"You're his mate."

I froze. Ice spread throughout my veins in fear.

"You're high on catnip. Mates don't exist anymore."

"Oh they exist," the cat said. "No one can *feel* the bonds because of the curse—but not even that could stop them from existing." He stood up, arching his back in a stretch.

I was at a loss for words. I was arguing semantics with a talking animal. Instead, I moved toward the window. Based on the lack of scenery around us, I could only assume we weren't on the first floor, but I wasn't sure how high up we were.

Peering over the edge, a pang of disappointment hit me. We had to be two, maybe three stories above a sloped roof. Too high to jump.

The cat insisted Vareck wouldn't hurt me, but I couldn't pin all my hopes on that. I'd heard the woman from the hall. Damon's mother. Eleanor. He'd been gone for a day and a half already. Eventually Vareck would have to do something if he didn't get information out of me, and the truth was, he couldn't. I was bound by the terms of the contract.

Something brushed up against my legs, making me jump. I glanced down to see the cat winding his way between them.

"What are you doing?"

"What's it look like? I'm sucking up on the off chance you'll take pity and feed me."

I opened my mouth to respond when the bedroom door suddenly opened again. My body jerked, arms flailing.

The cat between my legs merely purred as I fell backwards.

Glass shattered. Then I was falling.

CHAPTER 11

VARECK

"Oops." Corvo sat, staring at the spot where Meera had been standing.

My heart jumped into my throat, feet moving before I could even process what was happening. Grabbing the windowsill, I leaned over the edge.

Skid marks marred the smooth layer of snow, leading off the roof. I couldn't see over the edge. Panic gripped me.

I turned on my heel and ran.

The hallways passed by in a blur. Time seemed to skip as I got to the first floor. "Out of the way!" I shouted, as servants and nobles stood immobile in the hallways, watching me with curiosity.

I had to get to her. I had to—

The entryway doors burst open. Cold air pricked at my skin. I embraced the clarity, turning for the section of the grounds she would have fallen. Blood roared in my ears with every step I took.

What if . . .

No. I couldn't afford to think that way.

I turned the corner and nearly faltered.

In a windblown snowbank, Meera lay on her side, unconscious, her arms and dress dusted with snow. I collapsed beside her, my fingers going to her pulse.

My chest eased a fraction at the steady thrum.

Slowly I turned her body onto her back, searching for any visible wounds. A quick cursory glance didn't find any, apart from the smattering of bruises on her left side. She must have landed sideways.

Not wanting to waste more time, I scooped her up into my arms and started back toward the castle doors. Kaia met me halfway.

"Is she . . ."

"Breathing. I didn't see blood, but there's no telling what kind of internal damage she could have suffered."

Fucking Corvo. If he hadn't been wrapped around her legs, she wouldn't have tripped. My familiar and I were going to have words.

The second we crossed the threshold, I shouted. "We need a healer!"

People scrambled to get out of my way this time, not needing to be told. We made it halfway up the stairs when a high-pitched voice made me pause. "Is that her? My son's abductor?"

"Deal with her," I told Kaia, not even turning to address my brother's widow. She was a constant thorn in my side, but I would lose my temper if she so much as laid a hand on Meera.

Whispers followed us up the first floor, only giving way to silence by the time we reached the fourth. I was most of the way to my room when a healer came jogging down the hall, trying to catch up to me.

"My King—"

"Room," I barked.

"Y-yes, of course," he murmured, moving swiftly to my side. I didn't spare him a glance as I passed through the open door to my bedroom. With as much care as I could muster, I placed Meera on the fur blankets.

"Fix her."

"Tell me what happened."

I pointed to the broken glass. "Fell out the window. Landed in a snowbank." I stepped to the side, giving him room, but not moving far. Something feral stirred in my chest, restless and violent. With clenched fists at my sides, I counted the seconds while he looked over her. His hands hovered over her body, a slight glow emitting from his palms.

"Well?" I prompted, trying and failing to not scare the healer. He lifted one of her eyelids gently and used a light to look at her pupils.

"No concussion. That snowbank must have saved her head." He brushed his hands over a mark on her head, then moved back to her abdomen. "I don't sense any internal damage or broken bones, but there's a spot I'm unsure about. I'll have to remove her dress to get a better—"

"Do it."

Too slow for my liking, the healer dug a pair of sheers out of his bag and started to part the luscious material covering her form. I averted my eyes, while keeping him in my periphery.

I didn't trust anyone with her. Not with the crusade Eleanor was waging. I refused to stare at her naked body. She had panicked enough already. The last thing she needed was to wake up and have me standing and watching.

"Just heavy bruising, Your Majesty," he said at last. "That was a serious tumble. The winds changing yesterday turned out to be a good thing, it would seem. Without that snowbank, this could have been a very different outcome. My recommendation is food and rest. Nothing too strenuous for the next couple of days. I'll prepare a tea that should speed up the healing process."

I released a tight breath I didn't realize I was holding. A knock at the door drew my attention. Kaia slipped in without waiting for my reply.

"Thank you," I told the healer as he let himself out.

"Where's her bag?" Kaia asked.

"Bathroom."

She nodded once and disappeared to get it. I moved to take a seat in the armchair, my gaze falling to the shattered glass window.

"I'm going to wipe her down, then dress her." Kaia called from the bathroom.

"Thank you," I repeated. "I would but . . ." I grimaced as she stepped out of the bathroom.

"Trying not to be a grade-A creeper?" she snickered.

"Something like that."

Kaia set a bowl with water on the end table beside Meera and started the process of cleaning her.

"Think Corvo did it on purpose?" she asked.

"Unlikely. He's just a dick—" As if summoned, the asshole appeared.

"You called?" he said with his usual air of annoyance.

"What the fuck were you thinking?" I snarled, getting to my feet. He watched me with disinterest, then started licking his paw.

"You're going to have to be more specific."

I nearly saw red. "Meera. You tripped her."

"I was trying to get her to feed me. It's not my fault she's a klutz."

"Not your—" I ran a hand through my hair, my fingers tangling in the unruly strands. "Corvo, she fell out a window."

"Riiiiight," he drawled. "About that. How are you feeling? Anything magical happen since? Maybe a bond, perhaps?"

I leveled him with a glare. "What are you going on about now?"

He narrowed his eyes at me, then seemed to shrug it off as he flopped down on the blanket beside Meera. "Apparently I'll have to up my game."

"Wait—did you trip her *on purpose*?" I damn near roared.

"Um. I wouldn't so much say on purpose—"

"Why?"

"Why what?"

"Why did you trip her?" I asked through gritted teeth.

"I didn't trip her, but if I did, it would have been for ..." Corvo cocked his head. "Research."

I ran a palm down my face. This. Fucking. Cat.

"Get out."

"Vareck, baby, we can talk about this—"

"Actually," Kaia interrupted. "Before you go, can you fix the window? It's freezing in here."

"What do I get out of it?"

"Corvo!" we both said at the same time.

The cat groaned. "Fiiiine. We're even after this."

"She fell four stories. You're lucky I'm not re-homing you."

Corvo snorted. "As if. Who would fix all your problems if I were gone?"

"Given you cause most of them, that's a sacrifice I am willing to make."

He rolled his eyes. They glowed brighter for a second and his tail flicked like the snap of fingers. The pieces of glass rose from the ground and floated back to the window, resealing as if nothing had happened.

"Let it be known, I am a merciful god," Corvo declared. Before either Kaia or I could respond, he disappeared again.

"I should get a dog," I grumbled under my breath.

Kaia chuckled. "He would be an all-out terror if you did that."

"And he isn't already?"

She inclined her head. "Fair. What was he going on about with bonds?"

"No idea." I collapsed back in the armchair just as Kaia finished dressing Meera.

"Hm," she hummed. "We have to talk about this." She waved her hand in front of her, motioning to the unconscious woman.

"I'm not sticking her in the dungeon."

Kaia snorted. "Yeah. I gathered as much. Problem is, Eleanor isn't just some snotty noble. Her family has a lot of power—and Damon is missing. Like it or not, we need to figure this out."

I sighed. "I'm aware. I already told you what she said when I found her. When she wakes up, we can question her some more, but I wouldn't pin his safety on it. I don't think she knows much."

"Perhaps." Kaia stepped back, putting her hands on her hips. "But we need to get ahead of this. If word gets out that the prince was kidnapped out of the castle, people will question you as a leader."

I shrugged. "Let them. If they can do a better job, they're welcome to take the crown."

Kaia groaned. "We've been over this. You can't just

hand over your seat of power. Besides, we have dream girl now. Damon aside, you have the chance to get to know her."

I blew out a breath. "Yeah, because that's going to be easy when I kidnapped her. I'm sure she'll be feeling really talkative."

"Guess you'll just have to woo her."

"You sound like Corvo." It was not a compliment.

"Even a broken clock is right twice a day," she replied sweetly.

I rolled my eyes. "We're going to run into a problem there. Right now, she's injured and dealing with burnout. That's only going to last a few days though. Then we'll be right back to where we were at the ball when she persuaded me *and* Damon at the same time."

Kaia twisted her mouth, crossing her arms over her chest. "You've got a point. We need something that can stop her from persuading while she's here."

"Do you know where to get something like that?" I hedged.

"No," she answered. "But I know someone who might."

"The exiled one you mentioned earlier?" She nodded. "See if you can find him. He might be able to help us with Damon too."

"Will do. If he has a solution for us, it won't come cheap." She flexed her jaw. "How do you want me to proceed?"

"I trust your judgement."

She nodded. "Very well, I'll let you know when I find something." She turned to leave and paused. "Good luck with dream girl. I know she means a lot to you. Try not to put your foot in your mouth."

A smile quirked on one side. "Thanks, Ki. I'll do my best."

Silence descended at her retreat. I waited for a suspended moment to see if Meera would say anything.

Her breathing had changed while Kaia and I spoke. I didn't mention it because if she wanted to pretend to sleep while listening in, I'd let her. Now that it was just us though

. . .

"I know you're awake."

CHAPTER 12
MEERA

Falling out a window was a new experience.

My eyes remained closed, and my head throbbed more than it had before, but the king was right. I'd been awake. Right around the time my dress was cut off, as a matter of fact. My eyes had shot open, but the healer wasn't paying attention to my face, and Vareck had the decency to have his back turned.

Still, I didn't know what to say. Everything had happened at an alarming pace. Kidnapped. Dream man. Tumbling through snow and hitting the ground with a sickening thud.

"How long are you going to pretend to be asleep?" he asked.

"Hadn't decided. Feels safer if I keep my eyes closed right now."

"You're not in any danger." I peeked an eye open and the look on my face said it all. He added, "Not anymore, I mean. Just stay away from windows."

I sighed, sitting up and resigned to the fact that

ignoring the situation wasn't going to make it go away. This was not a dream, and the bump on my head proved it. That and all my dreams of him were *nothing* like this.

"Can we start over?" he asked, standing with his arms crossed and leaning against the bedpost.

Scooting back in the bed, I leaned against the down pillows at my back and smoothed the covers over my legs, avoiding the weight of his stare. "I don't know what that means. I woke up in a different realm, taken by the king himself."

"How about we start with introductions? What's your name?" I squinted my eyes as I looked at him in disbelief, and he shook his head. "Sorry, I know it's Meera. What's the rest of it?"

"Why? So you can hunt down my family and bring them here? They had nothing to do with my actions. That's on me, and me alone." Crossing my arms, I held my chin high. I would never let my family take the fall for me.

"I'm not after your family." He sighed deeply. "I'm Vareck Einar, which you already know."

I stared at him pointedly. Of course, I knew. Did he think I was an idiot? This was like a first date hell I couldn't escape from.

"Look, I'm just trying to get to know you," he began. "We have a lot to talk about."

"Like you sending Kaia off to find something that will nullify my powers? Because I heard that too."

He waved me off, not reacting to the accusation. "I said that to give her something to do. She's more concerned about finding my nephew. But she was right. This gives us the chance to get to know each other."

"What if I don't want to talk to you?"

He looked down at the floor, nodding like he understood my hesitation. "Then I guess I'll talk and hope you listen."

That wasn't the response I was expecting. Not from a guy in general, and definitely not from the king. "You aren't going to just persuade me for answers?"

"I could, but I'd rather not, if I'm being honest."

I stared at him in silence, trying to figure out his angle. Briefly, I reached for my persuasion, quickly discovering two things. One, my magic felt far away from me. More so than it had earlier. The exhaustion was too much. Two, that tiny attempt made my head start to spin again. I was well and truly stuck here until I could get back to full strength. Until then, all I could do was have a conversation the old-fashioned way. "Why don't you want to use magic on me?"

He raised a brow, tilting his head as he looked on. "Because you already view me as your enemy—"

"I don't think you're my enemy," I interjected, feeling a little defensive, but I couldn't figure out why. Maybe it was because he had come to my rescue after falling out of a window.

He chuckled, moving away from the edge of the bed to sit in an armchair next to a small round table. It had a pitcher and wine goblet set on top. He leaned forward, casually placing his forearms on his thighs and clasping his hands. "Well, you don't exactly think of me as a friend right now either, do you?"

Okay. He had a point there too. I grumbled my agreement.

"Right. Well, friends don't persuade each other."

"So," I began slowly, carefully thinking about which words to use. "You want to . . . be my friend?" Weird to bring a friend to your bedroom, but okay. I'd roll with it.

"I think it's a decent place to start."

"By your reasoning, friends also don't kidnap each other and hold them captive," I pointed out.

"Not generally, though our situation is rather unorthodox. You kidnapped the prince." My entire body stiffened, and I looked away. "I have to ask about that. Where is my nephew?"

I shook my head, speaking softly. "I don't know."

"Meera—"

"Really." I met his gaze, trying to show him that I wasn't giving lip service. "I genuinely don't know. Compel me if you want. None of this was supposed to happen."

"I'm afraid I don't understand."

"I told you, I took a contract for a job. I don't know who hired me. I didn't know it was for a person. I thought it would be for an object. You know, like a map or a compass or a stone? I'm good at finding things." I glanced down, playing with the gray fur that lined the blanket. "Once I accept the contract, I'm bound to it. I don't know the details as to why, and I can't tell you where I took him or who hired me. Magic prevents it."

Vareck scrubbed his hands down his face, exhaling deeply while thinking about what I'd just told him. "If you're telling the truth, Eleanor is going to lose her shit," he muttered, rubbing his hands over his beard.

"I am telling the truth."

"Have you tried to use persuasion since you woke up?"

"No." The lie slipped out effortlessly before I had time to consider the question.

"You think I didn't feel it earlier when you tried?" He grabbed a goblet, taking a slow, deliberate drink, his smirk practically daring me to try again. My jaw dropped as he called me out, and I attempted to defend myself, but a jumbled mess of incoherent words came out before I barely managed to speak.

"I—" Sighing deeply, I pinched the bridge of my nose. "I don't know why I lied. Self-preservation, I suppose. Yes, I tried to use it. I can't, okay? It makes me nauseous right now. That's the truth, and so is what I said about Prince Damon." I paused, thinking more about the emotional side of things. "I don't blame Eleanor, you know. My mom would be beside herself too, and she'd put someone's head on a pike. Is Eleanor your sister?"

Vareck recoiled with a quick, curt shake of his head. "Gods, no. She's my late brother's wife. My sister was. . . she died a long time ago." There was a great deal of sorrow in his voice, but he did his best to mask it.

I apologized softly, looking away at the fireplace. The flames twisted and turned, hypnotizing me while I thought about how much I should tell him. "I don't kidnap people. If I'd known, I never would have taken the contract. I had planned to get him back." Even if it meant beating Lou with a stick. Crafty shit. If I ever got myself out of this, he was a dead man. I'd never take a job from him again.

"What was your plan?"

"I hadn't entirely formed one yet. Step one was going to a safe place. Step two was laying out the plan for his rescue. I never even crossed step one off my list. You know, because you showed up."

"He does have impeccable timing, doesn't he?" The cat pushed the door open somehow, slipping in through the small crack. His tail brushed against the door, curling around it as he walked by. "Vareck, I mean. Not the nephew."

The king groaned. "Go away, Corvo."

He sat, looking between us as he ignored the dismissal. "So tell me. What'd I miss?"

"It sounds like you were listening in on us already," I said as my stomach rumbled obnoxiously.

The king huffed a quiet laugh. "You're probably starving. I wanted to have food ready for you earlier. I just didn't know when you were going to wake up. Corvo, will you see to it that the attendants bring lunch for her?"

"Seriously? I just got back, V."

"Yes, seriously."

Corvo let out a long, exaggerated sigh. "All right. But not for you. For the girl. She's crazy; I like her." I watched as Corvo waddled lazily toward the door.

Vareck turned to me, a teasing glint in his ice-blue eyes. "Well, he hardly likes anyone. It seems you have a fan."

"Can't be too fond of me. He practically pushed me out the window," I said flatly.

"I can't push someone out the window, Meera."

"Fine. You tripped me out the window. Better?"

"All-mighty powerful god, to cat, to alleged assassin. I'm moving up in the world, baby," Corvo called over his shoulder as he trotted out of the room.

Vareck pinched the bridge of his nose, exhaling slowly. "Sorry about him. He can be a little . . . catty."

Corvo peered his head back inside, glaring up at him with his ears perked up. "I heard that, and you should be ashamed."

"*Corvo.*"

"Right, right; the food. Don't talk about me while I'm gone."

Vareck slowly turned his attention back to me. The silence was awkward. Everything was awkward. Memories from my dreams flashed in my mind, except now instead of the blurred or faceless man I could never remember, it was King Vareck staring at me while he touched my body. I shivered just thinking about how good his hands felt.

He cleared his throat, breaking me away from my thoughts. "You're . . . uh . . . cold. I can put more logs on the fire."

"Wait. You didn't answer before," I began, and he nodded, sitting back down. "But why did you bring me here? To your room. You could have brought me to the dungeons and asked me the same questions." I pressed, scooting forward on the bed and swinging my legs over the side.

For a moment, Vareck just stared at me, lips parted like he wanted to speak but couldn't. I took the opportunity to ask what was really on my mind.

"Does it have anything to do with . . . the dreams?" My voice was little more than a whisper by the end.

"If I say yes, are you going to freak out?"

"I—"

The door creaked and swung open, with Corvo leading the way, his fluffy tail pointed up, high and mighty. He jumped on the bed, sitting with his chest puffed out and proud.

A servant followed, pushing in a silver cart draped in a white cloth. Two trays sat on top, each with a large dome protecting the contents beneath it. Two goblets and a pitcher of what I assumed was fae wine were sent up for drinks. A pot of tea steamed next to a single teacup. For the final touch, a small vase with a glass lily decorated the corner. He positioned it on the table next to Vareck.

The kitchen courier left with the king's thanks, and we were soon alone again, except now we had the company of the cat, and I didn't feel comfortable returning to my previous inquiry.

Not that I had time to dwell on what to talk about. When Vareck took the lid off each dish, my mouth instantly watered. A hearty looking stew steamed, the scent of root vegetables and herbs filling my senses and increasing my hunger tenfold. The second plate had fresh bread, some cheese, and slices of yellow winter apples. My stomach rumbled again; angrily telling me to hurry the hell up and feed myself.

"Your lunch," Corvo said, pawing at my leg. I leaned away, still slightly scared of the talking cat. His ears twitched, my best guess is that it was a sign of annoyance. "What? I brought the peon who brought you food. That was nice of me."

"It was. But as you recall, you also tripped me, and *I fell out the window*," I reminded him. "Forgive me if I don't trust you."

He rolled his golden eyes. "I said 'oops,' didn't I?"

"I don't know, did you? I was too busy tumbling across a rooftop and falling into a snowbank."

"But did you die?"

"That's not the point."

"Are you sure? Seems like a good point to me." Corvo licked his paw, and Vareck shot him a look.

"He's harmless, really. Just an asshole," he said, running his hand behind his neck and digging his fingers into the muscle. He gestured to the food. "You should eat before it gets cold."

"He is right about that. Everything gets cold in this hell-hole," Corvo muttered, leaving his spot and curling up a chair in the reading nook.

"You trust him?" I asked, sliding off the edge of the bed

and sitting in an empty chair across from the table. The stew tasted as good as it smelled. Maybe better.

"He's my familiar," Vareck confessed, though he seemed reluctant at the admission. "Do you have one?"

"A cat?"

"A familiar."

"Oh. No. Thankful for it now too," I muttered, side-eyeing Corvo. "I guess that means you have a spirit affinity." Tracing the petals of the glass lily with admiration, I shivered as their icy nature sent a chill through me.

Vareck watched me carefully. "I do. Do you have an earth affinity?"

I cocked my head to the side. I thought it was pretty obvious that I wasn't high-fae. My compulsion magic was strong, but the rest of me was decidedly *not*. I loved my curves, but it wasn't a feature high fae had. Ever. "No, I'm only half high-fae. What made you think so?"

He gestured to the vase. "You seem partial to the glass lily. You admire it in a way the garden caretakers do too, and their element is earth."

I shrugged, continuing to eat. "I just like them. They're my favorite flowers. Don't get to see them much in the Arcane District. My mom gets them for me on my birthday, though. The one time a year she comes back to Faerie." The king looked surprised that I had shared that with him. To be honest, I was a little surprised I shared it too. It was an intimate detail of my life, and somehow, I'd let my guard down enough to say it.

"What's your other half?" he asked, and I looked at him in question for further explanation. "You said you were half high fae."

"Oh, that." I paused, tilting my head. "Redcap, maybe? I don't know. My parents adopted me, and I don't think about it much. I'm not as hot-headed as my sister and brothers are, so maybe not." I shrugged, using a hunk of warm bread to wipe the bowl clean when I was finished.

"You mentioned you're good at finding stuff," Vareck started. "Is that what you do for work?"

"You mean in addition to my side gig as kidnapper extraordinaire?" I teased, and I was pleased my joke elicited a smile from him. "I actually have a shop, although it's more of a hobby at this point." That much was true enough. The store was really a money pit.

"What kind of shop?"

"Antiques. I like old things. Used things. They tell a story." It's a shame I was the only one interested. Most people in the Arcane District weren't. I just couldn't bring myself to focus the contents of my store on magic items only. The idea broke my heart.

"Do you collect any?"

I teased my bottom lip between my teeth. "Vinyl records and antique jewelry."

"How'd you get into that?"

I lifted my shoulder in a half shrug. "My mom had an old jewelry box with pieces from her parents and great grandparents. Me and my sister used to play dress up with them. When I got older, I found myself gravitating towards pieces with the same kind of character. Before I knew it, I had my own little collection growing."

"You sound like you're close with your family," he said, dancing around the subject.

"The closest," I answered, swirling the fae wine around in my goblet. "My sister is my best friend and my brothers are, well kind of overbearing, but they mean well."

Vareck chuckled. "Most fae men are."

An inkling of that tension from earlier started to bleed

into the atmosphere. After a large swallow of my wine, I pushed it away.

"Try the tea. It might help." Vareck poured me a cup, and I took a sip. The silence was awkward, and he must have sensed my discomfort because he changed the subject. "Tell me more about you. Do you have any hobbies?"

I snorted. "Hard to have hobbies when you're broke, but I do enjoy reading." I didn't mention my preferred material was straight up smut.

He perked up slightly, showing interest. "I have a library in the castle. We could go there sometime."

"Is that a pickup line? 'We could go there sometime?'" I asked, trying to stifle my laughter. "You don't date much, do you?" His shoulders jostled as he chuckled to himself, then tilted his head back to stare at the ceiling.

"Clearly not."

"Well, I have. That was a pickup line, and it was bad."

Vareck's attention snapped back to me, his features a mixture of confusion and surprise, but the way his nostrils flared and his posture tightened had me on alert. His grip on his fork turned white knuckled and my breath hitched. He couldn't possibly be jealous, could he? My mouth went dry despite the tea. "I hadn't thought . . . are you"—he swallowed thickly—"with someone?"

I barked a laugh, taking a sip of my drink and thinking about my recent date with Axton at his *mother's house*. "Hardly."

The king forced a smile, muttering, "Good. That's good."

"Is it?"

"If he's going to woo you, then yes, it's obviously a good thing," Corvo said dryly.

I blushed, recalling Kaia had said something like that

when she was leaving. Too much had been going through my mind to focus on that at the time.

"Thanks, Corvo," Vareck said through a clenched jaw.

"Just trying to be helpful."

Vareck shook his head, muttering something that sounded suspiciously like "*damn cat*" under his breath.

"What about you?" I said slowly. "I know you said you don't have much experience dating, but is there someone else? A betrothed, perhaps? I know you royalty like to do that sort of thing . . ." My words trailed and heat rose in my cheeks.

Vareck lifted a spoonful of the stew to his mouth and chewed slowly. "Why? Wondering if there's competition?" He smirked.

I blanched, not expecting that response. "What? No. Noooo," I repeated. "I was just . . . making conversation."

He snorted. "Sure you were. Relax, Meera. There's no one else. There hasn't been since . . ." He cleared his throat. "There hasn't been in a long time."

"Good," the word managed to slip out before I could hold it back. If I was blushing before, my face was on fire now.

Vareck lifted an eyebrow. "Is it?" He repeated my own question back to me.

Freaking hell. Why had I said that? I wanted to disappear into the bushes like that gif of Homer Simpson. Unfortunately for me, invisibility was not one of my talents and there were no bushes to be found. "I . . . it remains to be seen."

Vareck grinned teasingly as he took another bite. We didn't speak for the rest of our meal. In fact, I didn't even look at him.

That didn't mean I didn't feel his gaze on me.

And if I was being honest with myself, I liked it.

But that couldn't be. I was his captive. He was my captor. This was just a result of my long dry spell and too many romance books.

Right?

CHAPTER 13
LUCIAN

Smoke curled around my lips as I sighed, leaning back into the plush cushions. The Witching Hour sure knew how to make a fae feel comfortable. On a regular day, The Black Lounge was my preferred place to operate—dark corners, whispered deals, and enough shadows to swallow a man whole. The underbelly of the human world was where a leprechaun like me flourished.

Creatures weren't ruled by royalty or class barriers here. No, necessity ran this world, and wouldn't you know it—I was the lead supplier. All hail the King. Ancient artifacts, cursed scrolls, copious amounts of illegal glamour—you name it, I could get it. My connections stretched out like a spiderweb, intricate and inescapable, weaving everyone together in owed favors and good fortune.

My fortune.

And I seemed to have it in spades.

Today was not a day for The Black Lounge, but tucked away at a corner table in the main club was just as important. Blend into the background for a while and you eventually go unnoticed. Just another patron, sipping whiskey with a friend. A man like me learned a lot by people-watching. Listening. Knowledge was power, and with a little luck, it paid me well.

I flicked open the pocket watch in my hand, huffing on my pipe before setting it down on the table. The ornate gold piece was hooked inside my jacket, one side enchanted to show the current weather and any reminders for the day. A small trinket I'd lifted from Meera's collection. She'd been quite cross with me last time, but I had expected it. My friend wasn't motivated by money, only her desperate need for it. As long as I kept her luck in check, I had nothing to fear. She'd always come back.

"It's about that time. Finish your drink." I turned to my bodyguard, tapping the ash from my pipe into the tray. Sliding a small box from my pocket, I flicked it open to reveal dried lavender and tobacco leaves. I shook my head as I packed the bowl. "I got places to be, Frank. Items to sell. Money to make." Tapping the pipe on the table, I offered it up to him. The orc just shook his head, draining the rest of his scotch on the rocks. I shrugged, searching for my lighter when an unfamiliar voice made its way to my ears, making me pause.

A woman—high fae by looks of her—was at the bar, talking to Amelia. An angel if I ever saw one. Tall and lovely, with beautiful black hair tied in intricate braids and flawless umber skin. With weapons strapped to her back, her armor marked her as military, but the golden royal seal above her breast and the bold stripes upon her shoulders marked her as more. She was a personal guard to the king, and she was the commander.

A deadly angel, it would seem.

"Now what do you suppose she's doing here?" I whispered to Frank while I patted down my pockets. When I came up empty, I snapped my fingers a few times until a spark flared to life. The lavender caught, curling inward as it burned.

Frank grunted, rubbing at one of his tusks. A man of few words.

The lady guard, however, wasn't. She and Amelia's conversation spanned several minutes, their voices lowered until Amelia laughed, nodding her head and holding out her hand. The guard tossed a pouch of coins on the counter and Amelia turned, then pointed at me with a wicked grin.

When the woman turned, deep purple eyes found me. There was a delicate softness there, in contrast to the hardness of her demeanor. And that uniform—aye, I had a type. I thought surely I was in love. She approached, staring at me with a hefty amount of skepticism, but something caught her tongue. She appraised me head to toe, as much as she could see, but when I lifted my head, the shadows moved away, giving her a peak at my face. Her luscious lips parted, and she cleared her throat, adjusting her posture.

"You're the leprechaun who can get me anything I need?" she asked, standing across from where I sat at my table.

"That's an interesting way to introduce yourself," I said, puffing on my pipe. I gestured to the empty chair.

Her jaw tightened. "Are you, or aren't you?"

"Depends on who's asking. You see, lass, I don't do business with strangers. It's gotten me in trouble a few times before." I angled my head toward her shoulder. "And those stripes there? They sure seem like something that could cause me a bit of trouble. So I say again, my answer depends on who's asking. Is it you, High Commander of the Royal Guard, King Vareck himself, or someone else?"

She raised her brows. "You know I'm High Commander?"

"I can read a military uniform, love."

It looked as if she wanted to smile, but she remained stoic. "Yet you aren't afraid of me."

I shrugged, knowing damn well Meera and Amelia wouldn't have ratted me out. The guard didn't know about my involvement with the prince. She wouldn't be alone if she did, and I'd have already been captured and dragged back to Faerie in chains. "What's there to be afraid of? I've done nothing wrong." I tapped some of the ash from my pipe. "If I had, you wouldn't be trying to chat me up. Isn't that right, Frank?"

He snorted in confirmation.

"Are you going to sit or not?" I asked, glancing at the chair in front of me.

The guard's gaze flitted between me and the orc at my side. "I'll stand, thank you."

"Suit yourself." I laughed, rubbing a finger under my nose. A smirk curled at my lips. "Something tells me you're not at home here, lass."

"I go where duty leads me," she replied.

"How noble. Well then, let's try again. I'm Lucian." I leaned across the table, holding out my hand.

She hesitated before taking it. "Kaia."

I pulled her in, pressing my lips to the back of her glove, inhaling her scent. "Leather finger tab on your dominant hand. We have an archer in our presence, Frank."

Her breath caught, and she yanked her hand away, glaring at me before regaining her composure. I suppressed the desire to laugh at her indignation.

"Well, Lady Kaia, what can I do for you?"

"For starters, I'm not a Lady. It's just Kaia. And the barkeep said your name was Lou."

"Lucian to my friends," I said with a wink. My eyes trailed down her form, admiring the nice curve to her hips, especially in that tight-fitting black leather armor. She stared at me flatly. My angel did not find me charming. Nothing like a challenge.

Kaia tilted her head, then took a deep breath, finally taking a seat in the chair across from me. "Amelia said you were the man I've been looking for. She said you could help me."

I poured her a small drink into my empty glass, nudging it across the table. "The witch has a pure heart for all the darkness that surrounds her. My biggest weakness, that. A beautiful woman. Never could say no to a pretty face."

"Mine or hers?" she asked, taking the whiskey in one gulp and slamming the glass down.

"Yes," I answered vaguely, and a smirk tugged at my lips. "What exactly are you looking for?"

"I'm on a bit of a dual mission to find a what and a who," she said, placing her hand on the table and drumming her fingers.

"I'm listening." She watched as I tapped out the tobacco ashes into the tray, setting the pipe down to cool off. I laced my fingers together, setting my hands in front of me.

"I need to find Prince Damon," she said softly, meeting my gaze.

I chuckled. "I doubt you need me for that. I'd reckon the prince is in a brothel in Faerie."

"Normally, I would agree with you." Kaia's lips pressed into a thin line. "But we know he was taken. Brought back to earth through the public portal."

"That's a unique situation." I kept my heartbeat steady. A leprechaun was skilled with a great many tricks and could read through them just the same. She wasn't fishing for what I knew. I wasn't even a suspect. She genuinely wanted my help. It could pose a problem, but nothing I couldn't handle. "If it's a prince I'm after, I hope your pockets are as deep as your status."

"They are."

"Well that answers the who. Now the 'what.'"

Kaia looked to her side, checking behind her. Amelia was cleaning and working behind the bar, and still no other patrons were in our vicinity.. Returning her attention to me, she lowered her voice further, stretching forward as if to tell me a juicy secret. "I need a potion, or an artifact."

"I know a great deal about both. What kind do you seek?"

The guard rubbed her fingers together in what looked like a nervous gesture before placing her hands in her lap. "Something that can cancel a high fae's powers—specifically persuasion. *Not* permanent, just long-term."

The right dark witch could make a potion—still hard to find—but an artifact that could cancel another's powers? Lucky for her, I already had what she desired. She needed more than something as simple as a ring of nullification. With a single prick from the gem's barbed prongs, it would cancel out another's power for about an hour. Perfect for shaking hands or a close encounter. But something like this? That was trickier. And thanks to a fiery ginger, it was in my possession, ready to be sold . . . For the right price.

I let out a low whistle, sitting back. "Do you hear that, Frank? A rare request indeed..." My bodyguard nodded silently while I watched Kaia intensely, having measured her every movement. The way she'd lowered her voice further. The motion of her hands and moving them under the table. When she spoke of the prince, her posture was professional. Rigid. All business. But this? This was important to her in a different way. The secretive request. The curve of her spine as she leaned in closer. A smile curled up my lips. This was the ticket I'd been waiting for.

"Does something like that exist?" she pressed.

I nodded, grabbing the bottle of whiskey and pouring myself another three fingers before taking a long sip. The heat of it traveled down my throat, and I exhaled harshly, breathing out the spicy burn. "It does."

"Can you acquire it?"

"Already have it, love."

"What is it?"

I smiled at her, admiring the shape of her mouth and the way her eyes focused on me. "A necklace."

She frowned. "Can I see it?"

I laughed, shaking my head, tracing my finger over the rim of the glass. "You're truly lovely, Lady Kaia, but you're out of your element, aren't you?"

She stiffened in response, her jaw clenching as she gritted her teeth, but she didn't deny it. "You said you hoped my pockets are deep, leprechaun—"

"Lucian," I interjected, smiling even though she was clearly irritated with me.

She hummed in annoyance. "I understand everything comes at a high price but explain to me how I'm just supposed to trust you. Better yet, just tell me why I should."

I shrugged. "Do or don't. There's a reason I'm in business and I'm still alive, Kaia, High Commander of the Royal Guard. Going around and making enemies by taking money and not completing my side of the bargain is bad for the brand, you see? I have what you need. The rest is up to you."

"That's . . . fair enough." Kaia twisted her lips. "What's the cost?"

"Simple. I want to return to Faerie."

She sighed, sitting back and crossing her arms. "I had a feeling you'd want your exile lifted."

This time, it was me who'd been caught off guard. "You knew?"

Kaia nodded. "It's my job to know. It's been about, what, twelve years since you were exiled?"

"Thirteen," I corrected, grazing my hands down the side of my short beard. I chuckled. "Such an ominous number, people seem to think. Not me. No, I find it rather lucky."

Kaia considered my request for a moment. "I'll look into having your exile lifted."

"Just look into it?" I frowned, tutting while I shook my head. "I guess I misunderstood your level of authority. C'mon, Frank. The city calls us." I proceeded to put my hands on the table, indicating I was going to get up and leave.

"Stop," she said firmly, her eyes narrowing before she inclined her chin once in agreement. "The price will be paid."

"That's a lass." I smirked, keeping my seat and holding my glass. "Midday tomorrow. Don't be late."

"There's still the matter of finding Prince Damon," she said, reaching over the table and taking the whiskey from my hand. I let her, slowly releasing my grip as she took it over. Her warm skin touched mine, and I swore at that moment I'd do anything for that to happen again. She took a long drink, exhaling through her nose.

A strong woman with soft eyes who could also drink whiskey? I was smitten.

"Which one do you want first? The necklace or the man?"

Kaia opened her mouth to speak, but stopped, taking a pause before she sighed. With some reluctance, she mumbled, "The necklace."

I rapped my knuckles on the table twice. "The necklace it is. We'll deal with the matter of the prince tomorrow." I got up in preparation to leave, but her voice stopped me.

"Tell me one thing." I raised my brows in question and nodded once for her to continue. "Why were you exiled?"

My bodyguard grumbled, and I chuckled, rubbing my chin. "Ah, love, that's the question, isn't it? I thought for sure you'd know that, seeing as you already knew I'd been kicked out of Faerie."

"That part was redacted," she said simply, though I could tell by the way her left eye twitched that it bothered her.

"Redacted?" That was interesting. I considered why it had been erased, and more importantly, by whom. Shaking my head to clear the thoughts, I answered. "Accused of stealing. Falsely, of course. They had nothing on me but speculation and the word of a thief."

A dead thief, now.

Kaia tilted her head, watching me carefully. "The king doesn't exile people for stealing, and he certainly doesn't exile them without proof. What exactly were you accused of stealing?"

I picked up the pipe and tucked it into my trench coat pocket before pulling out my calling card; a golden coin. Precariously balanced on my thumb, I flicked it into the air, the metal singing as it flew up in rapid twists before descending. Kaia caught it in her fist, never taking her eyes off me. I met her steely gaze when I answered. "An amulet."

It took a few seconds for the gravity of the stolen item to register for the High Commander. Kaia's brows rose, and she stared at me in shock, her lips parting. *"Amoret's* amulet? The Faerie Queen's amulet?"

"That's the one."

CHAPTER 14
VARECK

I leaned against the doorway, watching her.

Meera sat curled up in my overstuffed armchair, her legs tucked beneath her. Her wild ginger hair had been pulled into a bun, though several strands had already broken free, framing her face in loose curls. On the table in front of her was a cribbage set. She was playing against herself.

"Is this what you did all day?" I asked.

She jumped, her wide hazel eyes flying to me. "Jesus, you scared me."

I chuckled under my breath and lifted my hands in mock surrender.

"To answer your question—yes. It's not like there's much else to do in here."

A tiny sliver of guilt tugged at me. Given that I was the reason she was currently holed up in my bedroom, it wasn't unwarranted.

Meera pushed the table away and got to her feet, placing her hands on her hips. Whatever guilt I felt quickly dissolved when she scrunched her nose in an expression I think was meant to be annoyance—but only came across as adorable.

I stepped into the room and softly closed the door behind me. "We'll have to get you something for entertainment, then," I murmured. "Maybe some books."

Meera snorted but didn't elaborate as to why she considered it funny.

I went to the bathroom to start my evening routine, well aware of the beauty standing just outside the door. I swapped the fine fabrics of my everyday clothes for casual wool pants that hung low on my hips. After brushing my teeth, I splashed cold water on my face.

I was apprehensive about this next part more than I wanted to admit.

When I stepped back into the bedroom, Meera paused mid-pace. I watched as she swallowed hard, her eyes dragging over my bare chest before snapping back up to my face. My lips twisted into a smirk.

"See something you like, siren?"

She licked her bottom lip, clearly trying to come up with a response. "Siren?" she asked casually.

I shrugged. "You're beautiful and your compulsion is unusually strong. Seemed like it fit."

She bit the inside of her cheek, fighting a smile. "Is that another one of your pickup lines?"

I grinned. "That bad?"

She shook her head, smoothing a hand over her hair in a nervous fidget. Then her gaze flicked down to my pants. "Why are you dressed like that?" she asked, gesturing toward me.

"Your game of cribbage must have been riveting for you to not realize it's nearly midnight," I said dryly. "I don't know about you, but I'm going to bed." I pulled back the furs and blankets on the bed.

Meera froze, her eyes going round. "Here?" she spluttered.

I cocked a brow. "This is my bedroom."

Her mouth opened then closed as she tried for words. "But there's only one bed."

I fought a smile. "I hadn't realized."

Her eyes narrowed in indignation as she crossed her arms over her chest. "I just meant, where am I supposed to sleep? No need to be an asshole."

I chuckled. "In the bed, presumably."

Her face turned beet red. "I think that's inappropriate given the ... circumstances."

I stood up and crossed my arms over my chest, not missing the way her eyes briefly dropped at the movement. "I don't bite."

"That's—" she practically choked on the word. "That's not what I meant. Or said."

"It's what you implied. I'm not going to take advantage of you. I would think if I've proven anything since you've been here, it's that."

Her lips pressed into a flat line. "I'm suggesting it's inappropriate because the ... ya know ... the ..." She swallowed. I knew exactly what she was talking about, but I made no effort to say it. Meera had pretended that she didn't have the dreams and had continued in her refusal to acknowledge it. If she was going to use that as an excuse, then I was going to make her say it. But when I didn't say anything to help her finish her sentence, she threw her hands up in frustration. "Whatever. I'll just sleep on the floor."

"If you insist," I replied, still fighting a grin. She

stomped over to the bed in a huff, dragging one of the thick blankets and a pillow onto the floor. I slid under the covers as she attempted to make herself comfortable. With a snap of my fingers, the overhead lights turned off, plunging us into darkness.

Meera let out a hiss, twisting this way and that. Ninety seconds passed before she spoke.

"This stone is freezing. Why don't you have a rug in here?"

"You do know I have a cat, right?"

"And?"

I snorted. "You've clearly never owned one. Corvo would throw up his hairballs on it if I put any kind of rug in this room."

Hearing his name, Corvo popped into the bedroom and curled up in the armchair Meera had vacated. "He's right. I so would."

Another couple of minutes passed before Meera let out an exasperated sigh.

"I give up," she groaned, getting to her feet. She bundled the blanket up and tossed it on the bed, followed by the pillow.

"That was my face," I said, pushing the pillow away.

"Oops." She said it like she wasn't sorry at all.

I chuckled again as she took tentative steps toward the bed. I couldn't make out her expression in the dark but the light from the moon made it easy to see her form.

"Just to be clear," she started. "There will be no cuddles, no feeling each other up, no touching—period. Got it?"

I arched an eyebrow she couldn't see. "There's no need to be nervous, Meera. I've seen you drool all over my pillow when you passed out from burnout."

"That's not what this is about," she squeaked, her voice going all high and breathy with panic.

"Uh huh," I hummed. "I'm not going to instigate anything. Now get in the damn bed and go to sleep."

"Fine." She acquiesced, gingerly lifting the covers before she curled up under them—keeping as much space between us as possible. I grinned, biting back a laugh as she rolled over to give me her back.

At first her breathing was heavy and labored, but as the minutes ticked by it slowed. For all the fanfare, she fell asleep well before I did. Meera wasn't the only one feeling some sort of apprehension about this set up.

For years, I'd dreamed of her.

Now we were sleeping in the same bed.

Would I dream of her still?

The thought didn't bring me the same comfort it usually did, but with the scent of blood oranges in the air, sleep claimed me soon enough.

Soft hands smoothed up the planes of my chest. My eyes snapped open. Darkness still blanketed the room, but there was no missing the feminine form pressed against me as I lay on my side.

I froze, my body forgetting how to respond as she trailed one hand up my neck to thread through my hair. Her fingers curled in a tight, too familiar grip.

She pulled me closer while arching her back, her lips parted.

"Meera," I breathed, mouth dry.

She groaned at the sound of her name, her chest

brushing against me. The feel of her crop top against my skin was both a blessing and a disappointment.

She was sleeping.

Of course she was sleeping. Meera would never do this while awake. She'd made that perfectly clear.

I cursed under my breath as I tried to pull away. She wasn't having any of it.

"Vareck," she said softly, tugging on my hair again. When I didn't move, she shuffled upwards. Her lips met mine, hungry as they ever were.

I grabbed her waist, trying to push her back. Meera moaned, tossing her leg over my hip. Her sharp teeth bit down on my bottom lip, hard enough to make everything hazy. When her tongue tangled with mine, I forgot what I was supposed to be doing.

Fuck, she felt good.

Her body was soft and warm and everything I'd ever wanted in a woman. Like every curve was made just for me. It was harder than it should have been to stop this. I trailed my hand down her leg and wrapped my fingers around the back of her knee, gently removing it from my body.

Meera growled, turning my blood to fire.

Fuck me.

"You need to wake up," I said, trying to extricate myself from her kiss.

"I am," she groaned. Meera opened her eyes, revealing dilated pupils blown with lust. She released my hair, placing an open palm against my shoulder and pushing. I fell back against the bed, unable to think past the woman who tossed her leg back over me. She moved her hands to my chest, sitting up to straddle me.

All complaints died in my throat.

My muscles refused to work when she grasped the

bottom of her shirt and pulled it over her head. A lacy bra cupped her full breasts, her hard nipples visible through the sheer fabric.

Meera grabbed one of my hands and moved it to her chest. I palmed her, feeling the heaviness while my thumb brushed over her peaked nipple.

Her hips jerked, pressing into my already hard cock.

"Fuck, I need you to touch me," she whined.

Any restraint I had snapped.

I gripped her thigh with my free hand, fingers pressing into her supple flesh. My grip on her breast tightened as she continued to rock against my length. I leaned up and pulled at the lace of her bra, lowering it so I could take her nipple between my teeth. She hissed at the pain, but that sound turned into a whimper as I lapped at the mark I'd left. When I sucked on the rosy bud, she bucked again, her head thrown back in pleasure.

"I want to fuck you so bad," I rumbled against her damp skin. I lowered my hand to press into the apex between her thighs where the material of her leggings was already damp. "Are you going to let me?"

"Yes," she moaned.

I rolled us. Her back hit the mattress as my weight came down on her. I moved my hands to either side of her face, caging her in. "I want to hear you beg."

A tiny whine slipped free from her lips. I rolled my hips, pressing into her just once before I pulled away. My fingers hooked in the band of her leggings. I dragged them down with ease, taking her thong along with them. "*Please.*"

I chuckled, sliding off the bed. I grabbed her ankles and pulled her to the very edge before sinking down on my knees.

I tsked. "You can do better than that."

She tried to speak, but only gasped as I licked her from her opening to her clit. I traced the tip of my tongue in circles around her little nub, stimulating but only barely touching. Meera arched her hips. "Pleaseeeee," she moaned. "Fuck me."

"Better," I hummed, my breath fanning over her slick flesh.

Meera shivered, but I didn't think she was cold.

In fact, it felt like she was burning up. I wanted to burn with her.

Without dragging it out, I plunged my middle finger into her tight channel. She clenched at the intrusion. Her fingernails scraped my scalp as she fisted my hair and tried to pull me closer. I gave in, lowering my head once more to suck her clit between my lips.

Her hips jerked again. "Yes, yes, yes!" She chanted, thrashing back and forward as I moved my finger in and out. "More. I need more."

"Greedy little thing." I pushed a second finger in her.

Meera climbed high, but just before she could find her release, I stopped. A sob left her throat. Her grip on my hair turned borderline painful.

I blew on her clit, then waited for her to come down before starting the process all over again.

Then again.

By the fourth time she was a sweaty, writhing mess. Just the way I liked her.

"Vareck, please," she begged.

"What do you want?"

"You."

I bit back my grin. "What do you want me to do?"

Meera groaned in frustration. "Fuck me. *Now*." She tacked on the end, her full lips pouting.

I got to my feet and removed my pants. My cock thickened, impossibly harder under her hooded gaze. Meera licked her lips.

"Scoot up the bed," I told her. For all her brattiness otherwise, this version of her, the one I knew all too well, listened beautifully.

She spread her legs wide without having to be told. Even in the low light, the wetness between her thighs glistened. I stroked my cock once before climbing up after her. Instead of crowding her body with my own, I lifted her hips to meet mine.

"Are you protected?" I ran my length through her slick heat, making her shiver.

"Y—yes," she stuttered out.

I notched my head in her entrance, pushing in the slightest bit. "Good." Then I filled her with a single thrust.

My teeth pressed together, threatening to crack. Godsdamn was she tight. She gripped me perfectly as I slowly pulled out then pushed back in. I took things slowly at first, using my hold on her lower half to guide her body up and down my shaft.

Meera wrapped her legs around me, her heels pressing into my lower back.

"Faster," she demanded.

"No," I replied through gritted teeth.

"Vareck—" she all but whined.

"I've been dreaming of you for fucking years. I'm going to take all the time I want to get acquainted with this body and you're going to be a good girl and take it."

Her pussy rippled around me as she tried, and failed, to find her release. I pulled out until only the tip remained in her before thrusting deep. Meera's labored breaths grew strained. Her legs trembled. Instinctively, I knew she was approaching a climax, no matter how slow I decided to take her.

"I—" she started. A beautiful flush crept up her soft, pale skin. "I need—" Her back bowed. "*Please.*"

"Shhh. I know what you need." I slid one hand across her hip bone, my fingers barely more than a caress as I circled her clit. Her body shook as she neared the edge. Her muscles twitched, squeezing the ever-loving fuck out of my—

I jerked, eyes flying open.

My heart was a riot in my chest, but there was no mistaking it. I was awake this time. For real.

Still on my side, my arm was wrapped around Meera's waist. She was pressed against me like a second skin, head cushioned by my arm. I rolled to my back, slowly disentangling myself. Unlike dream-Meera, this one didn't wake up and try to have her way with me.

I scrubbed a hand over my face. Gods, I was an idiot.

Too warm to relax and still hard as a rock, I climbed out of bed silently. Usually when my dreams ended, I would take care of business in the shower before going on with my day. This time, that felt . . . I shook my head. Everything was a mess, especially my thoughts.

I sighed, collapsing in the armchair. This was a problem.

A quiet moan sounded from the bed.

My eyes sought her before I could think better of it. Meera had moved to her back after having kicked off the blankets. Her thighs rubbed together, seeking friction.

The scent of arousal permeated the air.

I swallowed, fingers wrapping around the armrests in a white knuckled grip.

This was a new form of torture, having her right there

and yet so far. My iron clad resolve began to fracture when she whimpered in her sleep. Her brows puckered, like something was bothering her. One tiny hand slid across her belly, dipping beneath her leggings.

I bit my lip and tasted iron. Godsdamn it. I needed to wake her up. This was wrong. Right? And yet, I couldn't help but wonder if that embarrassment would be worse.

Meera rolled her hips. Her lips were parted, unintelligible sounds coming from them like the sweetest fucking music to my ears.

The wood cracked beneath my fingers. I flinched at the sound and Meera fell silent. Shit. I needed to leave. Even if I couldn't bring myself to wake her, I shouldn't be here.

I got to my feet then froze at the sound of my name. "Vareck?" Her voice was husky, like we'd done a lot more than sleep. "Why are you over th—" Her eyes flashed as they dropped down to my pants, seeing the very reason I needed to walk out. I could tell the moment it clicked. The sharp intake of breath only confirmed it.

Meera swallowed hard, looking away. I saved us from the awkwardness of addressing what we both knew. "I'm going to take a cold shower."

"I didn't know," she blurted out. I paused in front of the bathroom door.

"Didn't know what?" I turned, crossing my arms over my chest. I couldn't put my finger on it, but her continued denial was getting under my skin. It wasn't just because she was lying, but for the life of me I couldn't tell why.

Meera swallowed, still not looking at me. "That you were real. I just thought . . ." She didn't continue.

"That they were sex dreams," I finished for her. Meera dipped her chin in the tiniest nod as a deep blush spread across her face. "How long have you had them?"

I knew what I experienced, and it seemed like we were existing in the same dream, but nothing about this made sense.

Meera hesitated. "They started a few years ago. After the first time I visited Faerie." She slowly lifted her eyes to meet mine. "You?"

I nodded. "Four years ago. They were on and off the first year . . ." I trailed off, seeing what she would say.

"Then it was almost every night," she muttered.

Despite my raging hard on, I wasn't cutting this conversation with her short. Not when she was finally willing to talk. I retook my seat in the armchair, put a pillow on my lap, and rested my elbows on my knees, fingers clasped together.

"And it never occurred to you that I might be real?" I tried to keep the accusation out of my tone. On a logical level, I knew it wasn't fair to hold it against her. Hell, everyone assumed I was crazy for the last couple of years. Even my own familiar. Yet, I couldn't help the slight frustration that was there.

She narrowed her eyes. "You do realize that people have dreams all the time, and it doesn't make them real?"

I lifted an eyebrow. "Do you realize how unlikely it is to dream of someone you've never met for *years*? Always the same person. Always the same face."

"I never saw your face when I dreamed of you, but your voice was always the same. I thought I made you up," she argued defensively.

A thought occurred to me. "How old are you?"

"What?" Her brow puckered in confusion. "What's that got to do with anything?"

I sighed. This woman. She was going to drive me

insane. "I'm fifty-eight. I've been around long enough to know that this isn't normal."

"I'm twenty-five," she answered quietly. I nodded, suspecting as much. She was old enough to think it was odd, but not enough to realize just how much.

"Have you even gone through the passage?" I asked, referring to the time in a fae's life when immortality kicked in. Until that point, we aged just like humans. For most fae, it was around thirty. Some were younger, but I had a suspicion that wasn't the case here.

Meera confirmed it with a shake of her head. "I don't even know if I will. Only part high fae, remember?" I had no doubt in my mind she would. If she were this powerful before the passage, she would be a force to be reckoned with across the nine realms after. Something told me she didn't want to hear that.

"Small fae do too."

"I don't know if I'm small fae," she replied. "I only know I've got some high fae because I have persuasion. I might not even be half. I might be half human for all I know. It honestly wouldn't surprise me. I don't have any other characteristics. I can lie. I can't glamour. I don't—" Her mouth snapped shut, as if she just realized how much she was revealing. Meera's gaze narrowed again.

"I haven't compelled you since I brought you here," I reminded her. "You would know if I had."

"I still don't understand why not." She didn't sound bitter, only confused.

I shrugged. "I told you, I'd rather get to know you. I'm not going to force you to tell me anything."

"Outside of Damon?"

My shoulders dropped. "The situation with him . . . it complicates things."

"That's one way of putting it." Meera snorted. "I really was going to find him and bring him back. That was my plan before I even apprehended him, but then I saw you and everything went to hell in a handbasket."

"You were going to find him, yet you don't know where he is," I said slowly. While she admitted she could lie, I had compelled her to tell me his location when we were in her apartment. This didn't add up.

"I–" She broke off, biting her lower lip. I could tell she was debating something. I waited, giving her the chance to work through it. She took a couple minutes before finally saying, "I have an ability that lets me find things."

"Things?"

"Anything," she corrected. "I assumed it was just objects but then I got the job to take the prince. Turns out it works for that too. I was planning to complete the contract, then turn around and find him again."

"You told me you wouldn't have accepted the job if you'd known it was for a person. So why did you finish the job? Would they have been after you if you didn't?"

"Not exactly." She sighed. "I don't know how much I can tell you."

"That's not in the contract?"

She shook her head. "There isn't a fine print. It's magical. When I take a job, it activates. From that point I'm obligated to complete a job. I also can't talk about the job. That includes what I'm after, where I'm going, where the drop site is, who my broker is, or anything that could reveal another party involved."

"That still applies after the contract ends?" I asked. She dipped her chin. "Let's pretend this is the first time you were hired, when whoever it was approached you. I'm assuming they told you all this before you took it?" She nodded again. "Then tell me how it works. What you were told then, before you ever took a contract."

She pressed her lips together, tilting her head to the side. "That actually might work. Okay, so you asked why I completed the job. No one comes after me. To my understanding, the client hiring doesn't even know who I am. Only the broker. Once I accept, I have two choices: complete the job or become an indentured servant. Permanently. Doesn't matter what job it is, that's always the stipulation."

My brows shot for my hairline. "That's extreme," I said slowly. "Why would you ever accept one to begin with under those terms?"

Meera released a long breath. "Couple reasons. First, because I was broke, and I didn't want to borrow more money from my family. They would have done it, but I couldn't bring myself to ask if I had another option. They already supported my dream of owning an antique store, even though they didn't think it would support me. I can be stubborn sometimes . . ."

"You don't say?"

A slight smirk tugged at her lips. "I agreed when I was eighteen that I would give it three years to see if I could make it work. If it didn't, I'd look at getting another job. Well, at the three-year mark, I was only scraping by, but it was just barely enough to make ends meet, and I wasn't willing to let go. I didn't want to admit that 'enough' wasn't actually enough. So I told them everything was fine."

"But it wasn't," I said quietly.

Meera nodded. "I felt . . . feel like a failure." She lowered her head, picking at a loose thread on the blanket that didn't exist. Embarrassment heated her cheeks. "My contact heard through the grapevine I had a knack for finding things. Approached me right before I was going to be evicted if I didn't find money fast. The pay was enough to get me caught up. After that, the cycle just continued."

"Until Damon?"

"Yeah. After that I wasn't going to take another contract —even if it meant giving up on my dream. Stealing things from rich assholes is one thing, no offense. I'm not okay with ruining lives."

I tried to smother the grin on my face but failed miserably. "None taken. You said there were a couple reasons you took it."

"Right," she shifted her weight around to sit cross-legged on the bed. "I can find anything, even if it's in a different realm. I took the jobs because there was no real chance that I couldn't complete them."

"You still could have been caught," I pointed out.

Meera snorted. "I'm too good for that." She paused at the look on my face. "Or I was. As you experienced, I can usually persuade my way out of any problem."

"That I believe. I've never met a fae with persuasion as strong as yours."

She made a face. "Yeah right. I'm sure loads of people can."

I cocked my head. "You really don't realize how much of an anomaly you are, do you?" She shifted again, looking away. "I've only ever met two fae that could persuade me— and many have tried."

Her head snapped back. "Seriously?"

"Seriously. That you could hold both me *and* Damon at the same time?" I shook my head. "I don't know what you are, but I don't think it's human."

"I've wondered if I could be part witch. I don't know of a fae that can find things like I can."

I sat back in the armchair, lifting one leg to rest my

ankle on my knee, still keeping the pillow in place. "Do you have a mark?"

Her brows knit together in confusion. "A mark? Like a birthmark?"

"Sort of. You would know it if you had one. Witches are descendants of gods, or demons if you prefer to call them that. They're one and the same. Each god has a mark that is specific to them. Any witch born from their line could carry it."

"I've never heard that before."

I smiled, but this time it was sad. "It's not common knowledge. If a witch has a mark, they usually have remarkable powers, and they generally hide that brand. It can get them killed."

Her lips parted. "That's . . ." She shook her head, swallowing hard. "Why?"

"That mark makes a god vulnerable. If they find out a child has formed one, they put an end to it. If someone wanted to kill a god, they'd need to know their true name. And that's what that mark is: their true name."

Meera considered that, chewing on a hangnail. "If it's not common knowledge, how do you know about it? I mean you're the king, yeah, but I would think that out of everyone, powerful people like you are who they would especially want to hide it from."

I took a deep breath. The answer to her question had been a secret for a long time, but if I wanted Meera to trust me, I had to be willing to do the same.

"Because . . . my sister had one."

CHAPTER 15
MEERA

"Where are we going?" I side-eyed Vareck as we stepped onto the first floor of the palace. If he tried to take me to a set of stairs that led down to the dungeons, I would take my chances and run. I didn't care that I hadn't fully recovered from burnout or from my tumble out of the window.

"You'll see," he answered evasively.

I cocked an eyebrow. "You know that's not very encouraging given I'm a wanted woman, right?"

Vareck snorted. "If I wanted you locked up, you would be."

"And they say romance is dead."

He chuckled, the lines of his face softening. I wondered if he noticed the strange looks his court were throwing at us when they caught sight of me.

"Is that what's going on here?" he murmured, a twinkle lighting up his ice-blue eyes. "Am I romancing you?"

"You—I—shut up." I swatted his bicep when I saw a smirk crawling up his stupidly handsome face. My chest flushed with heat, creeping up my neck and onto my cheeks. "I'm a captive," I said, reminding us both of our reality.

His smirk dimmed, and part of me wanted to kick myself for saying something, but it was true. This wasn't a vacation. I wasn't here to get to know him or for him to court me. I was here because I kidnapped his nephew and then had the audacity to get caught.

We walked in silence for a few minutes, and not the comfortable kind. It was awkward, filled with unspoken truths and feelings that didn't belong. I barely noticed when we stopped outside a pair of double doors.

"This"—he opened the doors—"Is the royal library."

My lips parted.

The cylindrical room rose to a good four floors, every inch covered in white stone bookshelves. As cool as that was, it wasn't what stole my attention.

In the center of the library was a huge tree with white bark. The trunk had to be ten feet in diameter and the thick, heavy branches were easily wider than a person. They contorted with large, gnarled arms that swooped and stretched, reaching every side of the room with ease.

I stepped inside, my head tipping backward to take it all in.

"Is this . . ." I hesitated.

"The tree of life," Vareck answered. "When I was a boy it used to bloom with these long, hanging strings. The leaves on them each formed the infinity knot. Every strand was a different shade of yellow, orange, and red." There was no mistaking the sadness in his voice. "At night they would light up. Fae from all over the realm would travel to see it."

"What happened?" I was almost afraid to voice the question.

Vareck gave a bitter laugh. "My father. The curse. Eternal winter. Take your pick."

I pressed my lips together in understanding. With soft, shuffling steps I approached the great tree. The stone floors stopped a foot or so from it, giving way to a rich, dark soil.

I lifted my hand. "Can I...?"

Vareck nodded. "Go ahead."

My fingers brushed the white bark, half expecting it to crumble. Obviously that didn't happen, but given its fragile state, I exercised great care in how I touched it.

"Thank you for bringing me," I murmured as he stepped up to my side.

"This actually wasn't why."

I turned to face him, letting my hand drop. "What was then?"

Vareck swallowed, a nervous tell if I ever saw one. "You mentioned you liked reading. We have the most extensive collection in the realm right here."

I stared for too long. Vareck misread my silence and started to backtrack until I dissolved into an embarrassed chuckle.

"You—you thought—" Gods. I couldn't find the right words. It took a minute to gather my thoughts, and Vareck appeared wary. Definitely confused. I took pity on him and explained. "I read romance novels. Not . . . well, this." I motioned to the great library. There was no way my type of escapism existed in these walls. Not with how ancient this place was. Books written for women were decidedly modern—which Faerie was not.

"Oh."

I cracked a smile. "It was a kind gesture. Truly. There are books for everyone's taste. Mine just happen to be less . . . classic. Still. Thank you." I couldn't help the feeling that warmed my chest. Before either of us could say another word, a voice I recognized traveled through the open door, turning that feeling in my chest to ice-cold anger.

"So what's a pretty lass like you doing working for the fae king, eh?"

Immediately, my hackles rose. Kaia rolled her eyes, not deigning to answer him.

I knew I liked her.

"What is he doing here?" I nearly growled, crossing my arms over my chest.

Lou and Kaia drew to a stop just on the other side of the double doors. The leprechaun raised his hands in mock surrender that I didn't believe for a second.

"Mighty Meera," Lou said in greeting, ignoring my ire for him, as usual. "How is it that even in Faerie you still look like you stole clothes from a homeless person?"

I dropped my arms, looking down at myself. My mid-rise tapered jeans were cuffed at the ankles. I wore a plain black crop top with an unbuttoned black and red plaid flannel layered over it.

"It's called thrift store chic, you prick," I defended, recrossing my arms over my chest.

Lou snorted. "Sure it is."

"And who are you to crap on someone's life situation, hm? You don't know their stories, you judgmental asshole." There was a time when my family had nothing but the clothes on our backs. When we first came to earth's realm, we'd had to rely on the generosity of others. I was a baby when we arrived, so I don't remember it, but my parents never forgot. We all volunteered at soup kitchens to give back to the community that once helped us, and I refused to let him belittle anyone with his narrow-minded bullshit.

"I've only visited a few times recently, but crop tops are

coming back in style from what I can tell," Kaia said casually, as though she were reporting on the weather.

"Only visited the Arcane District to see me, is it?" he asked. "You should come for a longer visit. I could show you—"

Kaia scoffed, rolling her eyes.

"You know each other?"

I hadn't realized how quietly Vareck had been watching our interactions until he decided to speak. The gentleness and casual feeling we'd had before was long gone. In its place was something unreadable that I didn't recognize.

"You could say that," I grumbled. Lou merely grinned, neither confirming nor denying.

"Lucian has—"

"Lucian?" I questioned when Kaia said the name. "Since when do you go by Lucian?" I jutted my chin toward him, and Lou shrugged.

"I go by many names, lass."

"Spoken like a true criminal."

"Now, now," he tsked. "Haven't you heard? I'm turning over a new leaf."

I cackled like a witch on Halloween. "Since when?"

Lou waved a hand, twisting his fingers. A silver necklace appeared in it. "Since I have something His Majesty is keen on acquiring."

My heart dropped into my stomach.

No . . .

I whirled on Vareck. "Are you kidding me? You hired him?"

Vareck sighed, running a hand over his stubbled jaw. "Technically I didn't hire anyone. I sent Kaia to find a fae who might be able to help us."

I sniffed in indignation. "And that fae just happens to be this asshole?"

"Whatever history is between you, I promise I didn't know—" Vareck said.

I scoffed. "What's the necklace do?"

Vareck snapped his jaw shut.

Kaia didn't answer.

Silence settled in the air, filling me with apprehension. I knew the answer. They'd said it in front of me already.

"Right," I continued bitterly. "So much for 'I'm just keeping Kaia busy.' What a joke."

"Meera," Vareck started. "It's not like that."

"You're trying to render me powerless. Excuse me if I don't believe you."

He groaned in that rumbly voice of his and my lower abdomen tightened. Nope. Not going there right now.

"It's just a precaution. We can't have you persuading everyone the second you get your magic back."

My jaw tightened, teeth threatening to crack with the pressure. "So you're going to cut me off from my magic, making me basically human?"

"It's just until we find Prince Damon," Kaia interjected, trying to come to Vareck's aide.

I turned on her. "Oh really?" Then I pointed at Lou. "Why don't you ask him where Damon is?"

Both Vareck and Kaia whirled on Lou.

"I already agreed to help Lady Kaia once this business with the necklace is sorted," the leprechaun replied without missing a beat. I glowered.

"That is not what I meant."

"What did you mean?" Kaia asked.

"Yes, lass. What did you mean?" Lou asked mockingly.

Not that they knew it. He sounded serious, but the glimmer in his eye told me he was laughing on the inside.

Him and his damned contracts.

I couldn't out him as my employer, much as I'd have liked to.

"I'm going to kill you," I seethed.

"Promises, promises." He winked.

"All right." Kaia clapped her hands. "That's enough. Lucian, Lou, whatever your name is, give Vareck the necklace. Once we can verify it works, your banishment will be lifted."

I stepped back, my shoe sinking into the soil by the tree.

"I'm not letting you put that on me."

"Please don't make this harder than it needs to be," Vareck said quietly, taking the necklace from Lou.

I couldn't help it. I panicked. Reaching for my power, I nearly flinched as I called to it, feeling it struggle to fully surface. My eyes flashed green, glowing.

"*Break the necklace.*"

Vareck's hand closed in a fist. He lifted it over his head and—

"*Release him,*" Kaia commanded, and at this moment, she was far stronger than me.

My persuasion died quickly, leaving me light-headed and weak. My body shook. I tried to move away, but Vareck was faster.

"Forgive me," he said softly, words only meant for the two of us. "This is temporary. I promise."

I couldn't bring myself to speak as he slipped the chain over my head. All at once, a barrier slammed down, sucking the magic from my pores. My legs gave out, knees hitting the floor as I succumbed to the loss.

Vareck knelt beside me. I suspected he was speaking,

but I didn't hear it. My mind existed in a bubble, one that was void of sound, my soul crushing as reality settled in.

I was magicless.

Defenseless.

And at the mercy of the fucking fae king.

CHAPTER 16
VARECK

Days had passed since Meera locked herself in the bedroom, refusing to speak to me.

She claimed to not be as hot-headed as her redcap family, but the broken furniture, dishes, and vases in my room said otherwise. I wouldn't have been surprised if she had some redcap in her. A part of me expected her to be covered in blood each night when I snuck in there to sleep. I came in late, long after she'd fallen asleep, and I'd leave early, not willing to risk her ire.

That first day, she had screamed that she wanted space; to be left alone. I said the words no man should ever say. I told her she needed to calm down. The moment it slipped out, I realized my mistake. The wild rage in her eyes turned into a fury I'd never seen in a woman. Then a plate went flying at my head. Since then, I'd gone stir crazy trying to keep my distance. I dreamed of her every night, like usual. Except now they blended into reality. The dreams were so lifelike that I had trouble recognizing that I was asleep until I woke up. It didn't help that Meera knew my name now and would scream it every time she came in one of our dreams. On the third night, it had morphed and intensified, and a new hunger gnawed at me anytime I was away from her—the primal urge to break down the door and take her. The ways I longed to touch her, to make her mine, concerned me.

My study was where I spent most of my hours. I tried to focus on my work, scribbling away at documents, reading progress reports of my soldiers following trails in the Arcane District in an attempt to find Damon. They were all dead ends. The leprechaun kept his word, providing intel, but I didn't trust him. When I saw him with Kaia, I remembered exactly who he was. There was never proof he'd taken Amoret's amulet, but my gut said he did it. I still believed that.

Until we could figure out how to break Meera's contract and reveal who she worked for, all I had to go on was Lucian. Eleanor was breathing down my neck, and I wouldn't reveal the truth of it. At this point, I was concerned about Damon's wellbeing. He'd been gone almost a week, and there was no ransom. No message to get our attention.

My nephew was useless, a manchild with no sense of responsibility, but he was still my heir—not a great succession, but he was literally the only option. Basically I needed to not die.

I grunted as my quill snapped in my grip, ink blotting against the parchment. Damn it. Pushing away from my desk, I ran a hand through my hair, trying to shake off the restless energy that buzzed through me.

A weight landed on the corner of my desk, followed by a nudge against an open ink well. I barely caught the bottle before it tipped over.

"Must you?" I huffed, corking the ink and moving it out of Corvo's reach.

The demon cat stretched lazily, his ass up in the air, flicking his tail. "I must. You've got that thousand-yard stare again, V. I know your mind's running a million miles a minute—I can hear it *all*, you know." He sighed dramatically. "And frankly, I'm getting tired of how much you think about wanting to fu—"

I cut him off with a scratch beneath his chin. "You can also shut that connection off, furball. No need to listen."

"And deny myself the opportunity to goad you with it? Never."

"How in the world was I blessed with you as my demon guardian?" I muttered dryly.

Corvo purred, pleased with himself. "Hey, I do my best to keep things interesting."

"Please don't."

"What ails you, oh great fae king?"

"Oh, I don't know? I have a frigid, cursed kingdom. A smartass cat. Dead ends to a missing nephew." I flung a paper off the desk, and it floated to the floor. "Oh, and the woman of my dreams despises me."

"Boo-fucking-hoo. Whiny is not a good image for you. Where is the dark king? Ruthless lord of the land?"

"Make your point, Corvo."

"Look, you've tried talking to her, but she isn't going to listen. Maybe do the breaking down the door thing?" he suggested, settling into a loaf position. "Women like an alpha male, right? Like Drayden. Bang-bang on your chest and tell her she's yours."

"The thought has crossed my mind," I said, rubbing my temples with my elbows propped on my desk. "The likelihood of a chair flying at my face is usually how that scenario ends when I imagine it."

"Right? What is she? She *is* crazy strong for someone whose powers are nullified." He tilted his head the way he usually did when he was thinking. "Have you gotten her something? A gift? Women like things like that."

I arched a brow. "Since when are you an expert on women?"

"I observe. And I've decided the best advice comes from inexperience." He flicked his ear. "So? You gonna get her something or what?"

I leaned back in my chair, rubbing at the scruff of my beard. "I've been sending her books. I stopped sending flowers. The vases all ended up broken. I swear she dumped the glass lilies in the hallway and stomped on them."

Corvo's ear twitched. He looked wholly unimpressed.

"What?"

"You got her books. That's the best you can do?"

I flicked a wadded ball of parchment at him. "She likes books, and I got her the romance-kind she likes. I've been sending Lorne to the earth realm to get them."

"Did you read them?"

"No," I said quickly. "Why?"

Of course I read them. What else could I do with my time? The heat in the books was likely contributing to the increasingly intense desire to fuck her.

"You really are dense," he meowed, curling his tail around himself. "If she likes the books, maybe she likes what the guys in there do for romance."

Scenarios played out in my mind. I had a feeling if I told her to get down on her knees and crawl to me, I'd get kicked in the balls. What did some of those characters do? Killed an abuser. Tortured an enemy. There was some light stalking on occasion. We'd already done the whole kidnapping thing, and she didn't seem to be into it. What was actually considered romantic?

"Jewelry," I said suddenly, remembering a character that gifted a family heirloom to the woman he loved. "She told me she collects it."

"You already got her a necklace," he said with a feline cackle, and I glared at him. "It went over so well."

"Be helpful or I'm trading your tuna for some shit they feed cats in the earth realm."

He narrowed his eyes. "You wouldn't."

"Try me."

He hissed, swishing his tail sharply in annoyance, but he wisely—and reluctantly—chose to keep quiet.

Pushing myself back from the desk, I stood up, heading to the door.

"Where are you going?" he asked, sitting up.

"The family vault."

"You're going to get her jewelry from the family vault?" I turned, raising a brow in response to his tone. He chuckled. "Oh, wait until Eleanor sees her son's kidnapper wearing a family heirloom. She'll have a heart attack."

"We can only hope."

CHAPTER 17
MEERA

What could one do when locked in a room for days? Well, I'd spent the first two destroying things and crying, plotting the demise of a certain leprechaun. The necklace that had been forced on me? I knew all about it. I was the one who'd been paid to find it last year. I just didn't recognize it when I first saw it in the library. If that's not the consequences of my actions coming back to bite me in the ass, I don't know what is. Even though I knew what would happen, I still tried to take it off, hoping and praying that since I'd touched it before, it wouldn't hurt me. The burns on my hands proved that theory was wrong.

If I spent too much time focusing on my situation, the rage tears wanted to make a reappearance, and I was over the stuffy nose and swollen eyes. Besides a good long nap, the only thing that kept me sane was the company of a certain cat and reading romance novels.

Vareck was clearly trying to suck up to me. Flowers? What a generic, shitty gesture after binding my powers. Even though the lilies were downright beautiful, something as simplistic as a floral arrangement wasn't an apology. It was actually maddening that he could think something so shallow would win my affection or earn my forgiveness. Then he sent books. While it was still a shitty attempt, all things considered, he was at least sending me romance books. Stacks of them. I was devouring them like potato chips. Even though I was still pissed at him, the books did make for some interesting dreams. Weird how I could want to strangle him during the day, but each night my dreams were filled with him. Every delicious inch of him. An ache throbbed between my legs, and I squeezed them together.

Think about that damn leprechaun and how he did you dirty, I reminded myself. The thought of Lou, Lucian—the liar—sent ice through my veins and cooled any heat that had been building.

"Quit moving," Corvo mumbled, half asleep. His heavy weight pressed into my abdomen.

I groaned, trying to adjust my body and stretch. I had no idea how long I'd been asleep for, but now my bladder was full, and a fat cat was pressing on it. I had no reason to be tired. None. Physically I hadn't done much at all, minus some furniture tossing worthy of an Olympic medal. Emotionally, I was drained. The loss of my magic filled me with an exhaustion of hollowed sadness.

"Get up, Corvo, I have to pee."

He meowed in annoyance, a long and loud drawn-out sound, but he complied, and I ran to the bathroom. When I came out, he was curled up on the bed where I'd just been, hogging the warm spot.

"I have a question," I began, running my finger through my hair to comb it. "Why are you sleeping on me? That's the sixth time I've woken up and found you on top or curled up beside me."

"You were cold." He looked away, staring at the window when a small red bird landed on the sill.

"How did you know I was cold?"

He returned his golden eyes to me, giving me the most deadpanned look I'd ever seen on a cat. "You were shivering. Usually that indicates someone is cold. So I warmed you up."

"You're kind of an asshole ninety-nine percent of the time. Why are you being nice to me?"

"I like you. Don't tell Vareck." Corvo turned his paw upside down, nibbling on his nail and licking it afterward. "I'll deny it if he asks."

I huffed loudly. "I won't speak to him anyway, so you have nothing to worry about."

"You should know, I threw up in his shoes for you. You're welcome."

I chuckled, hoping Vareck stepped in it. Jackass. "Something tells me you like doing that for yourself, and not for my sake."

"Can't both be true at once?"

Laughing, I reached over and scratched Corvo behind the ear, and his eyes closed, pressing his head against my hand as he started to purr loudly. "You have the touch, Meera. Keep scratching my ear like this, and I'll trip him out the window for you too."

"I appreciate the gesture but maybe avoid the windows. Faerie needs a king. I wouldn't be sad if you shit in his shoes, though."

"I'll have a hairball for him later. Right on his favorite chair."

"Sounds perfect." I winked before asking, "What time is it?" I wished I hadn't broken the clock. I might have been able to get it working again had I not thrown it in the fireplace. Hope it wasn't important.

"Ooo, it's almost afternoon tea," he cooed, excitement in his voice.

I walked over to a crate that had been delivered the day before, and squatted down, balancing on my toes as I started sifting through the contents. It looked like an entire thrift store was in here, except everything was my size. He clearly had no idea how to go thrifting, or whoever it was he sent, so they just bought the lot, cleaned them all, and sent them to me. "You don't drink tea," I commented, pulling out a white turtleneck and an oversized, long black cardigan with deep pockets, holding them up to each other. What a killer find. Another pair of jeans, a black belt, and some black boots and this will look great. Leggings will have to go under the pants. It was simply too cold without them here.

"No, but I eat chicken, and they'll definitely send you some," he said, smacking his mouth and licking over his whiskers. He moved himself across the bed, closer to the edge as he observed me. "What in the nine realms did he send now? It looks like he robbed a rubbish bin."

I threw a shoe at him, and he ducked, though I purposefully didn't aim to hit. "Watch it, lord high-and-mighty. Thrifting is wonderful, and too many people don't appreciate it, looking down on it like it's some bad thing because it's not brand new. But let me tell you, cat, I have a seven-dollar cast iron pan that is better than any expensive name brand nonsense on the store shelves. It's a wonderful and cost-effective concept, and it lessens waste."

He tilted his head, considering me for a while. "You know, you could do a lot of good for Faerie."

I stopped sifting through the clothes, glancing at him for clarification. "Meaning?"

"When you're queen, of course."

I choked, causing me to bounce on my toes and then tip over with a thud. "You have some stash of catnip around here, don't you?"

"Of course I do, but that's beside the point."

Before I could argue with him any further, a knock at the door interrupted us. Normally, whoever was leaving something would knock and then leave. I usually waited for a while before opening it, just in case. This time was different. A familiar voice called my name from the other side.

"It's Kaia," Corvo said to me as if I couldn't tell. Then he turned in a circle and curled into a ball.

"I know that," I shot back, heading to the door and opening it just a fraction. I peeked through the sliver and raised a brow in question.

She was dressed in her royal blue uniform, leather armor layered on top as I would have expected. Did this woman ever take a day off? Her purple eyes softened when she saw me, and even though she was this badass High Commander, she smiled. I figured under different circumstances, we'd be friends. "I come bearing a gift," she said, holding a small box up so I could see it. "And I'm alone."

Swinging the rest of the door open, I let her in. I wanted to be mad at her. She was the one that found Lou. She was the one who procured this fucking necklace. Hell, it was her idea! Still, I was good at reading people, for the most part. I tended to go against my better judgement when it came to taking jobs from a certain trickster, but my instinct said Kaia was inherently good. Loyal. And honestly, there was a kindness in her eyes that couldn't be faked.

"I see you've redecorated," she said carefully, glancing around the room at the broken wreckage.

Crossing my arms, I shifted my weight to one leg. "Needed a woman's touch."

Corvo snickered, and Kaia frowned at him.

"His latest delivery, I presume?" She commented, gesturing to the crate of clothes. She assessed the sweatpants and sweatshirt I'd been in for two days before noticing the outfit I'd just picked out. "Looks like he made a good choice."

"Because he cares so deeply, right?" I turned around, heading back to the crate. Picking up the cardigan and turtleneck, I laid them out on the bed. "What do you want, Kaia?"

She stepped forward, her chin lifted slightly and her shoulders straight. "I thought about trying to talk some sense into you, but I see you aren't up for reason just yet."

I was completely taken aback, and my body stiffened, ready to verbally spare. "Excuse me? *Reason*? Because I don't find his gifts flattering? I was taken from my home, my magic was bound against my will, and I am being held captive. Please tell me how I should be acting right now, High Commander."

Kaia barked a laugh. "Oh, playing the innocent now, are we?" She shook her head. "Take some accountability, Meera."

My jaw dropped, and I pointed to the door. "You can see yourself out, Kaia."

"No." She took a step forward, the box still in hand. "Stop acting like a petulant child. Your current predicament is due to your actions. The king didn't take you captive for his own pleasure, so stop playing the victim. You came here and kidnapped the prince. What was he supposed to do?

Tell me. You have a sister, yes? Brothers? You'd go after them too." I inhaled sharply, caught off guard that she knew about my family. "You think I didn't research you the moment I found out who you are? You're smarter than that."

"This goes beyond Prince Damon," I argued, jutting my chin out.

"Of course it does, but the prince isn't a red herring. He's just the catalyst. The king has been looking for you for years, but only to know who you are. To find out if you were real. If Vareck had discovered your existence any other way, do you honestly think he would have just kidnapped you once he did?" She huffed humorlessly, shaking her head in disappointment. "The man has been obsessed with a dream for four long years. I can assure you; *this* was not how he expected it to go."

"He bound my magic. And it was your idea," I said through clenched teeth, my heart starting to pound with anger.

"I'd do it again. And you know what? If you were in my position, so would you." She tossed me the box, and I caught it before she continued. "You're incredibly strong, Meera. It's admirable, really. A good match for him. But the reality is you can't be trusted, and you know it. I won't have you persuading the king again. If you can't see how your choices led you here, I don't know what else to tell you other than to enjoy your self-imposed misery. Staying locked in here and bitching and moaning gets you nowhere. Frankly, it's tedious."

I wanted to blow up. I wanted to argue until I was blue in the face. The problem was, I didn't have a rebuttal. There was no defense. She was right. Every single stupid word was right.

"She's not lying, you know," Corvo added, jumping off the bed and coming to rub against my legs. "The Can Opener isn't really the kidnapping type. He's more like the guys in some of your books. Not the pastry kind. Like the other ones you like. The growly ones."

"Pastries?" Kaia and I asked in unison.

"Cinnamon rollies? I don't know what you called them."

I pressed my lips together in an attempt to suppress a smile while Kaia just looked confused. "Cinnamon rolls," I said, supplying him with the correct terminology.

"That's the one," he said, sitting down on his haunches and curling his tail around his body. He angled his head toward the stack of books and the crate of clothes. "Don't you find it interesting that you are still not in a prison cell? That he has allowed you to lock yourself in *his* rooms, safe, where a certain noble mother can't access or torture you?"

"Suddenly you're on his side?" I muttered.

"I'm on anyone's side that feeds me. I am particularly fond of you, though, and lying to you isn't going to get me extra scratches or your leftovers," he replied. "Remember that I'm also his familiar. I know him pretty well."

"I don't know what pastries have to do with anything, but Corvo makes a valid point, Meera," Kaia said, sighing, gesturing to the room. "You're being held in luxury, and believe me, he's getting heat for that."

"And he showers you with stuff," the cat added, walking over to the crate and jumping on top of the lid before pawing at it for effect. "Stuff that you like. That's how people worship gods. I would know."

Kaia rolled her eyes. "I think he means to say that Vareck isn't sending you mindless gifts. He's putting thought into it."

"He is," I admitted, glancing at my growing collection. I blew out a big breath, letting my body release some of the tension I'd been holding. "I'm sorry I snapped at you. You're . . . not wrong. About all of it."

"I know. Apology accepted," she said, and I could see in her eyes that she meant it. I'm not sure my outburst had even bothered her to begin with, at least not on a personal level. She looked at the box I was holding. "You should open that."

"Why didn't he leave it at the door?" I asked, pulling the string so it unraveled.

Kaia's gaze shot to the shards of a pitcher and a broken picture frame. "Guessing he wanted to make sure you didn't try to destroy this one."

When I lifted the lid, I saw why he'd be concerned about it. It was an antique hair comb, lined with rubies and diamonds that glittered as the light moved across them. I traced the outline of it in awe. "Where did he get this?"

"The family vault," Corvo and Kaia said at the same time.

My lips parted, and I blinked a few times, processing what I was holding in my hands. "I can . . . I can see why you brought it then."

"Meera," Kaia said, softening her posture slightly and lowering her tone from the chastising soldier she'd been earlier, "I say this as his friend, and nothing more. Just talk to him."

She inclined her chin, turning on her heel and heading to the door.

"Thank you," I said quickly, making sure to get it out before she left. I held up the box. "For this, yes, but for calling me out on my bullshit."

Kaia raised her brows in genuine surprise. "Not often I get thanked for that."

"Yeah, well, you haven't met my sister. Sadie is usually the one who calls me—or anyone else—out on our bullshit, and I needed that."

"Sounds like your sister and I would get along well."

"Scary thought, but probably true."

After Kaia left, I sat on the edge of the bed, staring at the family heirloom. It was *old*. At least two hundred years old, I'd guess, based on the design of the comb. While I collected antique jewelry, I certainly didn't have anything this old from Faerie. Most of what I found was from the human world, and even then, my oldest piece was Victorian.

"There's a note for you," Corvo said, breaking my train of inner thoughts. I looked under the comb, trying to see what he was talking about. "At the door."

There it was. A piece of parchment on the floor, having slipped through when I wasn't paying attention.

It was a formal request to have dinner with him, in what I assume was Vareck's handwriting as it was marked with his royal seal. "He's inviting me to dinner?"

"Are they serving tuna?" Corvo piped up, his whiskers twitching.

I pursed my lips at him. "You're worse than a hobbit."

"I don't know what that is, but if it likes food, we'll get along."

"You'd be a perfect match," I said in agreement, petting him absentmindedly. I thought about what Kaia and Corvo had said. While everything she said was right, there was something in particular that she'd pointed out that rang especially true. "I need to talk to him," I mumbled. "Before dinner."

"Then go talk to him."

"Pretty sure he's not on the other side of the door, eavesdropping. I don't know where he is."

Corvo looked away, staring blankly at the wall. His eyes glowed for a brief moment before returning to normal. "He's outside."

"How did you—"

"Familiar, remember?" He reached his front legs out, pulling his back up into a deep stretch. Claws emerged while he let out a little groan. "Get dressed. I'll lead you to him without Eleanor seeing you. And I have a surprise for you."

CHAPTER 18
MEERA

Wrapped in the warmth of the fur-lined cloak I hadn't seen since the night I had left with Prince Damon, I walked through a garden hedge of indigo snow dahlias.

Once Corvo led me outside, it was easy to follow Vareck's footsteps in the snow. Snowflakes fell in an unremarkable way, slowly coating the lands in a new layer of white. No storms or howling winds tore through Faerie. Other than the brutally cold temperature, the atmosphere felt calm.

A stone mausoleum had been built about two hundred yards from the castle. As I approached, the winter hedges came to an end, the ground opening up to a fenced graveyard. Headstones and sculptures lined the open grounds uniformly, and to the side of the crypt entrance, Vareck stood in front of two large feminine statues.

He kept his back to me as I cautiously approached. "Corvo mentioned you were coming."

"I don't want to interrupt . . ." I paused, and he turned to look at me over his shoulder. I angled my head at the statues, suddenly feeling like this was the worst idea. When Corvo said he was outside, he didn't mention *this*. Invading a personal time of respect and grief to make it about myself? That felt gross, and it wasn't my intent. "I should go."

He returned his attention to the women in front of him, not responding to what I had said. "This is my mother and sister," he said, holding his hand out to each one of them as though it were a true introduction. I took it as an indication he wanted me to stay, so I walked up beside him and admired the carved faces that looked down on us.

The taller statue had grand wings and soft eyes, small lips, and round cheeks. Her intricately braided hair draped over her shoulder and came down to a deep curve in her hourglass waist. Gentle hands looked as though they were conjuring a spell, but instead, a carved glass lily sat in one of her palms. There was a delicate nature to the way her features had been portrayed. The second statue was just a few inches shorter. She had no wings, and her features were stronger. Beautiful, but in a harsh way. Her hair was long and flowing in waves. It was the only soft thing about her. She'd been given high cheekbones and sharp eyes. Fuller lips curved into a smirk that likely held many secrets when she'd been alive. The names Lore and Maeve were etched beneath each figure, respectively.

"They were beautiful," I said quietly, clasping my hands together in front of me.

"Yes, they were," he agreed, the words barely audible.

I glanced to the left, wondering why they hadn't been buried in the family tomb. I hadn't noticed it when I initially arrived, but now that I was paying attention, new details stood out. The mausoleum doors had charred marks around the edges, traveling from the sides and marring the stone in what looked like black flames. The surname *Einar* had been carved above the entrance, each letter filled with a similar shadowy film.

"That's where my father is buried." Vareck's darkened tone startled me, and when I looked at him, a different man stood beside me. One I hadn't seen yet. His jaw was clenched, and his icy blue eyes were filled with unspoken hatred. "I burned his coffin and everything else on the inside. I haven't opened the door since that day."

Even having grown up in the human realm, I had been taught about his father. The Mad Fae King. He was the reason the land was cursed and the people suffered. The lands had once flourished, experiencing seasons and bountiful crops. Rumors spread about how it had all happened, and how he was killed, but my mother said no one knew what had actually happened or why he chose to curse the lands. The tales were only spoken in hushed whispers, and she would remind me that some secrets aren't meant to be told.

"I'm sorry." It was all I could say, and it was a weak consolation considering the kingdom was now Vareck's to govern. It was his people that endured the continued effects of that day.

"Why are you here, Meera?"

I flinched at his coldness. He didn't even look at me when he said my name, still focusing on his mother and sister.

"I . . . got your invitation." I said stupidly, wishing I could suck the words back in the moment they left my mouth.

He turned, raising a brow as he looked down at me. "Don't tell me you came all this way to tell me that?"

I sighed, shaking my head. I couldn't fault him for being distant. "No, Corvo said you were outside, and I didn't realize . . . now really isn't a good time. I didn't mean to intrude."

"Well, you're here now. What did you want to say?"

This wasn't going at all how I planned, in so much as you could call it planning. I took a deep breath and tried not to lose my nerve. "I came to say that I'm sorry. Not sorry like I just said a minute ago about this," I said, gesturing to the graves in front of us. "I meant I'm sorry for how I've been acting."

Vareck rubbed his gloved hands together, fighting against the cold, but he made no move to leave. "What brought this on?"

I hesitated. "Kaia ripped me a new one, and Corvo agreed with her. She made me see something about this that I wasn't willing to admit. So basically I decided to pull my head out of my ass and come talk to you."

Vareck huffed a small laugh, muttering, "Of course she did."

"Look," I began, turning to him slightly. "You have every reason to not trust me. I've done nothing to earn your trust, and she helped me realize that. Quite bluntly, I might add. I knew it already, but I got so caught up in us . . ." My cheeks heated, but I forced myself to keep going. "I lost sight of the reason I was here to begin with. I thought I was justified in my rage. It felt like a betrayal, but none of this would have happened if I hadn't kidnapped Damon. So I might have overreacted a little bit. Or a lot. I've never had my powers bound before and I don't like it. The feeling . . . it doesn't matter. That's not why I'm here. I just wanted to say I'm sorry I've been blaming you for it, when I should be blaming myself."

He looked down, nodding softly. "I didn't want to take your powers from you. That's not the man I am. You left me with no choice."

"You had a choice," I said, tilting my head at him, giving him a tight smile. "You just didn't have good options. And if I'm honest, I would have done the same thing if I had a nephew and he'd been kidnapped. I would burn down the world to find them. It's part of the reason I've been so angry."

"I don't quite feel that way about my nephew. But I see what you're saying," he said, rubbing the back of his neck.

"I can't imagine that. Truth be told, I'm surprised my own family hasn't shown up and tried something crazy. They'd need to know where I am though, to do that." I pulled my cloak tighter, swallowing the emotion that formed a knot in my throat. "I told Sadie I'd meet her at the safe house, but then I never showed. They're probably worried sick." Guilt ate at me, because this really was my own damn fault. I knew better than to work with Lou and yet I took every job he offered.

"You never said anything about wanting to get word to them."

"I hadn't thought . . ." I paused, thinking about my words carefully. "None of this was meant to happen. That's why I kept testing my powers. It wasn't really to persuade you. I needed to know when they returned to full strength so I could find Damon and bring him back."

"You were going to say you hadn't planned on staying." When I didn't respond, he scoffed, looking away. "Still not telling the entire truth. You were going to leave. Once you gained the use of your powers, you were going to disappear without saying goodbye."

Vareck returned his gaze to me, waiting for a response. I

bit my bottom lip. No matter how uncomfortable it was, Vareck deserved honesty from me. Looking away from him, I nodded. "Yes, I was going to leave."

"Would you have compelled me to stay if I caught you?"

"Yes," I said quietly.

"And there's the truth." He sounded bitter with hurt. I hated it, but I understood it. There was a reason I lost sight of why I was here. Vareck hadn't treated me like a prisoner. While Kaia had been searching for Damon, Vareck had been . . . wooing me? Getting to know me? Whatever it was, feelings had started developing, and he wasn't the only one.

"I would have come back."

Vareck glanced over, his expression unreadable. "To drop Damon off before you left again?"

I shook my head. "I . . . I want to know you too. But I want to do it without my actions between us. I know I can't undo the past, but I guess I thought maybe once Damon was back we could move forward." I pressed my lips together in a self-deprecating smile. "I suppose that's stupid now that I say it out loud. Even though you haven't thrown me in the dungeon, you're still a king and I'm still the asshole that kidnapped the heir to the throne."

Vareck stared at me with an intensity I didn't understand. Part of me wanted to hide from it, but the other side won out. The side that wanted to be brave.

"Why are you telling me this now?" His voice gave away nothing. "I've made it painfully clear how I've felt since the moment we met, and you've fought me at every turn. Why admit this now?"

"Because I want you to trust me. I want to trust each other. Being honest seems like a pretty good place for me to start."

Vareck turned to face me, his shoulders releasing the

tension they'd been holding, his body language finally changing for the first time since I'd arrived. "This isn't how I imagined it," he said, gesturing between us. "You and me."

"Me either. To be fair, I didn't know you were real. But when you found me, it was under the worst possible circumstances and everything since has spiraled out of control." I smiled, thinking about the four years I'd dreamed about him. "I think the way that we met in our dreams was a much nicer introduction than what reality provided us."

His eyes darkened for a moment, and when he spoke, there was a small growl in his voice. "On that we agree."

An idea formed. I wiped the palms of my hands against my pants as nervousness followed it. "What if we started over? Like you tried when you first brought me here." He raised a brow in question. I held my hand out to shake his, and said, "I'm Meera Wylde. I was born in Faerie, but my family moved to earth when I was a baby. I'm the youngest of six kids. Kinda. Sadie and I are the same age, and we don't actually know who was born first." I let out an awkward laugh because I was totally rambling like a damn middle schooler trying to talk to her crush. "Anyway, Twizzlers are my favorite candy. Blue is my favorite color. I have a somewhat unhealthy addiction to romance books, especially the morally gray kind. I own a failing antiques store and my favorite thing to collect is antique jewelry." I turned my head slightly so he could see the antique comb that he had given me, tucked away in my hair.

"Vareck Einar," he said with a playful smile. "My affinity is spirit. I have an annoying cat as a familiar. I've never had Twizzlers, but I love a good red velvet cake. I've never thought much about having a favorite color, but it would be anything other than white. I'm sick of white after being surrounded by it for so many years. I don't really have hobbies. It's hard to, with the realm and all. When I was younger, I enjoyed horseback riding and archery. Kaia was better at both and never let me forget it." He chuckled, smiling with fondness at the memories. "My talents lie more with strategy and problem solving. Useful in ruling a realm, but not very flashy. When I'm not in meetings or reading proposals I've been searching for this woman I've been dreaming about for years."

"That's so weird. Me too." I placed my hand on my chest, enjoying the moment.

"You've also been dreaming about a beautiful woman with red hair?"

"No, I see her in the mirror every day." I pressed my lips into a coy smile. "I've been dreaming about this guy. He has the sexiest voice I've ever heard. I never knew what he looked like, though. Not until recently."

Vareck chuckled. "I hope you weren't too disappointed upon that discovery."

I snorted. "Not at all. Tall, dark, and handsome—he's really the perfect cliché."

"Cliché, huh?" He scratched jaw then ran a hand over his short beard. "Never heard that as a compliment."

"Well it is. He also gives very thoughtful gifts."

"That so?" Vareck grinned.

"The books were really nice, by the way. Good selection. I read all of them. And the clothes fit well," I said, opening my cloak slightly to show him the new pieces I was wearing.

"I'm glad you liked them."

"I'm sorry about the flowers," I said, feeling my cheeks

flush with shame as I looked at the glass lily in his mother's hand. I felt like I had dishonored her somehow.

Vareck reached out and grazed the side of my cheek gently with his knuckles, the supple leather caressing my skin. "She would have liked you." When I tilted my head in question, he elaborated. "My mother. Glass lilies were her favorite flower too. That's why I have them everywhere. They remind me of her."

"Well, now I feel worse for having stomped on them in the hallway," I muttered.

Vareck shook his head gently. "Don't. You were upset. Even if I had good reasons for the necklace, you're allowed to be angry about it. She never wanted anyone to feel guilty for their emotions. Not even when we reacted to them poorly. She said it was part of growing and learning."

"She sounds like my mom. There has never been a point in my life that I felt adopted. Sometimes I forget that I am. But there were times in my youth when I wanted to rebel in anger, you know, say stupid, hurtful things like 'you're not my real mom,' and she accepted that from me without shaming me afterwards. She said discovering where I fit into the world was part of growing and learning too." I glanced at the statue of Lore, thinking they might have been friends. "It didn't take long to realize I fit in just fine with all of them. Since then, I don't even think about where I came from, or why."

He listened without judging, letting me talk freely.

"She was a good teacher. Redcaps are spirited and reactive, but she taught and encouraged us to have a range of emotions, never giving into just one. I think it's what helps my sister win fights. Sadie isn't ruled by her anger, even when provoked."

"And you? How does it help you?"

"It lets me see outside of myself. Think about others." I huffed a laugh. "Helps me recognize when I'm wrong, despite the fact no one enjoys being wrong. I think there's strength in that though. Doing the hard thing."

Vareck's eyes flick to my lips briefly before returning. "I'd be lying if I said I didn't admire that about you. My mother was similar. Where my father lashed out and couldn't care less, she owned her mistakes and actually worked to do better."

"She sounds like a good mom," I said, feeling an ache in my heart for his loss.

He smiled faintly. "She was. Everything that is good in me, I learned from her. She was the one that believed in equity among the fae and abhorred the elitists who looked down on others. She reminded us that we were all specks of dust in the vastness of the nine realms, and only for a blip in time."

"I wish I could have met her. Maybe all this wouldn't have happened if . . ." I motioned to the snowy landscape, then fell silent. "I'm sorry. Again. Shit, I'm saying that a lot right now, but I didn't mean to imply—"

"I know," he cut me off, saving me from sticking my foot in my mouth again. "How much do you know about the curse?"

"Very little," I admitted. "My parents said it came on very suddenly shortly after the Mad King died."

Vareck nodded. "There was a prophecy about him. It's what started everything, but no one could have predicted how it ended." His gaze was a thousand-yard stare. I didn't know for certain, but I suspected he was seeing the past.

"You don't have to talk about it," I murmured, giving him an out. I wanted to build trust, but it was too much to ask him to relive that for my own curiosity.

"My mother insisted he wasn't always mad. That paranoia poisoned his mind. I don't know if I believe that, though. My mother saw the best in people, and someone like my father . . . you don't become a monster overnight. Deimos Einar was cruel. Power-hungry. Long before I was born he had made a name for himself." Vareck clenched his hands at his sides, the leather of his gloves pulling taut. "He was quick to anger and fast to kill. The few times a coup had been attempted ended with him making a horrific and inhumane example of the traitors. For better or worse, Faerie bowed beneath his power. My father wasn't content with simply ruling this realm."

"He tried to overthrow another?" I asked, unable to help the question from bubbling up. My parents had taught me the history of Faerie, but this . . . I'd never heard this version of events.

Vareck laughed coldly. "No. He tried to overthrow them *all*. Deimos believed that they were a threat, and in time that they would turn on us. He claimed they would steal his throne. In truth, I don't know if he actually believed that. My father lied as often as he told the truth."

"He could lie?" I frowned. "How? He was high fae."

Vareck glanced sideways at me, his ice-cold stare heavy. "He was also a descendant of the goddess Amoret. The first Queen of Faerie. Most aren't aware that my bloodline has certain abilities other high fae don't—including the ability to lie."

I struggled for words. "Why would you tell me that?"

Vareck didn't look away. I felt like a spotlight was shining down on me, revealing every part of myself to him. "Trust has to start somewhere."

My lips parted. "So, your father," I said, steering us back

to the history lesson at hand. "He wanted to lord over all nine realms?"

Vareck nodded. "Powerful as he was, he couldn't go up against a god—let alone eight. That left him with a problem to which he scoured the lands to answer. When his search came up empty, he went to oracles, thinking that they might be able to lead him to what would bring him that power." He looked me up and down, huffing through his nose. "Good thing he never found someone like you. If there was an artifact out there that could have done it, he'd have enslaved you for your power." A shiver wracked my body, but I didn't comment. "Eventually he found a banshee who claimed to have the answers he sought. She didn't. When he brought her to court, she laughed at him and told him his search for power was all for naught." Vareck's jaw clenched, old anger rising to the surface. "She prophesied that he would never become a god and instead meet his end by a fury's sword. We knew he was depraved, but no one realized the extent of his evil until then." Vareck swallowed, his Adam's apple bobbing with the action. "He ordered the execution of every fury in the realm. No exceptions."

My jaw dropped, and I looked at the statue of Lore. The wings. "But..."

He nodded solemnly. "My mother was the last."

I swallowed thickly, feeling my mouth dry. "And your sister? Was she . . . a fury too?"

"Yes. She was a hybrid. Part witch and part fury." He trailed off, his eyes becoming distant.

"The rumors say you killed your father . . ." I paused, not sure if I should finish my question, but half of it was already out there. "If that's true, you are also . . ."

"Part fury," he answered.

"But the wings." It wasn't phrased as a question, but Vareck understood.

"Unlike my mother and most other furies, I can summon mine at will."

"I thought you were full dark fae. I had no idea." All high fae fell on one side of the spectrum or the other. Some were light, others dark. There was no gray.

"What I am is rarely discussed anymore. I'll ask you not to repeat any of what I just told you."

"I won't," I whispered, looking at his sister's grave. "She died that day as well, didn't she?"

"Maeve was incredibly gifted, even as a child. Her power was the kind that hadn't been seen in living memory. When she started to go through the passage, my father gave her an amulet. No one knew that it was spelled," he said, staring at her statue. The way he looked at her made me think he was reliving that day. He cleared his throat. "He siphoned her power to kill the furies. With a single command, the entire race went extinct, apart from my mother and myself. He didn't believe I would harm him, and he'd chosen to poison my mother instead. He claimed it was because he loved her and wanted her to have the chance to say goodbye. My sister wasn't given the option. Once he killed the furies, he could have stopped, but instead he chose to drain her to the very end. It was her power that allowed him to curse the land as he died."

My heart broke for him. I could have sworn there was a crack that sounded. "But why? If he killed all the furies . . ."

Vareck shook his head. "As the only living Einar, I would inherit the crown. He died at the end of my sword, and he cursed Faerie to punish me."

I let out a stuttered breath. My eyes blurred as water filled them. I tried to blink back the tears, drawing him into focus again. "It's not your fault," I whispered. "The curse. Their deaths. None of this is on you. If anything, you were the greatest victim of all. To lose your family all at once," I shook my head. One of the tears fell and turned to ice partway down my cheek. "I'm so sorry."

Vareck kneeled down, wiping the snow off the plaques with their names. He remained there, his arm resting across his thigh while he stared at the quote beneath his mother's name.

Spring will come on shadowed wings.

"Is it a part of a poem in her honor?"

"Those were her final words to me. She said it was how to break the curse." My heart jolted. If the curse were broken, the entire kingdom wouldn't be on the brink of starvation. My family could come back home. That tiny ember of hope winked out when logic kicked in. If he knew how to break the curse, he would have, and the sorrow in his eyes told me what I already knew.

"Nobody knows what it means, do they?"

With a single shake of his head, he stood up, dusting the snow off himself. "I've sought out fortune tellers, soothsayers, oracles, and witches. Not one of them understands it and I don't know how to find the answer."

A thought occurred to me. It was a stretch, but worth trying.

"What if I could help?" I murmured, thinking through it as I spoke. "I don't know if it's possible. But at first, I thought my powers could only help me find objects. Then I learned it could find a person. Maybe there is a way for me to use my power to find the answer? It's not a concrete thing I can search for, but maybe if I figure out how to ask the right questions, it can lead me to where we need to go."

Vareck's eyes were cautious as he thought about what I'd suggested. "Would this be something we do together?"

I bit my lip. "After we find Damon."

"You're trying to leave again."

I shook my head, trying to find the words to explain. "I am used to working alone. I took a job I shouldn't have simply because I wasn't willing to ask my family for help, and I wasn't willing to throw in the towel on a business that's been sucking me dry. I'm the epitome of 'I can carry my own fridge.'"

"You've lost me now."

"It's just a saying in the human realm. It means that something is heavy, and you shouldn't be lifting it by yourself, so you should ask for help from people you trust. It's a metaphor. Instead of asking for help, I am more likely to find a way to carry it myself."

"What's that have to do with you leaving?"

"I've always done things by myself. It's not meant to be an excuse. It just is. To find Damon, I will need to leave again. But I'm coming to realize I may not need to carry the fridge on my own." I gave him a sad smile. "Damon's the fridge in this scenario."

"So we would do this together?"

I nodded. "Assuming you wanted to come with. I know you have kingly duties, but given you're not keen on me leaving you behind, I'm guessing you do."

Vareck stood slowly. "I do." He dusted the snow from his gloves. "You can't find him with the necklace on."

I inclined my head, sensing his wariness. "I need my powers. Otherwise I'm no better than an amateur sleuth."

"I want to trust you, Meera. I have a duty to my people and my kingdom, and he's the heir. I don't want to bring him back because I'm related to him. He's a twat and his overbearing mother has put him on a pedestal where he can do no wrong. Honestly, this might do him some good. Introduce him to hardship in the real world. Until he's willing to act like a man, he wouldn't make a good king. But he's the only other Einar alive. I swore..." He stopped, looking up at the statues of Maeve and Lore before finishing his thought. "I swore I'd take care of our people. That I would put them first. This is difficult at the moment, because every instinct I have tells me to fuck everything and not let you leave. That if I remove the necklace, you'll leave without a trace, and I'm not willing to let you go."

Part of me wanted to rebel against the notion that he could keep me, and yet another part of me melted over the possessiveness of his admission. I blamed it on my romance books, bleeding into my reality. I had to shake it off. It was doing funny things to my decision-making skills.

"You're not the only one with a promise to keep. I owe it to you and everyone else to bring Damon back. But I can't find him without my power. "

He glanced down, rubbing his thumbs over my hands. After a suspended moment, he nodded to himself. "What if there was a way to do this?"

"Remove the necklace?" I was confused. He should be able to take it off me. The only one that can't remove it is the one wearing it.

"That, but also ensure that you didn't go back on your word."

"I'm listening."

"You're not going to like it," he warned.

"Something I like less than wearing this? Doubtful." I squeezed his hand playfully, but when he met my gaze, he didn't smile. "Ah hell, you're serious." I blew out a sharp breath. "Okay, what is it?"

"A blood oath."

I squinted at him. "What's a blood oath? I'm not familiar with it."

The intensity of his stare made me want to squirm, and not because I was uncomfortable. "It's a vow forged with blood magic. You can only form two in your life, and they are permanent."

"As in lasts the entirety of our incredibly long lives?" My voice sounded breathy, even to my own ears. The warmth that was coiling low in my belly dissipated beneath the anxiety.

Vareck nodded. He released my hands and tugged off one of his gloves. The red tattoo I'd noticed before took on a new meaning.

"I've already forged one—with Kaia. You would be the only other person I would have this with, if you agreed."

A minute passed, then two. What he was talking about sounded serious. I mean, it was permanent. You don't get much more serious than that. Marriages could be undone, even tattoos could be removed, but this couldn't.

I should say no. Damon needed to be found, but this was asking too much.

I opened my mouth to decline, except those weren't the words that came out. "What exactly does this do? Will I still have free will?"

"Of course," he answered without hesitation. Something dark flashed through his gaze and he looked away. "I would *never* take away your will. I want you to trust that, just like I want to trust you. This lets us have that." He turned back to me, and whatever ire he felt about my question wasn't in his eyes anymore. "A blood oath prevents us from betraying each other or knowingly causing harm."

"That's very . . . broad."

A slight smirk quirked his lips. "Much like your contracts. It's a magical binding that is set around intention."

"Would I be forced to tell you the truth about every-thing?" I knew how it sounded. Guilty as fuck. But there was more than just our situation with Damon to consider. If this lasted forever, it would surpass our partnership in finding his nephew.

Vareck hesitated. "Yes and no. Inconsequential things, trivial lies, those usually aren't affected because it's not a betrayal. Something larger, like telling me you won't disap-pear on me—that would require the truth. Blood oaths aren't an exact science. Magic rarely is. But let me ask you this, could you honestly see me and Kaia doing one if it would take away our choices or trap us?"

"No." I didn't even have to think about it. While I'd only met Kaia a few times, it was pretty clear that she would never let someone take advantage of her that way. "Just to be clear, this won't let you control me in any way? I can't betray you or do something that I know would hurt you, but that's all?"

Vareck dipped his chin. "You want the necklace off. This would allow me to do that without having to question your motives or what you'll do when it's gone."

I mulled that over. "What about after we get Damon back? What does this sort of oath look like then? Does it prevent me from returning home?"

"No. Kaia has traveled to earth and a few other realms several times over the years. It doesn't force a certain proximity."

I blew out a breath. This is a terrible idea. Sadie would

tell me to let Damon rot before committing to something like this.

But I wasn't my sister.

And for reasons I wasn't ready to acknowledge, I wanted to trust Vareck. The oath went both ways. I couldn't lie to him about important shit, but he also couldn't lie to me.

Fuck it.

"Okay. Let's do it."

CHAPTER 19
MEERA

Something went wrong.

I paced the room furiously, back and forth. I had folded all of my clothes, arranged all of my books alphabetically, changed my outfit twice, and ran my hands through my hair so many times I'd probably need to wash it again soon.

"I'm tired just watching you." I jumped in surprise and Corvo laughed.

"When did you get here?"

"A few moments ago," he answered, slowly blinking his golden eyes. He sat primly in front of the armchair, his long fluffy tail wrapped around him. "I convinced one of the kitchen staff that Vareck didn't feed me breakfast. Now I have a full belly and a desire to sleep it off. Instead, I've been watching you talk to yourself while you walk around in circles."

"No one's making you watch me."

"No reason to get snappy with me. You're the one who did a blood oath with him."

I sighed. "He said it didn't work. What does that mean? Why didn't it work?"

I walked over to the bed and started pulling the covers up and fluffing the pillows. I needed to keep my hands busy, and cleaning was the productive thing to do whenever my head was in a different place.

Corvo hopped onto the covers, enjoying the rewards of a freshly made bed.

"Seriously, cat? I just straightened up," I muttered.

"Beds are made for napping, Meera. Why else would you make it if not to use it?" he replied with his usual smugness.

"I can't argue with that," I sighed, surrendering to Corvo's logic. I kicked my boots off and crawled onto the blankets.

My entire body was buzzing with anxiety. It wouldn't hurt anything if I tried to rest. As I leaned against the headboard, crossing my ankles and trying to settle in, Corvo curled up on a pillow next to me.

"What are you doing?" I asked, gesturing to the rest of the bed.

"What's it look like I'm doing? I'm going to sleep on Vareck's pillow. He hates it when I do that. Makes it all the more satisfying. Especially when he sneezes."

"The two of you are something else, you know that?" Reaching over, I ran my fingers through his fur, and he started to purr. "We made a blood oath, or tried to at least. It didn't even occur to me that it could go wrong. I'm an idiot. Why did I do that, Corvo?"

"Is this a rhetorical question, or do you actually want the answer? Frankly, I'm happy. Maybe the two of you will finally fuck and see what everybody else sees."

I yanked my hand back, and he protested with a loud meow.

"What do you mean, 'what everybody else sees'?"

"Well, me and Kaia. That's everybody that matters. Bring back the pets, please." I lowered my hand back to his flank, brushing the soft fur there.

"A blood oath is forever," I said, not expecting him to respond. "I don't know what went wrong, but I can only assume this one is too."

"So?"

I rolled my eyes. "What part of forever did you miss?"

Corvo slowly blinked at me. "Why did you do it?"

"I literally just asked you that question because I've been asking myself for about an hour now."

"No, what was your reasoning when you said yes?"

"I . . . I don't know. I wanted him to know that he could trust me." When I said it out loud, it sounded a tad bit desperate. Embarrassment made me look away. I stared at the ceiling instead.

"So . . . you entered into a lifelong bond with him, so he'd take off a necklace? Nah, I don't buy it. This doesn't have anything to do with one of your romance books, does it?"

"No," I said quickly. Then sighed. "Maybe? I don't know. It just all happened so fast."

"You knew what it was, and you agreed to it."

I opened my mouth to speak, but nothing came out except a sigh. On the surface, it didn't scare me. I'd been dreaming about him for four years. In a way, I felt like I knew him better than I actually did. I weirdly trusted him, even though I had nothing to base that on—especially considering he had essentially collared me. With a blood oath, we couldn't control each other. That felt safe to me.

"But?"

"We formed a bond somehow, but it wasn't a blood oath. I don't know what that means now, and it's for life,

Corvo. I should have thought about it more. Considered all the outcomes."

"It could be worse. It's not like it's marriage. That would be the worst."

"I feel like you have your priorities backwards."

"No, my priorities are food and a good place to nap. My priorities are exactly where they need to be. Maybe you should think more about food and a place to nap."

My stomach growled as though it had heard him and wanted to be part of the conversation.

"I don't know why I'm talking to you." I scrubbed my hands down my face.

"Because I'm pretty good at being the voice of reason," he said, reaching his paw out to gently touch my arm. "You're overthinking this. Trust me. The two of you have been dreaming about each other for years. If you think about it, you're both already bound to each other somehow. Almost like mates, you know, if they still existed."

I tilted my head toward him with an incredulous look. "You're hyper-focused on mates, you know that?"

"Maybe you're not focused enough," he huffed.

"But I can see where your logic is coming from," I continued, ignoring his last comment. "There's something that has connected us already, and even if I don't know what it is that I've agreed to, I know Vareck wouldn't abuse it. Maybe that's why it didn't scare me as much at first. I'm just not usually one to make rash decisions so quickly. That's more Sadie's thing. I like to think about my options."

"And yet, here we are. You trusted your gut, then got cold feet after."

I sat up, eyes narrowing on him. "You make me sound fickle."

He yawned, stretching his mouth and showing his

teeth. "Look, either you trust him, or you don't. Either way it's too late, but if you claim he wouldn't abuse it, maybe you should believe that and stop worrying."

I opened my mouth, then closed it. "You're right."

"Of course I am. No need to sound so surprised. Now that my work is done, I'm going to take a nap. My belly has expanded, and the food coma is taking over."

I scratched him behind the ear while he laid his head down. The soft vibrations of his purr changed to rhythmic breathing, his sides rising and falling.

"Wish I could fall asleep that fast." I leaned back, trying and failing to relax enough for sleep. I let out a huff and got to my feet, quickly shoving my feet back in my boots and lacing them. Vareck said he would do some research about what kind of oath we made. If cleaning didn't help me chill out, and sleep was out of the question, I might as well help him.

The door creaked open. Two brownie servants entered, pushing a cart with a large sterling silver dome. My hand instinctively reached for the spot on my leg where my dagger would normally rest, even though it wasn't there and hadn't been for some time now.

What surprised me was the servants' failure to knock. All the other attendants had done so. The only ones who usually entered unannounced were Vareck, Kaia, and Corvo. I glanced between the two nervously, unsure what to make of them.

"Hello, dearie! We didn't mean to startle you. Hope you're hungry," the first brownie said, her simple gray dress fitting her form, black buttons running down the sides, and an apron tied around her waist.

"I'm supposed to be having dinner with Vareck."

"Right you are. The king sent us ahead and said to not

wait for him but that he'd be back soon," the other brownie said, his outfit similar with gray slacks, a matching vest, and a white dress shirt. They were only slightly shorter than me, and without the clothes, it would be hard to tell them apart. They looked *exactly* alike, down to every crease and wrinkle and beauty mark. I'd never seen anything like it before. They must have seen the confusion on my face.

"We're twins. I'm Gertrude, and this is my brother, Gin." The girl had brown pigtails that bounced as she spoke, while her brother was more put-together, stoic, his short brown hair neatly cut, gloves covering his hands.

"Hi," I said, smoothing out my cardigan, feeling a bit more at ease at their introductions, though servants didn't usually come in and start chatting with me. I walked over to the table and took my seat. "I'm Meera."

"We know. You're the pretty fae woman His Majesty has taken a liking to." Gertrude laughed, pressing her hand to her chest as Gin removed the silver dome. The heavenly scent made my stomach riot, eclipsing any embarrassment I might have felt about her comment. Gin decorated the table with bowls of stew and silvery cutlery. Gertrude walked around the cart, filling two goblets of wine, handing one to me directly.

"Thank you," I mumbled. The smell of root vegetables and herbs filled my nose, and I noticed the slightest hint of a new herb I couldn't place.

With the food laid out, the twins stood back on either side of the table, giving me a small bow. "We hope you enjoy your meal," they said in unison.

"I—yeah, thanks." I wrapped my fingers around the wine goblet. The twins smiled back, their hands resting in front of them. The odd thing was they kept standing there. Staring. Waiting. What did they want me to do? Were they waiting for me to eat? Did Vareck tell them to keep me company until he got here? "This is all very kind," I said, breaking the silence.

"Of course," Gertrude replied, her tone still perky.

Gin put a hand on his chest. "If there's anything we can do to assist you, please let us know."

"This is perfect. Honestly," I said, setting the wine down on the tray. I grabbed a piece of warm bread, dipping it into the stew and taking a big bite, letting out a pleased groan. "This stew is so good. It's my favorite thing here."

"Oh good, I'm so glad you think so. There's a lot you can do with a root vegetable, if you know what you're doing." Gertrude grinned, clasping her hands together.

The tiniest of snores escaped Corvo as he slept. I rolled my eyes, finishing my bite, then took a swig of the wine. But instead of the familiar warmth alcohol usually brings, there was an odd cold that began to seep into my veins. At the same time, my face started heating up quickly, a burning numbness crawling over my skin.

I set the glass down, noticing my vision blurring at the edges. Was this the oath I took? Holding my palm up for inspection, I saw that nothing had changed. No mark that Vareck had mentioned.

"Something is wrong," I mumbled, looking at the twins. I blinked, trying to shake it off, but it was getting worse. Anxiety flared, mixing with the growing numbness. Everything felt too fast and too slow at the same time.

"Everything seems to be working just fine," Gertrude said, reaching into her pocket for something I couldn't see clearly.

"Did you poison me?" I slurred, trying to push myself up, but barely made it half a foot before I had to hold on to the side of the table. I tried to call for Corvo, but only a quiet slur escaped me.

"Oh, don't be so dramatic," Gin chided, tilting his head to face me.

"Don't worry, we didn't poison you," Gertrude giggled.

"We just need you to go to sleep for a while," Gin finished.

Slumping over, I fought to stay conscious. I swallowed dryly, begging internally for the world to stop spinning. When I fell to my side, I knew it was over. Gertrude repeated words I couldn't understand, and what looked like a portal appeared in the middle of the room.

"It'll all be over soon." Gin tapped me, and I felt like I was floating.

I didn't know what "it" was, but I didn't want to find out. My thoughts went to Vareck. If I'd see him again. How long would I be gone before he knew I was missing? My heart ached when I realized he would think I left him, right after telling him he could trust me.

The thought crushed me, simultaneously giving me enough energy to let out a choked sob. As the world faded into oblivion, Corvo's eyes shot open, and he looked directly at me. I think I might have mouthed the word 'help,' but the portal closed around me just as my consciousness faded.

CHAPTER 20

CORVO

Shit.

CHAPTER 21
VARECK

"There you are," Kaia said. She swept her gaze across my office, then arched an eyebrow. "What's with all the books?"

Several stacks were piled high on my desk and on the end table by my reading chair. Any other visible space had open books with random items wedged in the spines to hold the place.

"Research," I muttered. My jaw tightened as I scanned the rest of the page I was reading, only to find nothing of use.

"The History of Blood Magic," Kaia read aloud. She picked up the book off the stack and read the one below it. "Bonds and Bindings." Her voice dropped an octave as she picked that one up too. "Blood Oath Case Studies."

My head snapped up. "Hand me that one—"

"What the hell? Please, please do not tell me you're considering entering a blood oath with her."

"I'm not considering anything."

"Then why are you—" Kaia tilted her head, lips parted.

"You didn't." She dropped the books back onto my desk, a tiny plume of dust rose in the air, catching in the light.

"We're going to find Damon."

Kaia barked an unamused laugh. "How do you plan to do that with the necklace on her?" I didn't answer. "Godsdamn it, Vareck. Tell me you didn't do a blood oath with her *and* take off the necklace. I know she's the dream girl, but come on. She's the one who abducted him and can't even tell us who hired her."

"I didn't take the necklace off."

"Oh good," Kaia deadpanned. "You didn't take off the trinket that was *temporary* and instead entered into an *unbreakable* vow that will last till one of you dies. Yeah, that's so much better."

I sighed. "This is why I didn't ask you."

"Because I would have talked sense into you," she snapped. "Maybe that should have been your first hint it was a bad idea."

"I trust her."

"Clearly not if you did a blood oath."

I bit the inside of my cheek. "Meera has a unique ability to find things. She can find Damon, but she can't do it without her magic. The necklace was only on her to begin with so she couldn't persuade me. The blood oath runs deeper—"

"Because it's permanent!"

I leveled her with a glare. "We have no leads. Meera's bound to a magical contract. There isn't a trace of him. The longer that goes by—"

Kaia threw her head back and laughed. "She's been here all of what? Eight days? Nine?"

"We have to find Damon. You're the one that told me sometimes sacrifices have to be made."

"About being king, not this!" she snapped back. "You may be able to lie to yourself, but not me. This has nothing to do with Damon and everything to do with your obsession with her."

I slapped my hands on the desk. "If you're just here to lecture me, you can leave."

Kaia pressed her lips together, crossing her arms. A tense minute passed before she spoke again. "Why are you researching if you already did it?"

I ran my hand along my jaw. "Something went wrong."

She dropped her arms immediately. "What do you mean wrong? Are you okay?"

"I'm fine. The oath just didn't take right. It's weird and I probably wouldn't have questioned it if I didn't know what it should feel like."

Kaia glanced down at her left hand briefly, where the binding from our own blood oath was embedded in her skin. Deep red lines twisted around her wrist and down the back of her hand. They met on her palm and formed a jagged crown. Most people would mistake it for a tattoo.

My own binding matched hers but sat on my right hand. The only difference was that instead of a crown, mine became a sword.

We'd been kids when we did it. Teenagers who thought we knew everything. I remembered us being confused about why the bindings took the forms they did. They were supposed to represent us in some way and back then, I wasn't the heir. Back then, she wasn't a soldier.

Yet somehow, it seemed fate knew. We were always meant to end up here. I had no regrets.

"What's different? Explain it to me."

I tugged off my left glove, revealing my bare skin.

Kaia frowned. "So it just didn't work?"

I shook my head. "I feel her. Flickers of emotion. Where she's at."

Kaia took the seat across from me, pushing the books out the way so we could see each other. "Neither of those things happened with ours. I don't feel your emotions, thank the gods, and I definitely can't track you with it."

I nodded. "Same. I would assume it didn't work if not for that."

"Hmm." She tilted her head back, looking off into the distance. "Do you think you formed a different kind of oath?"

"No idea. Hence, the research." I motioned to the book in front of me.

"The lack of a binding mark makes me think it could be temporary," she said. "So that's good."

I kept my face neutral, not betraying how much that idea bothered me. I knew it was insane to want something permanent with a woman I'd only known a little over a week. But I did. Badly.

"Hey guys," Corvo said, making his presence known.

"Not now. We're busy."

"You might want to—"

"What if you made her your familiar?" Kaia interrupted. "You feel Corvo's emotions and can kind of sense where he's at right?"

"I already have a familiar."

"Well you clearly made some sort of weird bond with her and the familiar bond doesn't have a binding mark."

"V, my man, you need to listen." I looked over at the window, but he wasn't on his usual perch, sunbathing.

"Where are—" I caught the flick of his tail in my peripheral. He was scrunched up on one of the high bookshelves. "Why are you up there?"

"Because I don't want to be turned into a hat."

I got to my feet, pushing the chair back. "What did you do now?"

"I didn't do anything."

"But you're hiding," I growled. "From me."

"You're a little crazy when it comes to Meera—"

"Did you push her out the window again?"

"No," Corvo groaned. "Fuck's sake. I didn't push her the first time. I told you; she tripped."

"On you," Kaia added, picking her nails clean with the blade end of a dagger.

He narrowed his eyes on her. "Not helping."

"Corvo." I ground my teeth together. "The point. Find it."

"Right, so, I know you're all focused on the necklace, but you don't need to worry about it anymore."

Kaia and I looked at each other. "Why?"

"Because she's gone."

A second passed where I froze. A single breath. The beat of a heart.

Time held still.

Then the spell broke.

"What do you mean by gone?" My hands clenched into fists. I stepped around my desk. If she ran . . .

"She got dragged through a portal by some brownies."

"WHAT?" I exploded, sending books flying across the floor.

Corvo cocked his head. "And that right there, is why I'm up here."

I couldn't listen to this. Without wasting another second, I took off down the hall. My blood rushed to my head as my steps quickened. I didn't let myself hesitate when I got to my door.

"Meera!" I yelled, storming through the empty chamber to the bathroom attached. There was no sign of her. No nothing. It was like she disappeared into thin air, or through a portal.

I paced, taking in the scene around me. Nothing seemed out of place. Her food was barely touched, but other than that . . .

"Vareck." Kaia stepped into the room. She did a quick sweep of the room and frowned. "Doesn't seem like there was a struggle."

I lifted the stew to my face. The aroma was strong and slightly pungent. Almost like it was disguising something.

"Valerian root," I spat. "She was drugged."

Her lips parted to form an 'O'. "You said you could feel where she was though, right?"

I focused on that feeling in my chest. The thread that was distinctly her. I felt a pull somewhere to the north, but that was it.

"It's not exact. I can sense the direction she was taken, but Faerie isn't small, and they could move her at any point. If they take her out of the realm . . ." I shook my head. There was no way that was happening. I wouldn't let it. There had to be another way.

I'd never heard of anyone being able to track the way that Meera could, but even with her ability, it could take months. A lot of Faerie was inhospitable. Even a draft horse would struggle with the deep snow. No. I needed something that could find her and take me to her now.

I made for the door and was halfway down the hallway when Kaia called, "Where are you going?"

"To find a witch."

CHAPTER 22
VARECK

"There are no witches in the castle," Kaia said, eating up the distance between us with long strides.

"There is at The Witching Hour," I replied, taking the steps down two at a time.

"Most aren't powerful enough to create a portal between realms, let alone one that can find her across the veil. You're better off finding someone on this side." My mouth twisted. She had a point, much as I loathed it. The portal to The Witching Hour was in the palace gardens. Finding someone in Faerie would take longer and every second she was missing, my anxiety mounted. I wasn't this torn up over my nephew's capture. Not even a fraction. Not sure what that said about me.

"I need one quickly. If I have to drag them through the portal to Faerie first, so be it."

Kaia sighed, keeping pace with me. "You're asking for help by pissing off a witch? Not a great way to go about it."

I growled under my breath. "If they won't bargain, I'll compel them."

Kaia cursed. "You're just asking to get cursed. No, I

know of one here. She's not too far from the castle. Only half a day's ride."

I paused at the first floor. "Half a day? That's too long." I shook my head. "She could be anywhere by then." Kaia stepped in front of me. My jaw pressed together, teeth grinding. "Move."

"No," she said without hesitation. "I'm not going to let you be stupid about this. If you try to force a witch, they will retaliate. That's assuming you even can. We both know they ward themselves to prevent persuasion. You want her back. I get it. Be smart about it . You can't help her if a witch subdues you."

My chest tightened. I didn't like it, but Kaia was right and not just because she couldn't lie. "Fine."

I turned for the stables without another word. Kaia followed, slightly behind as we traversed the grounds in silence.

"Belfor!" I called out to the stable master. He stood outside the structure, grooming one of the mares.

"My King," he answered in greeting. "What brings you here?"

"Ready Dealanach and Toirneach. Quickly, please."

"Of course." He tossed the brush he was using aside and stepped away from the mare. Kaia and I stopped just outside the stable. The scent of hay and horses might have calmed me under different circumstances. Instead I paced, biting back my impatience when it threatened to snap.

It felt like hours but was likely minutes before Dealanach was guided out to me. His thick white coat had spots of dappling gray, making him blend in with the snow. Both he and Toirneach were Vetr Horses, named for the north-most city in Faerie. Before the winter, we'd had many kinds of horses, but once the realm froze only a few breeds remained.

I mounted my steed as Belfor appeared with Kaia's. The two were brothers, but where Dealanach was mostly white, Toirneach was grayer.

"Thank you, Belfor," I tossed out while I waited for Kaia. She didn't waste time, directing us toward the west side of the castle. I followed after her, gripping the reins between numb fingers. We started at a trot that quickly turned into a gallop once we exited the castle grounds.

From there, it became a waiting game. With every second that passed, my emotions rioted. Desperation coiled in my stomach, twisting it into knots. Fear was a hand around my heart, squeezing the beating organ in my chest. It pounded painfully in my sternum, making my breaths short and quick. Neither of them silenced the rage. It built the longer we rode, drowning out everything else. I tried not to think about what might be happening to her right now. If she had the necklace off, I knew she could protect herself, but with it on she might as well be human.

The only thing that kept me in check was the sliver of a bond we shared. I wasn't sure what went wrong with the blood oath but whatever we had done at least allowed me to feel her. If she weren't alive, that thread would sever.

"Up ahead," Kaia said, pointing toward the tree line.

We slowed back to a trot when we crossed it. While I didn't recognize the area, the white willow trees told me we were in the Everwood Forest. A plume of smoke sifted through the bare branches up ahead. I pulled ahead of Kaia and came to a stop once we hit a small clearing. In the center was a small wood cabin with a thatch roof. A small barn that had seen better days sat behind it, doors open and swinging on the hinges. The creak of metal grinding against metal painted an eerie picture. No other sounds carried on the wind and no lights were on in the cabin. If not for the smoke coming from the chimney, I would assume no one was home.

"How did you find this woman?" I asked while we dismounted.

"I was looking for your dream girl. One of the servants was talking about a witch who made her a love potion."

My eyebrows rose. "Those are illegal."

"So is stalking," she replied. "Besides, the information turned out to be good. She's the one that told me about Lucian." Kaia motioned to the cabin.

"I don't trust him."

"The broker?"

"Yeah." The steps creaked under my weight. I half expected a plank to snap on the way to the door.

Kaia snorted. "He's a leprechaun. No shit."

We shared a look, then I raised my hand to knock on the door. Before my knuckles could meet the wood, it opened. A woman that didn't appear a day older than thirty stood in the doorway. Her hair was snow white, but her eyes were black.

"Hello, High Commander. I didn't expect to meet again so soon." Her voice had a soft, lilting quality to it. "I see you've brought our king. What can I do for you, Your Majesty?" Her unnerving eyes settled on me with an intensity that bordered on uncomfortable.

"I need a portal."

She lifted a dark brow. "That so?" The witch stepped back, holding the door open. I stepped inside, surveying the cabin.

It was one room. Beside the door sat a long table with a mortar and pestle on top. Herbs were spread across the surface along with various unnamed bottles holding different colored liquids. Beside it was a small bookshelf with several leather-bound tomes. Apart from that, the room only hosted a small cot, two rickety chairs with a table between them, a fireplace, and a hanging basket with bread in it.

Kaia followed me in, and the door closed on its own behind her.

My shoulders tensed. This place was setting off all sorts of alarms, but I was desperate.

"Where are you looking to go?" the witch asked, turning her back on us as she pulled a kettle off a metal grate in the fireplace.

"It's complicated," I said.

The witch chuckled. "You wouldn't be here otherwise. Tea?" She glanced back, and I shook my head.

"There's a woman. I'm . . . bound to her. We attempted a blood oath, but something went wrong. I'm trying to find her."

The witch hummed under her breath while she poured the water into a chipped cup. "Wrong how?"

"I'm not sure exactly."

"But you're bound?"

I nodded. "I can feel her. Her emotions. Where she's at. I don't know what happened or what kind of bond we created, but I know there is one."

The witch blew the steam that was rising from her tea, silent for a moment. "If you can feel where she's at, why do you need me?"

Frustration bled into me and my hands fisted at my sides. "She was taken north through a portal. That's all I know. Can you help me or not?"

She nodded absentmindedly. "I can," she murmured. "But it's going to cost you."

I reached into my pocket, pulling out a heavy bag of coins. The witch laughed. "I wasn't talking about money, Your Majesty."

"Name your price."

She watched me with a strange, dark gaze. A lesser being would have fidgeted under her attention. I would not.

"A favor now for a favor later."

"Absolutely not," Kaia bit out. "Name a different price."

The witch's eyes flicked to my best friend. She lifted one shoulder in a shrug, her shawl falling partway to reveal dark red lines that another might have mistaken for tattoos. I knew better. This witch dealt in blood magic.

"No," she replied. "You want my help. That's the cost."

I worked my jaw. "What's the favor?"

Her smile was beautiful and horrifying at the same time. "You'll know when I ask it."

I glanced at Kaia. Her lips were pinched, expression unreadable to most. I knew her well enough to tell when she was displeased.

"We can find another way," she said quietly.

"We can, but how long will it take? She's out there—powerless—because of me. I don't know who took her or what they want."

Kaia sighed. "This is a terrible idea. She"—Kaia hooked her thumb toward the witch listening to us—"could ask for anything. If she's not interested in money, and she won't say what favor she wants, you know whatever it is won't be good."

I ran my palm over my jaw, thinking. "What if there were stipulations on the favor?" I asked, turning to the witch.

She took a sip of her tea, considering it. "What sort of stipulations?"

"You can't ask for my kingdom. No ownership of a person. You can't ask someone's execution." I looked at Kaia. "Am I missing anything?"

Kaia rubbed at her forehead. "I still think this is a bad idea."

"I'm aware. That's not what I asked."

She blew out a tight breath. "Off the top of my head, that seems like the most important things. I'm sure there are others, but I would need time to come up with a list."

"We don't have time."

Kaia pursed her lips, glancing back to the witch. "Would you accept those terms?"

"I would."

It was too easy, and yet there was nothing simple about it. I would have paused and taken more time to consider if I had it, but time was not on my side.

I opened my mouth to agree, but then hesitated. Kaia looked at me, holding my stare. After a short pause, she dipped her chin.

"You have a deal."

The witch's blood-red lips curled up in a close-mouthed smile. "It is done." A frown tugged at the corners of my lips. I didn't feel any different. There was no wash of magic. Hm. Perhaps it wasn't the same with every witch.

"Now." She set her tea on the table and reached into a hidden pocket in her dress, withdrawing an athame. Kaia moved in front of me, her hand going to one of the swords strapped to her back. A wry smile crossed the witch's face. "I mean no harm to our king, Commander. But if he has a bond with this woman, I will need his blood for the portal to find her."

I put a hand on Kaia's shoulder. "It's fine."

"She's a blood witch," Kaia hissed under her breath.

"We already made a deal. She's bound by the terms as well."

Kaia narrowed her eyes, still not looking at me. "One wrong move, you die."

The witch let out a cackle. "I think you will find I am no easy kill, but that's neither here nor there. I agreed to make a portal to the woman, and I will." She extended the athame, hilt first. I stepped around Kaia, taking it.

Without fanfare, I dragged the blade across the meat of my palm. Blood welled at the cut. The witch grabbed my wrist and muttered a spell under her breath, in a language I didn't recognize. Her free hand pressed against mine, palm to palm, then she extended it away from us.

Black smoke poured from the bloody print, creating a sibling vortex in seconds. The witch stepped to the side and motioned to the portal.

"As requested."

Kaia grabbed my arm when I moved closer to it.

"Until Drayden returns, someone needs to be at the castle while the search for Damon is underway."

"Stay." I nodded. "Corvo can find me. If there's trouble, I'll send word."

Her hand dropped away. "Be careful, Vareck."

"Always."

Then I walked into the portal, and I didn't look back.

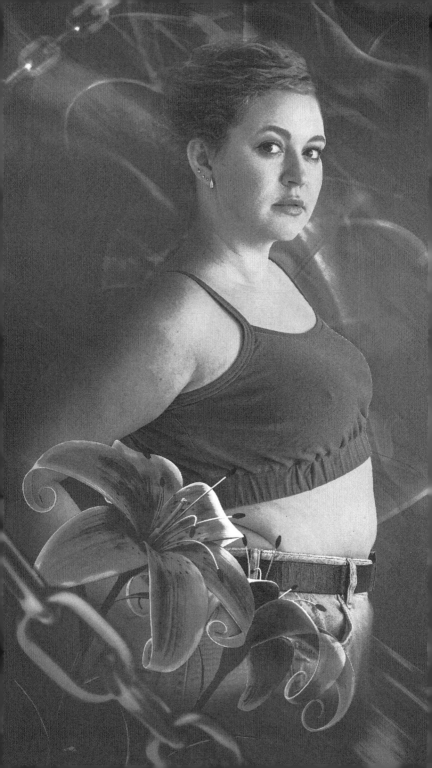

CHAPTER 23
MEERA

The unsteady motion of the covered wagon jolted me awake from my groggy state. I flinched as a wheel dipped into a rut in the road, then groaned as my head hit something hard behind me. I tried to focus, pushing away the nausea, but it was no use. I felt as though I were hungover, unable to distinguish one blurry shape from the next. I closed my eyes, hoping this was all just a bad dream.

Time crawled slowly, taking what felt like an eternity before I was willing to peek through my eyelids again. I moved my hands up to rub at the corner of my mouth when I realized both hands were bound.

The lead up to my predicament came crashing back to me. The twins. The food. The overwhelming loss of my motor functions, all while my mind was intact, knowing I was being dragged from the safety of the palace.

Vareck.

Did he know I was gone? Did he think I'd left him? No, Corvo saw me right before the portal closed. Or was that something I had imagined as I'd lost consciousness? Now I wasn't so sure.

I could officially say, what goes around comes around. There was a cosmic sort of irony that after kidnapping someone, I got to be on the other side of it.

I glanced up, catching sight of one of the twins sitting across from me. Gin was sketching something in a book, his left hand loosely holding a piece of charcoal.

"You," I groaned, fighting against the pull of sleep. I touched my neck, feeling the chain of the necklace still wrapped around me. Of course it was still there. Whatever they wanted me for wasn't so they could steal my jewelry. Still, no magic meant no persuasion, which translated to a whole lot of nothing. So much for rescuing myself.

"Welcome back," Gin said, not bothering to look up from his sketch. He was out of his royal servant's clothes now, dressed mostly in furs with a deep green cloak. He finished one final line, closing the book and setting it next to him before pulling on his glove. "How are you feeling?"

"I'd probably feel better if you hadn't drugged me and knocked me out," I mumbled, wincing at the pounding in my head. The small fae chuckled, leaning back.

"It's all business. Sorry about that." Gin searched his belt, pulling out a canteen. He tossed it across the wagon, and I managed to catch the flask between my tied hands, eyeing it suspiciously since the last thing he'd given me led to our current arrangement.

"It's not drugged," he said, rolling his eyes.

"That's what all the captors say." He stared at me while I considered my options. My mouth was dry and sticky and being dehydrated wouldn't make my odds of escape any easier. Taking my chances, I unscrewed the top and took a swig of the water, silently praying to the gods it was clean and that I wasn't about to pass out again. I gulped down more, coughing before I spoke up.

"Told you it was fine."

"That remains to be seen." I shook the canteen, gauging how much was left. "You plan on telling me why I've been kidnapped again?" The question wasn't something I expected him to answer, but it was worth asking. I swished another mouthful of water around, letting it soak onto my parched tongue before closing the flask and tossing it back to Gin.

He quirked a brow as he caught it with his gloved hands, then placed it back at his side. "What do you mean, again? Is getting kidnapped a normal occurrence for you?"

I shrugged. "It's a long story." It wasn't, but I wasn't sharing anything with Gin, if that was even his real name. I pivoted the conversation, trying my luck with a different question. "So, where are we going?"

Gin tilted his head, eyeing me for a moment. "We're on our way to the Summer's Heir."

"Yup. Summer air. Cool. I have no idea what that means or where it is." I looked around at the covered wagon, making notes of a few small bags of what I assumed were supplies, two sleeping rolls, a lantern, and a few skins of water. They traveled often. "I'm guessing your portal wasn't strong enough to just take us to wherever summer air is? I don't recall seeing that on a map."

"It's not a place."

Portals could still get close to a location where someone was, so my assumption that they didn't have a strong enough portal was probably right. "Can you elaborate?"

The brownie shook his head, chuckling at my response. "You'll see when we get there."

"And when will that be?" I asked, but Gin didn't answer. Instead, he took off his glove once more and reopened his journal, continuing to sketch, ignoring my question. I sighed in frustration.

No wonder he had to stop drawing. It was freezing. He needed time to warm his hands back up. I didn't have gloves, a cloak, or any winter wear. A long-sleeved shirt, leggings, and a cardigan. That was it. I was lucky I had put my boots on before they arrived. I had a feeling they wouldn't have been thoughtful enough to grab them on our way out. They'd at least brought a thick blanket for me, but it was barely enough to keep the bitter air from seeping into my bones. I could feel the burn of the cold eating away at my exposed skin. This whole eternal winter thing was a real bitch and a half when you were stuck outside in it.

The painful silence was only broken by the creak of the wagon wheels, the horse's hooves crunching through the snow, and the scratching of charcoal on parchment. It was almost like a form of torture. The slow kind, meant to drive you crazy. Not like using a stun gun, for instance, which I would kill for right now. I'd jam it right in that stupid little brownie's throat.

I tilted my head back, closing my eyes as I hummed. Soft words followed; the lyrics of a song my record player had spun a hundred times before. I sighed, letting the tune fade.

"You have a good voice," the brownie mumbled, glancing up from his drawing. "Why did you stop?"

"The entertainment will continue with one small payment of freedom," I suggested, lifting my bound hands, fluttering my lashes as I tilted my head.

"Forget it," Gin said with a shake of his head.

"What about the necklace I'm wearing? Given to me by the king himself." I waggled my eyebrows. "You could sell it. Make a lot. Let me go. Everyone wins."

Without answering, he shut his book, setting it next to him, and let out a long sigh before closing his eyes.

I breathed out slowly, wondering if I could wrap my hands around his neck and choke him, then sneak out the back of the wagon. Flexing my fingers, I stretched and tested what kind of reach I had, and the results were less than stellar. It was unlikely I could hold him long enough when my wrists were bound. If I couldn't finish the job, I had a feeling I would end up clubbed upside the head.

The carriage slowed before the wheels ground to a halt. The front cloth lifted, showing Gertrude's face.

"Oi!" The peppiness in her voice at the palace had vanished. A hoarse snarl replaced it when she shouted, "Get your ass out, Brother. We're in Warwick."

I blinked, staring at the spot where her face had disappeared. Gin's demeanor had changed for the better, and he seemed more subdued and less cranky than the kitchen servant I'd met. His sister, on the other hand, had the temperament of a wild boar. I slowly turned to him, my eyes wide. I mouthed, "what the fuck?"

"Charming, isn't she?" He smiled politely, offering no further statement on the issue. I shook my head, trying to shrug off the emotional whiplash. Gin moved forward to take the blanket from me and placed his gloved hand on my shoulder.

"Meera, is it? Stay here. Don't try to escape." His brown eyes glowed as I felt the power of his persuasion settle in. Small fae didn't have persuasion, which meant he had high fae blood in him. Go figure. Apparently hybrids were a dime a dozen around here.

I gave a tiny nod as I looked into his brown eyes, my gaze flickering to the hand on my shoulder. Gin smiled before pulling himself up, pocketing his sketchbook. "We're just getting some supplies for the road. We'll be back soon, and I'll return your blanket."

As he exited from the back, the cloth flapped closed and my body shook. The air was freezing. I had to make a quick decision. Staying in the back of the wagon wasn't an option. I had no knowledge of why I was taken, or where I was going, but I wasn't extended an invitation. Being drugged and bound didn't lend toward good intentions. Though, if I didn't find a safe place quickly, there was a good chance I would freeze to death.

There was an upside. We were in Warwick. I knew nothing of the city except it was a town somewhere in the northern region of Faerie. More buildings meant more places to hide.

Gin wasn't nearly strong enough to keep me under his control for long. While my own magic was bound, my will was not. I felt my body relax, smirking as I began to scoot myself toward the flaps at the back of the wagon.

"Pair of fools, they are," I whispered to myself, using one of my small fangs to start breaking threads on the rope. I didn't have time to fully unbind myself though, not if I planned to escape.

A door jingled nearby, and I waited, listening to the noises outside the wagon. Gertrude's shrill and angry voice filtered outside as she argued with a shopkeeper, trying to haggle down the price of whatever she was buying.

I peeked out, spotting them through the window of a shop, their backs turned, her arms flailing as she yelled.

Slipping out, I bolted, dipping immediately into an alley. The winds cut through my shirt and sweater, threatening to stop me in my tracks, but adrenaline kept me going.

If ever I made a revenge list, those two goblin shitheads were on top.

CHAPTER 24
MEERA

My fingers were going to get frostbite and fall off. I was sure of it. Tearing through the streets with no gloves, no cloak or jacket, and my exposed hands sounded like a good escape plan, right up until the howling wind turned my skin red and raw in a short period of time.

Part of me wanted to call for help, but I didn't trust a damn soul. I didn't know if Gin and Gertrude were from here or if they had friends and connections. Gin might have, but I doubted his sister could make friends with a porcupine.

I'd managed to weave my way through some alleys. Only a handful of people saw me. A few strange looks were thrown my way, but no one attempted to speak to me or offer assistance.

"Warwick, Warwick . . ." I muttered through chattering teeth, trying to scrape my mind for anything useful.

All I knew was that Blumary and Habberton were the two closest settlements to the palace. Warwick was much further north, but where did the portal come out? We'd been traveling for over a day, at least. Probably? I had been cold in the back of the wagon, but not hypothermic. It was hard to judge. I wasn't familiar enough with the land to calculate distance and time for travel. How long had I been unconscious? How many stops had we already made? My shoulders shivered, my body burning with exhaustion as I ducked into an alcove behind some buildings. I paused to catch my breath, bringing my hands to my mouth to warm them up.

Walking around with my wrists bound was going to draw attention. I resumed trying to saw through them with the edge of my fang. It was a painstakingly slow process, and the taste of rope was disgusting. A hot bath and Vareck's bedroom seemed like a faraway dream now.

A noise made me freeze. My eyes narrowed as I leaned out of the alcove only slightly to scan my surroundings, heart hammering. There was no way Gin and Gertrude had caught up to me. I had a hell of a head start, and the streets and alleys here were frequented enough that footsteps would be hard to follow unless they were expert trackers, which I highly doubted. Biting into the rope harder, I pulled my wrists apart, and with a sharp snap, the cord broke.

Relief flooded me. At least now I could use my hands. One step closer to safety.

I turned a corner and slammed right into a figure just over half my height. Stumbling backward, I found myself staring at a group of three kids, all ragged, dirty, and armed with daggers. Fantastic. Safety just took one step forward, then two steps back.

I spun around, only to see another four figures blocking my way—these kids were younger but still armed.

"Oh, you've got to be kidding me," I hissed, swiveling my head between the two groups. They looked more desperate than dangerous, but that didn't make them any less of a problem. "Do your mothers know where you are?"

"'Ello, miss," one of the older boys said, stepping forward. "I'm afraid there's a toll ta' pass through these back ways."

I held my hands up, slightly shrugging. "No can do, Artful Dodger. You can pick my pockets, but I have no money."

The ringleader looked insulted and spit at my feet. "My name ain't Dodger."

"Not much of a reader, huh?" Tough crowd. I continued to assess the way they'd closed in around me. Hand to hand combat was really more Sadie's style. I could hold my own for a while. Usually. I was currently weaponless . . . against this many kids with knives? Eh. . . I wasn't making bets, that's for sure.

"She's lyin'," one kid whispered.

"Maybe not. She don't even have a cloak. Coulda been picked over already."

"Maybe she's just stupid?"

"You know I can hear you right?" Two boys shot me a look in surprise before they narrowed their eyes like I'd bewitched them. And they thought I was stupid. "Here," I said, opening my cardigan. I shivered as I exposed myself more to the cold and tried to stop my teeth from chattering. "Search for yourself."

The older boy, Not-Dodger, grinned, a glint in his eye. He glanced down at my chest and back to my face. "We'll take that necklace there, and ya' can be on your way."

The necklace.

I looked down, suddenly aware of the weight of the artifact against my sternum. The cold had nearly made me forget about it. My lips curled into a grin as a laugh bubbled up. How perfect.

"Take it. It's all yours." I smirked, shaking my head. Gods, I hoped they could take it off. They should be able to, but luck didn't seem to be on my side.

The boys exchanged uncertain glances.

"What's your deal?" another one asked, eyeing me suspiciously. "If you're up ta' any tricks, you'll get cut." He swiped his dagger through the air, clearly never having used it in his life.

Holding my hands out, I knelt down, throwing on a faux look of uncertainty. I had instant regret, but it was too late to change my position without scaring them. The cold bite of the snow pierced through my leggings and into my knees, the fleece lining doing next to nothing to create a barrier. "Look, I'm serious. I'm cold, and you all seem very dangerous." My voice wavered just enough to sell it. "I'll hold my hands out. You can take it off me yourself."

One of the younger boys didn't wait to be told twice. He rushed forward, fingers fumbling as he yanked the chain from my neck. The metal snapped easily.

And the moment it did, magic surged through me.

I sucked in a breath, warmth blooming in my chest, flowing through my veins like molten fire. The boys were already sprinting away, their feet kicking up snow and mud as they disappeared into the shadows.

"Let's get out of here!" one yelped.

"Go, go, go!"

I barely heard them. My entire focus was on the energy flooding back into me. My head tilted up, a breathless chuckle slipping from my lips.

"Oh, hell yes." The words purred from my throat like honey.

I stood, flexing my fingers, feeling my power thrumming just beneath the surface. If I ran into the twins again, I was more than ready to give them a run for their money. What it didn't give me was the power to stay warm, but free of the rope and free of that necklace, my odds of survival were much better.

Stalking out of the alley, I turned my head toward the sound of music and laughter. Dusk was settling in, and a tavern loomed ahead, warm light spilling onto the frozen street. In a town smack dab in the middle of a frozen wasteland, it figured that thriving businesses would be ones that served ale.

I pushed through the door, making a direct line for the roaring fireplace. Heat licked at my fingers as I stretched them out, listening to the hum of conversation around me. The place wasn't packed, but it wasn't empty either. A few tables were full, and several patrons lingered at the bar. Eyes flicked toward me, curious, assessing my clothing.

Let them look. I just needed to find someone to help me out of this town after my body returned to a normal temperature. Spotting an empty seat by the fire, I dropped into it, rolling my stiff shoulders.

The bartender walked over, drying a mug with a cloth. "Lookin' for summer in those clothes, are ya'? Ya' must be freezin'."

"Yeah," I muttered. "Just a little. Got anything to warm me up?"

"'Course," he said, nodding. "Wouldn't be a bar without brown liquor and ale. Comin' right up."

I exhaled, sinking further into the chair, my body still thrumming with the return of my magic. It seemed I'd already become accustomed to Vareck's luxurious bed, blessedly forgetting what it was like on my springy mattress. Spending time in a wagon had done a number on my back.

"There ya' go. I'm Galpin. Gimme a holler if ya' be needin' anythin'." He gave me a nod before moving on to another customer behind the bar.

I took a gulp of the brown liquor, wincing at the burn when I swallowed. The warmth of the alcohol spread through my chest and flowed through my veins. After another few sips, the heat settled, and I no longer felt like a popsicle.

Now I just needed to find a way home. The thought made me pause. Home. Was Faerie home? I meant that I needed to find a way back to the castle. Back to Vareck. But I'd said back . . . *home*. I shook my head, convincing myself it was just a slip.

I'd find my way back to him, find Damon, then what? What *were* we? Weirdly, I was pretty sure I missed him. And not in a 'I miss the safety of your castle and not being taken hostage in a freezing wagon' kind of way. Both things were true, but a piece of me missed *him*. His company. I wanted his arms around me, keeping me warm.

"Excuse me," I said, walking up to the counter and taking a seat on an empty stool at the bar. I placed my glass in front of me. The bartender came over, waiting for me to speak. "I need to find a ride out of here."

"Where ya' headed?" he asked, throwing his towel over his shoulder.

"Brumlow. Is there a public wagon or something that would take me that way?"

"What in the nine realms is a 'public wagon'?" Galpin asked, his brows scrunching deeply.

"You know, like a bus?" I said, realizing quickly the barkeep had likely never left Warwick. "Never mind. I mean a wagon that would take several people at one time to that location?"

He continued to stare at me, as if I would have a better explanation. I sighed. This was why I liked the Arcane District. Public transportation.

Galpin took the towel and wiped it over the counter. "If ya' don't have yer own horse, the only way to Brumlow is by catchin' a ride with a tradesman." He turned to look at a parchment on the wall while I took the last gulp of my brown liquor. "They just got back yesterday, so . . . looks to be about two weeks before another scheduled trade."

I almost choked on my drink. Coughing, I pounded a fist against my chest.

"Two weeks?" I repeated hoarsely, trying to think quickly. That was way too long. I could walk faster than that. I'd freeze, but that wasn't the point. There had to be another way. "What about a portal? Are there any portals?"

If I tapped into my power and followed the trail, I had no way of knowing how far it would be. The frozen lands were holding me hostage. But if one was close enough . . .

"None 'round here, I'm afraid."

"You don't know of one, or there isn't one?"

"Isn' one," he confirmed, giving me a wary look. "Ya' all right?"

I ignored his question for a more important one. "What about sending a message? Do you have pigeons or something?"

"Don' know what pigeons are. Mail goes out with a tradesman," he answered, though he did look like he regretted having to give me answers I clearly didn't like.

The human realm sometimes cursed cell phones and claimed they were a distraction. Usually I would agree. Now I'd give my entire apartment just to have the option to use one. If I ever got back to Vareck, I planned to ask why the hell his kingdom didn't have a better system for communication. This was ridiculous.

"It is really, *very* important that I get back as soon as possible. Is there someone—*anyone*—who could get me out of here? Even if it's to a place that leads to another place that maybe, just maybe, leads to Brumlow?"

Galpin let out a slow sigh, glancing around the tavern before tossing his rag over his shoulder again.

He crouched forward, leaning his elbows on the counter, lowering his voice. "Ov'r there." He subtly nodded toward a door in the far back corner. "Ask for Irene—"

"Thank you," I said quickly, and he grabbed my arm before I could stand up.

"Wait, now. Be careful 'n there. If anyone can get 'ya home, it'll be her. But she's a trickster. Keep yer wits about 'ya. Dealin' with Irene is trouble. . . 'ya might wanna wait the two weeks."

"I'll take my chances." I patted his hand, feeling guilty that I was going to have to persuade him to give me the drink for free. Before I even had to, he glanced at the glass, then back to me.

"On the house. Ya' need all the money ya' have once ya' walk through that door."

I thanked him with a tight-lipped smile and prepared myself for bargaining.

The door was black and carved with symbols I wasn't familiar with. The golden knob sparkled when I approached, as though it were expecting me. When I swung it open and walked through, I didn't predict finding a two-story tavern filled with patrons.

A huge bouncer suddenly obscured my view. He towered over me, arms crossed. When he looked me up and down, his tongue darted out to wet his bottom lip. I did my best not to roll my eyes.

"Galpin said I should ask for Irene," I told him confidently, holding my chin up.

He pointed to the back of the crowded room, and I began walking in that direction. A thin haze of smoke permeated the air, and I prayed to the gods it was nothing more than tobacco. If it were any other kind, I was already breathing it in and it was too late. I needed to stay alert.

As I passed through the throng of people, I noticed the tables were almost all full. Card games were being played. Dice were rolled at some. It looked like an old saloon from westerns, except there were women in scantily clad outfits draping their arms around customers—

My eyes darted around the room. The hidden entrance. The flirting. The ample cleavage. The rows of doors on the second-story balcony.

I was in a brothel.

If I didn't stick out like a sore thumb before, I certainly did now. As I approached the back table, men and women stepped aside, appraising me openly. I waved awkwardly, dipping my chin in greeting.

The woman I assumed to be Irene sat in a plush red velvet chair at a private table . She wore a tight black dress that dipped down only enough to show her cleavage. I assessed her quickly, taking in her pointed ears, dark red hair, and blue eyes. She had a large gold earring through the conch of her ear, and she wore a medallion that sat nestled just above her breast, stating loud and proud her family clan. I cursed internally. I'd seen medallions like it before. She was a fucking leprechaun. No wonder Galpin had warned me.

A part of me wanted to turn around. The last time I

made a deal with a leprechaun didn't go so well. But I needed to make it back to Vareck, and I had very few options.

She leaned back and smirked at me. In one hand, she flipped a coin over her knuckles back and forth, while she used her other hand to pet the stomach of a very large, and very familiar, black and silver cat who was sprawled on his back snuggled on a pillowy cushion next to her. The cat opened his golden eyes and looked at me through a foggy feline smile.

"What the hell, Corvo?"

CHAPTER 25
MEERA

"Hey, Meera," he purred. "What are you doing here?"

"Me? What are *you* doing here?"

His back leg twitched, and he turned his head side to side, scratching his neck on the pillow. "They worship me here. As they should."

I stared at him incredulously, crossing my arms and huffing. His golden eyes met mine, and for a brief moment, they glowed. In an instant, they were back to normal, and he was wiggling around for more belly rubs.

What that meant, I wasn't sure. I didn't speak fluent Corvo, but I had a feeling that it was my warning to be sparse on details about myself. No problem. I didn't trust anything about this lady.

"You two know each other? How interesting." She brought a cigarette to her lips, inhaling deeply before blowing out a ring of smoke.

I blinked. Her accent sounded *nothing* like Lou's. Thank the gods. Fate was already taunting me by throwing another leprechaun in my face. I just hoped she was easier to deal with. Considering Galpin's warning and glancing at

259

my surroundings did little to encourage that thought. She just might be worse.

A group of fae at a large table were hitting their limit, sloshing ale over the sides of their mugs as they sang and clanked glasses, groping their paid partners. Women sat on their laps, rubbing their client's chests, and laughing with fake enthusiasm.

I waved away the cloud of smoke as it neared my face, keeping my tone casual. "We're acquainted. Didn't expect to run into him here."

Irene's eyes sparkled, and she tapped the cigarette against the edge of an ash tray. "So, Meera, is it? Tell me. Why did Galpin show you in? Are you"—she waggled her brows—"looking for work?"

"What? N-no," I spluttered, utterly shocked at the proposition.

"Oh, I see. It looks like we have a judgmental princess in our presence." She turned to an associate that sat next to her, his face obscured by the incline of his brimmed hat, speaking to him in a low voice while looking at me.

I shook my head quickly, taking a seat at her table. "Not what I meant. I'm not judging anyone's profession here. Honest work is honest work, as long as it's what they want to do," I said, pinning her with a look. "It's just not for me."

She chuckled, her cleavage jiggling as her chest moved. "Okay, princess. Enlighten me. What can a madam like me, do for a chaste girl like you?"

Chaste. Hmpf. I officially didn't like her. If she kept calling me princess, I was going to pick up that ashtray and throw it at her.

"Galpin said you might be able to help me find a way back to Brumlow."

"Brumlow," she cooed. "So you *are* a princess."

It was irritating simply because it was condescending, but now it felt uncomfortable, if only because Vareck was royalty, and we were . . . I don't know. Together-ish? How would one label our relationship? The way that Corvo looked at me indicated I needed to move on.

"I don't know what you mean by that." It was an odd assumption truthfully. I didn't look anything like a noble, and there were plenty of impoverished fae living in the main city.

"A lady from Brumlow with your beauty has money."

I chuckled, adjusting my second-hand cardigan in an effort to draw her attention to it. "I can assure you I don't."

She looked me up and down, assessing. "Well you're not dressed like you're from the King's city; I'll give you that." She waved at a waitress and pointed at the table holding up two fingers.

She had a mocking laugh when she'd said it, but it didn't bother me. It was true enough; I just thought it was rude.

"I'm from the human realm, but I was on business in Brumlow. I need to get back."

The server came back, setting down a tankard of ale, a small glass of brown liquor, and a small board with bread, dried meat, and cheese on it.

Corvo jumped up to the table immediately and began walking between the glasses wrapping his tail around the mug that sat in front of me, caressing it as he walked by. I could have sworn his eyes changed color again in a deep glow, but at this point, my mind could have been playing tricks on me. The smoke and haze that settled in the room was heavy. He pawed at the board, speaking in a pathetic voice. "No treats for me Irene?"

She reached beneath his chin and scratched, baby-talking to him when she said, "Haven't you had enough chicken treats?"

"I thought you wanted to spoil me," he said, curling up on the table and nudging my hand. I petted him absent-mindedly.

Irene sipped her liquor, gesturing for me to take a drink. "Business, huh? How did you end up all the way out here in Warwick?" Her tone was skeptical, like she was trying to catch me in a lie. I didn't like it. Her questions felt like bait.

I considered my words carefully. I was capable of lying, but was she capable of sniffing that out? It wasn't worth the risk. It'd be better to give a vague, but partial truth.

"Another business deal. That one fell through." I took a gulp of ale and swallowed, remembering to take it slow. It wouldn't be long before the effects hit. I'd already had one drink, and my stomach was still empty. I grabbed a hunk of bread that sat on a cutting board on the table, wrapping it around a piece of cheese and eating before I continued. "Galpin said a trade cart won't be headed for Brumlow for another two weeks, and there are no portals around. So, I need your assistance."

"I can't make a portal, princess," she said, tilting her head to the side. She picked up the coin again, rolling it over her knuckles.

I sighed. I don't know why she thought she was crafty. She was just playing hardball. Irene had no idea I worked with a leprechaun more times than I could count. So, I played along. I placed my hands on the table, pretending to stand up. "Sorry to waste your time—"

She held her hand out. "Sit down, princess. I didn't say I *couldn't* help you."

Settling back in, Irene gestured for me to continue my

meal. I grabbed more food, taking sips of the ale to help me swallow each mouthful. "So how can you help me?"

"I think the question is, how can you help me?"

"I don't follow," I said, glancing at Corvo. He narrowed his eyes, shifting his glance slightly. The bouncer sitting next to her chuckled, his body shaking. He snorted, leaning back as he tipped his hat forward.

She picked up her cigarette again, taking a drag. "I didn't think you would. See, you don't have any money."

"How do you know that?"

"She wonders how I know that," Irene said to her bodyguard while tapping ash into a tray. Pointing at me with her cigarette in hand, she gestured to my body. "Look at you. You're not dressed for winter, princess. Almost like you fell off the back of a wagon," she said with a smirk.

My heart stuttered, but it appeared to be an off-hand remark. She had no idea how spot on she was. "I don't have money, but I can—"

"Then what you're asking for is a favor. You and everyone else in this realm. You know what I want, princess?"

I ground my teeth at the nickname. "Do tell."

"I'm a businesswoman, Meera. I only want one thing. Money."

"If you'd had let me speak I was going to tell you that I can get you money. However much you want." I didn't know how much a transaction like this would cost, but I did know that Vareck would pay it, and if worse came to worse, I'd give her my money. Technically, I was a hundred thousand dollars richer the moment I handed Damon over, even if I hadn't seen the money yet, it was magically transferred as a part of the contract.

"That just means you're desperate. We haven't started

negotiations, and you've already told me that you're willing to pay me whatever I want." She tutted in disappointment.

Shit.

"Desperate only to a point, Irene. I said I'd pay you whatever you want because I want to cut through the bull-shit. I figured as a businesswoman you would appreciate that I wouldn't be wasting your time."

"I don't know that you can afford my services."

"Try me."

"I'll get you to Brumlow." I breathed in, my heart starting to race with excitement. "In one week," she finished.

"One week?" I asked. "Why not now?"

"Because you don't have payment now." She wrapped her painted lips around the cigarette, narrowing her eyes at me while she inhaled, tendrils of smoke coiling around her face.

My stomach twisted. The sounds of the brothel roared in my ears. Corvo was facing me, his backside turned to Irene and her bodyguard that sat on the other side of the table. I looked down at him, hoping the fear that was coursing through me didn't show on my face. His eyes glowed briefly, and then I heard his voice in my head, and I damn near jumped out of my seat, my hands gripping the edge of the chair.

"Vareck is on his way."

"How did you do that?"

"Keep them talking. Don't persuade her."

"Why—"

Irene laughed. "You okay there, princess? You seem a little jumpy."

"Cold chill. I have those a lot here." I swallowed thickly, trying to stall for time. Frustration filled me, but I tried to tamp it down. My powers were finally accessible, and I'm told not to use them. "I'm a pretty decent bartender. I think a week's wages would be enough for a portal? I'm assuming you were going to connect me with someone who can make a portal, yes?"

"Bartenders are a dime a dozen. You have two options, princess."

"Really? It seemed like you were only going to give me one," I muttered.

"You're pretty, but those curves are something else. Voluptuous is a hard quality to find in Faerie. Makes you *exotic*." Her voice dropped in a sultry tenor, accentuating the last word for effect, though I wasn't sure why. I wasn't flattered. She smacked her lips, eliciting a little pop. "All the clients would want a taste. You'd make me a pretty coin here, Meera. Keep quite a bit for yourself too."

The grip I had on the edge of the chair increased, and I shook my head. "Hard pass. What's option two?"

"I give you back to the brownies you escaped from. Either way, I get paid." A cruel smile formed as she dropped all sincerities.

My lips parted, my mouth feeling intensely dry. Bile rose to my throat, and I glanced around the room, quickly assessing the patrons to see if I spotted Gin and Gertrude.

She waved me off. "Relax. They're not here, but they're certainly waiting for you on the road out of town. The one that leads to Brumlow, as a matter of fact, as if they knew which way you'd be headed. In the meantime, they've put a reward out for you. Not the smartest pair."

"Yeah?" I propped my elbows on the table rubbed at my temple, trying to keep her talking while I waited for Vareck to find me. "How so?"

"What could a couple of brownies want with the likes

of you? Someone paid them for you, that's what. Which means you're worth much more than they're offering."

I had no idea how much money was being thrown around on my behalf, and at this point, I didn't want to know. I figured it would just give me anxiety. "Is there an option number three?"

"Afraid not, dearie."

"And if I refuse your offer?"

She pointed at my tankard. "That ale you've been drinking? It's going to make you lose consciousness soon, and then I get to make the decision for you. Guess which one I'll pick?"

I glanced down at the mug, not feeling at all woozy or like I'd been poisoned or drugged. Since I'd recently been knocked out that way, I was accustomed to the feeling. On the contrary, I felt better with hearty food and a thick ale in my stomach. All I could do was stare at her. Was she bluffing? Was I moments away from falling over?

Corvo's voice entered my mind again, startling me. *"You're fine. Keep talking."*

"But—"

His eyes flashed quickly, glowing as he wrapped his tail around the tankard again, and that's when I understood. I was stupid enough to drink without considering the woman in front of me, but he knew who I was dealing with. Desperation had made me careless, and I was grateful he was around. Perhaps I had more luck on my side than I'd realized.

I sniffed, rubbing at my nose before crossing my arms and leaning back. "Something tells me you're going to go for option number one, but something also tells me it's going to take longer than a week."

Irene winked at me. "Smart girl."

Shaking my head, I leaned back in my chair a little more, almost tilting it on two legs. "I'm more of a behind-the-scenes kind of girl. You know, like mopping floors and doing laundry." Which was not a fun thought, but it beat the alternative. I angled my head toward a table to see a woman tracing her finger down a client's jaw before she planted a lingering kiss on his lips. "The ladies here look like they're really into their job. Which is great for them, but I don't want to."

"Oh, they're into their work, but you know, sometimes it just feels like work. Not every day can be your best day. That can be said for any job." She reached into her dress and pulled out a small pear-shaped glass bottle topped off with a small cork. The contents looked like silver glitter. "That's where the pixie dust comes in. They put a little bit of this on their bodies and it makes them feel *good*. It's one hell of an aphrodisiac."

I felt disgusted by the way she so nonchalantly spoke of sexually enslaving me. "So you give them the choice, yet you want to take away mine? That's kind of backwards."

She shrugged. "Money talks, princess. You're a wanted lady and you do have a nice price on your head. But you also have a rather lovely look to you, and I play the long game."

"I don't like games, Irene, and I don't think I'll agree to the arrangement."

She glanced at my empty mug with a curl of frustration at the corner of her mouth. With a single angry snap, her bodyguard got up and took a step toward me.

"I wouldn't do that," I said, and she held a hand up for him to stop.

"You change your mind and want to do this the easy way?"

"No, I just don't want your man here to lose a hand."

He cracked his knuckles and sniggered. "You gonna cut me, girlie?"

"No, but my boyfriend will."

"Who's your boyfriend?" Corvo asked, his eyes filled with mischief. I had a feeling he was starting to enjoy this.

The volume of chatter in the room softened, and heads turned to look at the entrance of the brothel. I kept my focus on the leprechaun. A few wolfish whistles pierced the air, women catcalling the newest patron. Turning to glance over my shoulder, I saw a familiar figure walking toward us, lowering his hood.

With a wide grin, I nodded my head toward the king and stared straight into the madam's eyes.

"He is."

CHAPTER 26
VARECK

A favor now for a favor later.

The price I'd paid echoed in my head as I traveled across the barren winter to find her. Images of her suffering had burned into my mind. Every time I closed my eyes, the fear of what could have happened to her haunted me.

Making a deal with a blood witch and throwing myself into an unknown portal, all for the chance to find her and bring her home. Back to me, where she belonged.

And here she was.

In a brothel.

Jealousy coiled through me. I could see the way men were looking at her, licking their lips and practically salivating, though I doubt she even noticed.

The moment I entered Warwick, I felt her presence again. Now that I'd entered the tavern, it buzzed stronger. With her in front of me, my soul felt content that she was near again, but restless for a reason unknown.

Corvo had already filled me in on the current situation, and while I scanned the premises, I noticed several bouncers and bodyguards. We didn't have the upper hand. Nowhere close to it. This was a problem.

Meera glanced at me, a cute smirk on her face, but I couldn't match it. She had no idea what was about to happen. She was so focused on my arrival, she didn't realize a crucial detail.

"Well, well, well, who do we have here?" the leprechaun asked, giving me a full appraisal head to toe. She bit her bottom lip and raised an eyebrow. "This is your boyfriend, princess? Well done."

"Irene, I presume," I greeted, inclining my chin. Standing behind Meera with a hand on her shoulder, I squeezed it lightly. It was partial reassurance to her, and partial for myself, feeling the warmth of her beneath my palm, knowing she was real, and unharmed.

"My boyfriend," Meera said, her tone filled with snark. She had her arms crossed when she added, "King Vareck."

I exhaled, waiting for the inevitable. Irene's brows rose, and she looked at her bodyguard next to her. He chortled, lifting the brim of his hat to take a look. After a moment's pause, they both laughed. Meera's face filled with confusion, and she shifted in her seat.

"Sure. And I'm the Faerie Queen," Irene said, snickering. She tossed back a glass of liquor, audibly sighing after she'd swallowed.

"I don't understand," Meera said, looking between Irene and me.

"You think that's the king?" she asked, shaking her head. "Child, please. He bears no royal seal, no crown"— she made an effort to look behind me, then searched the room dramatically before holding her hands out, palm up —"and walks into a tavern and brothel with no royal guard? I don't know who he is, but King Vareck wouldn't come to the likes of Warwick, and he certainly wouldn't be here alone."

"But he *is* the king," she argued, sitting up straight, and putting her hands on the table. "And we're leaving."

The bouncers in the room had taken note of our interactions, having heard the exchange. In my periphery, I assessed their positions. Their stance. The way the tension in their shoulders intensified. The danger had increased substantially.

"Meera," I said softly, and when she looked at me, I shook my head ever so slightly. Her hazel eyes searched my chest, my arms, my hands, looking for some sign, only to find I had standard riding leathers and gloves. They were high quality, but all that could mean any number of things in Faerie. A noble. A thief. But not a king. When she understood, her features dropped.

Corvo reached over the edge of the table, stretching his paw and aiming for a piece of sausage. "Don't mind me," he purred. "I just came for the food."

"Have a seat next to your princess, 'your majesty'," Irene said mockingly. "Ale or liquor?"

"Neither," I replied flatly, ignoring her offer and choosing to stand while we stared at each other. "You have a penchant for spiking drinks, so I'm told."

"On occasion. When it suits me." She narrowed her eyes, quickly glancing at Meera and wondering why her tricks hadn't worked. Meera was none the wiser, but Corvo knew the dangers from the moment she'd arrived.

"Of course I knew the danger. You owe me." His eyes flashed at me while he gnawed on a piece of meat he'd taken from the tray.

I resisted the urge to roll my eyes. "Owed" him for protecting Meera from being drugged? *"Consider us even."*

"For what, pray tell?"

"She was drugged on your watch once already."

His whiskers twitched, and he licked his paw while his tail flicked. *"Agree to disagree."*

"Well, it doesn't suit me," I said to Irene, resuming our conversation.

"And what does, handsome?"

"Leaving."

"You're free to go."

"With Meera."

"Ah, see, that's going to be a problem."

"Excuse me? I fail to see how that's a problem." Meera waved her hand toward me. "He's here. I'll hitch a ride back to Brumlow with him. No need for your services, so no need to pay your exorbitant price."

"See, that's where you're wrong, princess. You accepted my food and drink, seated so graciously at my table. And you think you can just get up and walk away? That's not how things are done in Faerie."

"We'll pay you for the meal," I said, watching a bouncer carefully as he moved to block doors. The chatter in the room had shifted to a softer hum as everyone listened in on the tense situation we'd found ourselves in.

"I don't think you want to do that," Meera said to me softly, pulling her hands back from the table and setting them in her lap.

"Oh, he wants to," Irene replied, not taking her eyes off me. She took a new cigarette from a silver case and tapped it twice on the lid. Bringing it to her lips, the man next to her lit it without being asked. After she blew out a cloud of smoke, she continued. "He just doesn't know the price yet."

Corvo sat in the middle of the table, curling his black tail around him tightly. He patted a pear-shaped bottle, scooting it across the table, nearing the edge. It was such an annoying habit of his. "Things are all so tense here. Can't we all just get along? You could take turns scratching my chin. Wouldn't that be fun?"

"Not the time, Corvo," Meera grumbled, scrubbing her hands down her face. It wouldn't be long before he would get temperamental. He was a cat, through and through, and he disliked it when people ignored him.

"Your princess here was just about to make a deal with me," the madam said.

"I was not!" Meera stood up quickly, gesturing to the second balcony. "You were going to force me into prostitution, you twat. That's not a deal. That's trafficking."

My fists clenched, the sound of my leather gloves creaking at the pressure. The tension in my jaw pounded in my ears as I gritted my teeth to keep from losing control. The simple thought enraged me. Knowing that was exactly what would have happened had I not shown up was about to send me spiraling.

"It's business," Irene said flatly.

"Screw your business," Meera spat, her eyes glowing a brilliant green I'd seen before. Before I could stop her, that sweet and sultry voice issued a command. "You're going to let us leave *now*."

Irene glared at her, her cheeks reddening with anger. "Bad move, princess." She rapped her knuckles on the table twice.

Fuck.

Meera realized her mistake too late. Irene couldn't be persuaded. She was either immune, rare as it was, or paid a pretty penny to a witch for a talisman that would do the

275

trick—and even Meera wasn't strong enough to break through.

Bouncers closed in on us, and I sighed. Corvo bounced across the table surface, knocking the tray of food as it clattered, and the contents went flying in different directions. The pear-shaped bottle tipped over the side, crashing onto the floor as he darted under the table.

A silver glitter exploded into the air, fanning across the room like a dust storm. Meera barely had time to register what had happened before the shimmering flecks settled over every inch of her exposed skin, peppering her face like freckles before she sneezed and cursed.

"Oops!" Corvo meowed, and honestly, he didn't sound the least bit sorry.

The patrons scrambled to get away, hiding behind the bar or banging on locked doors.

A man twice Meera's size went after her, and she held her hand out, yelling for him to stop, and this time, her compulsion worked. I grinned. "Stay close," I said to her quickly.

When a bouncer took a swing at me, I moved out of the way, his momentum causing him to lose balance when he missed. Grabbing him by his arm, I reared back, smashing my knuckles into his face in quick successions. Blood sprayed from his broken nose as he stumbled backwards, crashing into a table. A pitcher of ale tipped over, spilling across the wooden surface before pouring onto the floor.

Two more came for me, and with one swift kick, chairs went flying as a bouncer flew across the room. His cohort tried to sway to the side, and I grabbed him, yanking him close enough to wrap my hand around his neck.

"Wait, wait, wa—"

I squeezed. "Enough of this."

His muscles flexed beneath my fingers as I lifted him, slamming him against one of the inn's brick pillars. His feet dangled, claws scraping uselessly at my grip. I watched as his eyes rolled back, his face darkening to a sickening shade of purple.

A bouncer grabbed Meera's arm, jerking her toward him. She yelped, caught by surprise when her compulsion on him failed. It was the man who'd been sitting next to Irene. His grip caused her to whimper. With more fight in her than I expected, her hand curled into a fist and swung. The crack of it echoed through the brothel. Pride swelled in my chest, but was quickly squashed when the brute slowly turned his face back to her. His free hand wrapped around her neck.

"You're going to regret that, girlie."

"Not the face," Irene commented. Meera reared back as much as she could to spit on him.

"Fuck you."

"I plan to."

Something inside me snapped.

"Aw, shit," Corvo said.

I dropped the man I'd been choking, and he slumped to the floor with a thud. A low, guttural snarl ripped from my chest before I could stop it. The noise startled everyone in the room, but everything around me felt like a blur. Grabbing the man's wrist, I twisted it sharply. His fingers opened as the bone fractured beneath my strength. Fae were strong. Dark fae even more so. But a fury? He never stood a chance.

I wrenched his hand away from Meera, slamming it down on the table near us. I stared into his eyes and growled, "Don't. Fucking. Touch. Her."

The bouncer's shock wore off quickly, and he reached to

his side, going for his dagger, but I got to mine first. In a swift motion, I slammed the blade into his hand, effectively nailing him to the table where Meera had just been sitting. He shrieked as the metal sliced him open and burned the skin around the wound making whatever supernatural healing he possessed worse than a human's. His body stiffened as the gravity of his mistake came crashing down. "No one touches my fucking woman, and make no mistake— she's *mine*."

Several feminine screams echoed in the room. Meera's hands clapped over her mouth. "Oh shit," she gasped, the words coming out muffled.

The man I'd stabbed crouched over the table, trying to breathe through the pain and holding his arm steady with his good hand. Anytime he moved, the burn spread, and tendrils of smoke curled around the blade. Irene's gaze fixed on the hilt of the dagger, holding her hand up in a motion to instruct the rest of her bouncers to halt in their oncoming advancement.

The royal seal was branded into the handle. I pulled a matching dagger from my side, twirling it in my hand.

"What did you say your name was again?"

"I didn't."

"That's a fancy trick your blade is doing," she commented, pointing at it as she spoke. "Burning his skin that way. Steal that off a royal guard, did you?"

"Does it matter? I'm either capable enough to defeat them, or I am one. Either way, I may not be able to kill all of your men, but I damn sure can make it across this table to slit your throat before they can save you."

She pursed her lips and swallowed, seething at the threat. "And your girl here would die in the process too."

Meera turned her head, touching my arm gently and

mumbling through the side of her mouth. "I would like to not die."

"I'm guessing all three of us would die," I said, motioning my hand in a circle to Irene, Meera, and myself. Then I shrugged. "Can't do much business around here as a dead woman, can you?"

She smirked, taking a deep drag of her cigarette, though I could tell I had her concerned. The way her gaze shifted ever so slightly. The twitch at the corner of her mouth. She was weighing the risk. Self-preservation ran deep in all of us, but a leprechaun would use anyone to shield them if it meant staying alive. They only looked out for number one, and I'd never known them to truly care for another person.

"You wanted payment, didn't you?"

She nodded, watching the weapon very carefully as I expertly twirled it.

The entire room had gone silent. You could hear a pin drop, but all I focused on was the sound of Meera's ragged breathing as the silver pixie dust settled into her pores. The feel of her palms holding onto my arm encouraged my mind to wander, to think of how she would taste, yet I remained in control. We were both on borrowed time with the drug working its way into our systems, but she was more so than me.

"Then let's negotiate," I said calmly, swallowing through the discomfort. "Meera, how long did Irene want you to work here?"

"Um, a week, she said. . . before she, uh . . . said it would be longer." Meera swayed, holding my bicep for stability. She rubbed her nose, muttering about being allergic to the silver shit.

"A week," I repeated, keeping my eyes firmly on the

leprechaun. "How much would she have made you in a week?"

"Two hundred golds, easy," she answered, keeping her tone even and waiting for me to respond. Did she think I would be surprised? Insulted by the cost? Meera was priceless, and Irene was a fool.

I reached beneath my cloak, pulling a pouch and tossing it onto the table. It landed with a thud, the coins inside clanking. The sound of money made her eyes shift, her pupils dilating in excitement as she quickly glanced at it and then back at me. "There. That's five hundred. You've been paid more than double what you would have made. If you accept the payment, you agree to call this off. No one dies. I let you live. Meera and I leave this place alive, and none of your associates can follow us. The debt is settled. Forever."

She reached for it, pulling out a gold and biting it. A smile curled up her lips. When it came to a leprechaun, money would always win. She nodded, and a contract formed between us, magic sealing us to the terms with a small pop.

"Good." After sheathing the dagger I held, I reached forward, yanking the other one from the bouncer's hand, the squelching sound more audible than most patrons were comfortable with as a few of them gagged. He grunted, staggering back, or tried to anyway.

I wrapped my fingers around his wrist once more. "Before we go," I forced his hand back to the table and slammed the knife through his wrist, tearing through muscle and tendon and bone. He screamed and the smell of piss followed. I wrenched the knife to the side, mutilating his hand. Without bone to keep it from falling, the appendage dangled by the remaining muscle and skin. I released him and wiped the blood on my trousers. He fell to the floor, cradling his wound close to the chest.

I pointed the dagger at Irene, who watched me with narrowed eyes. "Try to find a loophole and I'll have this piece of shit establishment ripped apart for kindling and you'll be tossed into the fire first."

With that, I reupholstered the blade, and I wrapped my arm around Meera's waist, pulling her into my side as we turned to leave. Everyone watched us in silence; fear, disbelief, and uncertainty still permeating the air. Only our footsteps could be heard as we took leave, Irene's people forced to follow the terms their boss had agreed to. The man at the door pulled it open, his nostrils flaring at me in anger.

"Fucking leprechaun," Meera said, flipping Irene off before we walked through the exit. "I hope you find hair in your soup . . . and I hope it's a pube."

We didn't bother to stick around for a reply. The door shut behind us, and we stood in what felt like another world. The sounds of the tavern were a stark contrast to the brothel. No one in the pub heard past the sound barrier. People were drinking merrily, chatting to each other, completely unaware of what had just happened.

Meera's hold on me tightened, and her walk was unsteady. She turned to me, her eyes dreamy as she bit the corner of her bottom lip.

"We need to leave here quickly," I whispered to her, cradling her cheek carefully with my gloved hand. The silver sheen covering her face and neck was already affecting her, and it was starting to affect me too.

"Something is happening to me," she muttered, pressing her hand to her chest. "I think I'm having a reaction to that dust. I feel hot. Is it hot in here?" She started to fan herself.

"Yes, it's just hot," I lied, pulling her toward the bar. I flagged down the man I'd spoken with when I arrived. "Galpin, was it?"

"Who's askin'?" He came over with a smile but quickly took a look at Meera and his skin paled, guilt causing him to lower his gaze. "No . . . she's such a nice girl. I should'na sent her 'n there."

"No, you shouldn't have," I replied through gritted teeth. Lashing out wouldn't help us now. "But we both need your help now."

"Name it," he said, straightening his shoulders.

"We need a place to stay. An inn. A barn. A room. Anything. Somewhere that isn't *here*," I said, gesturing to the brothel door.

He nodded, yelling at someone in the back to come out and cover the front. He grabbed his cloak from a hook on the wall, wrapping it around himself. "My brother. He owns the inn. I'll take ya' there myself." He quickly assessed Meera's clothing, and he looked around to see if there was another one hanging. He began to remove his own. "Ya' need this ta' stay warm."

She swallowed thickly, shaking her head. "Too hot," she said, licking her lips, and I swear the sweep of her tongue was in slow motion. A low rumble vibrated in my throat.

"I understand." Galpin's eyebrows knit together, and he refastened the cloak. He turned to me and quietly added, "It's on ya' too, mate. The dust."

I nodded, my jaw clenched. "I'm aware."

He waved us to the door, pulling it open. "This way."

The wind howled, swirling flakes of snow in spirals. The moment the crisp night air reached me, my senses were assaulted by something new. I inhaled sharply, my muscles locking into place as a new heated desire coursed through me. The scent of her filled my lungs—heady, intoxicating—utterly *ruining* me.

Arousal coiled between us, pulling tight and trying to take control.

Thick and powerful and all-consuming.

But it wasn't mine.

It was hers.

CHAPTER 27

MEERA

Everything burned. A tingling heat swept from my legs to my fingertips and everywhere in-between, making my skin feel too tight, too sensitive. My mind reeled back to the fight in the brothel, the heat intensifying as I recalled the way Vareck moved. The way he *fought* for me.

I knew he was intimidating. I'd heard tales of his ruthlessness. After spending time with him, I'd begun to wonder if they were even true. Now there was no doubt in my mind.

Instead of scaring me, it had the opposite effect. Fricken romance books.

I lifted a trembling hand to my throat, wondering what it would be like to get on his bad side. To feel those strong fingers wrap around my neck, pressing just enough to make me shiver. Would his hands be calloused like they were in our dreams? Would he hold me firm and take me from behind? Maybe he'd shove me up against this wall and—

"Meera?" His rumbled tone pulled me from my fantasies. "How are you holding up?" He'd ended up a few feet in front of me, but doubled back when I didn't move. I bit my lip hard, shaking my head. "I can't . . ." *What's wrong with me?*

"It's the pixie dust," he said quietly. I must have asked my question out loud.

My throat felt rough when I tried to swallow, like sandpaper rubbing together. "Never been on it. This is . . . something else."

Vareck let out a strained chuckle, holding out his gloved hand for me. "Come on, we need to get to the inn. We'll talk there."

His fingers wrapped around mine. We weren't even touching skin to skin, but it didn't matter.

A fresh wave of heat pooled between my thighs.

I groaned, my knees buckling as I collapsed into the snow. The ice seared into me, bypassing the fabric of my pants, but I barely felt it. I just needed a moment—just one moment—to clear my head. But it wasn't working. My thoughts spiraled, filled with images of Vareck—of us—of the things we had done in our dreams.

Lust throbbed in my veins, making me dizzy.

"Fuck."

The word was both a whisper and a curse coming from his lips.

I forced myself to look up, eyes hazy, chest rising and falling in shallow breaths. He knelt beside me, all traces of anger from earlier gone, replaced with a hunger that should have worried me. His gaze burned as it roved over me, his breath slow and controlled.

"How much further?" Vareck asked our guide, his voice strained. I whimpered at the cold pressing against my skin, my nipples peaking painfully beneath the fabric of my shirt and sweater. Everything *ached*. Everything burned.

"Three minutes, give or take."

His chin dropped, head bowed for a suspended moment. "I need you to stand up, Meera." His grip on my hand tightened, pulling me up on shaky legs. I swayed instantly. Vareck lunged, pulling me to his chest with an iron grip around my waist.

We were surrounded by winter, yet when his scent washed over me it was like the snowy landscape around us was a pale comparison.

A long, breathy moan escaped me. I melted into his touch, pressing tighter against him. I arched, my fingers hovering over my lips before biting down on my knuckle, desperate to curb the wicked thoughts tearing through my mind. But it wasn't enough. I needed *more*. My hand twitched, ready to slip beneath the band of my pants—

"You have to walk." The voice sliced through my haze, and my breath hitched. Vareck frowned and gently moved my hand from my face. A soft whine left my lips.

"How"—I swallowed again, trying to focus on the words—"How are you still . . ." Functioning? Not affected? I wasn't sure how I planned to end that sentence, but he seemed to understand.

"I've been through the passage. You haven't." His voice was rough, but it sounded miles away.

I blinked up at him, my vision blurring at the edges.

I wanted him.

Oh, how I wanted him.

Right here. Right *now*.

I wanted him to shove me onto the ice, to claim me against the cold, to drag me up by my hair and—

"We need to get out of the snow," he said. I heard the words, but my feet didn't move. They couldn't.

I didn't care.

"You had me so turned on back there," I admitted,

breath hitching as I trailed a hand down my own chest. I pinched one of my nipples, arching into my own touch.

"Gods be damned," Vareck cursed. His heat pulled away. The pressure against my body was no longer there. "Siren, I'm barely holding on here. I *can't* carry you. You have to walk."

My body shook like a leaf in the wind, but it wasn't from the cold, even if my fingers were numb.

A shadow loomed over me as Galpin stepped up beside us. "I can carry her. It'll be faster—"

He made the mistake of reaching for me. Vareck reacted before I could even process what was going on.

"*Do not* touch her," he all but snarled, persuasion steeped in every word of his command.

Galpin stepped back, lifting his hands in surrender. "I wasn't goin' ta' do anythin' unsavory, friend. Yer lady is goin' to freeze in these temperatures if we don't get her inside." The muscle in Vareck's jaw tightened, but Galpin continued, wrapping his scarf around his face. "I'm covered head ta' toe. She won't get any dust on me, n' even if she did, it's not the first time. I've had plenty of encounters. Don't affect me much anymore."

A shudder ran through me. Without thinking, I leaned toward Vareck, reaching for him. He caught my wrist in a gloved hand, fingers flexing against my skin.

"Vareck," I whispered, trying to break his hold.

He didn't budge.

Didn't even *flinch*.

"Do it," he said quietly. "Just know if you touch her inappropriately—"

"I'm happily mated. Only woman I want ta' touch is my wife." He and Vareck stared at each other for a second, then the king nodded. He released my wrist and stepped back. I was too busy watching the man who'd occupied my thoughts for years to notice the bartender move. My world tilted as he knelt to bend me over his shoulder. A strong arm wrapped around my legs, just above my knees.

A growl rumbled in my throat.

"Put me—"

"Do not compel him," Vareck cut me off. My eyes narrowed. I couldn't see him; only the back of the man carrying me. He must have sensed what was coming because he quickly added, "*or* me."

My sexual frustration turned into a new irritation. Logically, I knew this was probably the best route. I clearly couldn't walk. Vareck was struggling more than I'd origi-nally thought. We were both trapped by the pixie dust and needed to get somewhere safe, or as close to it as we could manage.

Unfortunately, because of said dust, logic was not going to win.

"You—you asshole!" I yelled, fisting my hands to keep from beating against the nice man's back. Or butt. I couldn't make out much through his cloak, but the body beneath me was warm and hard. The pressure on my lower abdomen wasn't helping matters either. "Put. Me. Down." My demand turned into a low moan. One I tried to stifle. This was why I didn't want to be carried, especially by some stranger. Frostbite seemed less embarrassing, though significantly more problematic.

The man holding me didn't react, but Vareck did. A rough growl sounded from somewhere close to my left.

"We're here." Galpin opened a door with his free hand and stepped inside. Wood groaned beneath his boots. My skin started to burn with the sudden temperature differ-ence, and not in a good way.

My body was gently lowered to the ground. A strong hand held me up with a grip on my bicep. "Farris!" he called out in greeting. I was too out of it to turn and see who he was speaking with. "These two got caught up in . . . a situation. They're goin' ta' need a room. Not above anyone else, if ya' know what I mean."

The room blurred around me. Everything became distorted except for Vareck. He wasn't touching me with his hands, but his eyes—I'd had fucks that didn't feel as deep or sinful as his gaze. My lips parted.

"Sure thing. It'll be—"

Metal clinked as Vareck tossed another leather pouch on the counter.

Galpin whistled under his breath. "They had a run in with the dust," he explained to the other man, presumably his brother.

"Ahhh," Farris hummed. Something hard scraped across wood. "Here's yer key. Second floor, turn left, last door on the right."

"Ya' need any help?" Galpin asked. His question was directed at me, but it was the man looming over his shoulder he looked at.

The muscle in Vareck's jaw flexed. "I've got her."

Gravel had less roughness to it than his voice did, and gods was I here for it.

The hand on my bicep dropped away. Before I could sway, Vareck scooped me up, carrying me bridal style toward the stairs.

"Have fun!" Farris called.

"Don't forget ta' bathe," Galpin's voice followed behind. Their good-natured chatting continued, slowly quieting as Vareck led us away.

I wrapped my arms around his shoulders, my lips

grazing his neck. His scent—dark and masculine—ruined me. I kissed his jaw, nipping at his skin, wanting him to break.

He quickened his pace, but otherwise didn't respond. We came to a brief stop, but he didn't put me down. Maneuvering the arm bracing my back, he shoved the key in the lock and twisted. The door swung open silently.

Vareck stepped inside and kicked it closed with his foot. The arm beneath my knees dropped away. My legs fell, but he slowly eased me down, dragging me against his body as he reached behind him and flicked the lock back in place.

I reached up, my hands skimming his shoulders, moving to wrap around the nape of his neck and through his hair. I pulled, trying to make him lower his face to mine, but the king remained as immobile as a statue.

The frustration from earlier resurfaced. A low keening whine built in my chest. "What in the nine realms are you waiting for?" I demanded.

Gently, he reached back to wrap his fingers around my wrists, prying them from his body. "Bath first." He jutted his chin toward the door to my right.

"No."

"Meera, this isn't a negotiation."

"Either you fuck me or so help me gods, I will find someone else—"

"*Do not* finish that sentence," he snapped. His voice was ice-cold yet burning with fire. I growled under the compulsion, wanting to fight it, but unable to with how the pixie dust was affecting me.

Vareck reached around me, opening the bathroom door. He pressed one hand to my hip and the other to my lower abdomen, pushing me firmly toward it.

"This is ridiculous," I groaned. "I want you. You want me. It's not like we haven't done this hundreds of times—"

"Strip."

My hands dropped, pulling at my shirt and cardigan without hesitation. Any stubbornness I had died a swift death now that he was speaking my language. I didn't even need the compulsion to obey, but I'd be lying if I said it didn't do something for me.

My leggings clung to my thighs, damp from my arousal. Vareck turned on the bath, testing the water temperature before stepping back. Once naked, I reached for him again.

"Get in."

"But—"

"Get in," he repeated, this time using persuasion.

Unable to fight his commands, I stepped into the claw-foot tub and sank to my knees. The water was only a couple of inches high but filling quickly. I leaned back, gasping when my bare skin touched the cold cast iron.

Vareck paused, tugging off his gloves, his dark gaze zeroing in on me. His eyes, usually so blue, were nearly black from how dilated they were.

My breath hitched.

He resumed undressing. "How familiar are you with pixie dust?"

I licked my bottom lip. "Heard of it. Never used it. My brother had a problem with it for a while, and I didn't want to touch it after watching him go down that road." Lust made it hard to focus but easy to talk.

He nodded, hanging his cloak on one of the mounted wall hooks. "It hits hard and fast, but unlike drugs you consume, the effects of pixie dust don't start to wane until it's off your skin." Vareck glanced at the tub. "Which is why we're both going to wash up before I take you to bed."

My heart rate ratcheted up. My hand touched my throat, then slowly descended my naked form. Water dripped from my fingertips as I circled one of my nipples. They were already sensitive, and I had to bite back a moan.

Vareck let out a harsh breath as he quickly unbuttoned his shirt. His focus was locked in on where I touched myself, expression feral.

I loved it. I needed more.

He whipped off his undershirt, revealing the gleaming muscles of his bare chest. Without hesitating, he started on the laces of his pants. "You're toying with me."

"I'm horny," I corrected. "And you're holding out on me."

Vareck grunted, leaning over to tear his boots off, then his socks. My hand slid between my breasts and down the soft swell of my stomach. "I'm making sure we don't end up in Warwick for a week because we can't stop fucking. I'd love nothing more than to lose myself in you." His pants dropped, revealing the lack of boxers or any type of under-clothes. "But if we're going to do that, it won't be under the influence of pixie dust." My hand slipped beneath the water, traveling toward the apex of my thighs. Vareck wrapped his fingers around my forearm, stopping the descent.

I lifted my chin, meeting his eyes in a challenge. A sexy smirk curved up his face. "Scoot forward. Let me take care of you."

Despite the lust drowning me, my heart stuttered in my chest, constricting uncomfortably tight. Vareck settled in behind me, his legs braced on either side of my body. A strong arm wrapped around my waist and pulled me so my back met his chest. I tried to ignore the thick shaft nestling against my backside, but it was almost painful from how turned on I was.

Instead of touching me, like I wanted, Vareck dipped a washcloth in the water before pouring some sort of soap on it. The smell was floral, but light and not overwhelming. While the cloth was likely soft, it felt rough against my sensitive skin as he began the process of washing me, and first up was my face and neck. He gently wiped and re-wet the cloth over and over, removing traces of silver.

"Is there anything you don't want to do?" he asked quietly, cleaning one arm, then the other.

"I, uhm, no." My back arched when he started on my chest.

"Nothing?" He paused. "I know it's hard to think right now, but I need to know your limits."

I groaned, arching my back against him when he stopped moving. The breath hissed between his teeth. A sharp pain made me gasp, then moan. He bit me.

He bit my ear lobe, and I should have been alarmed.

Keyword: *should*.

Biting between fae wasn't the same as with humans. All it took was a slip of control for our fangs to break the skin and a mate bond would be formed.

Sure, Faerie lost true mates because of the curse. Chosen mates, though? Happened all the time.

"Behave," Vareck ordered gruffly. It didn't escape my notice he hadn't used persuasion. Maybe he didn't actually want me to behave . . .

I leaned back, tilting my neck to the side in an open invitation as my hands settled on his muscular thighs. "I'd rather we didn't."

He muttered something under his breath that sounded like he was asking for a god to give him strength.

Ha. There were no gods in Faerie, not since Amoret's demise.

"Meera, if you can't focus, I'm going to have to compel answers out of you and I *really* don't want to do that." I lightly ran my nails up and down his thighs, making him shudder. "Please."

That word made me pause.

He was a king. Royalty didn't say please. They didn't beg. Except, he did. For me.

I took a deep breath, trying to pull together my jumbled thoughts. "You asked me something. What was it?"

Vareck laughed softly, but it was tight. I wasn't the only one feeling the effects of the pixie dust. He was just better at controlling his reaction.

"Your limits. What are they?"

"Um." The scenarios that flashed through my head had my blood boiling. I clenched my teeth to keep from making a sound. Except to answer him, I had to speak. "I'm okay with most things."

Vareck groaned as he resumed washing me. "That's not an answer. I don't want to take things too far."

He had good intentions. I knew that. He was trying to do this the right way. And sober, uninhibited Meera appreciated it. She, however, was not here. "Anything we've done in dreams is fine—other than biting."

The idea of it made my body flush with arousal, but I wasn't making a decision like that while under the magical equivalent to ecstasy.

"I can work with that. If at any point you want me to stop, all you need to do is say it. Okay?"

"Yes. Now can you—" My words died a quick and lustful death when the washcloth rubbed one of my breasts, then the other. His strong fingers circled my nipples. Pleasure shot straight between my legs.

"Tell me something." His warm breath fanned my ear, sending a wave of goosebumps down my arms. "That first night we were together, what would you have done if I were in bed when you woke up?"

"I . . ." His hand traveled down my stomach, to the junction between my thighs. "Oh gods." My back bowed, pushing my hips forward.

All too soon, his hand slipped away, washing my legs instead.

"Words, Meera. I want them," he growled.

A whine built in my chest, threatening to pass my lips. I bit down hard, tasting blood. "I wanted you."

"I know, but that's not what I asked you." A calloused hand wrapped around my shoulder, bending me forward so he could wash my back.

"I don't know." My voice didn't sound like me. It was deeper, sultry, and breathless. "When I woke up and saw you . . . I was embarrassed."

Vareck paused. "Why would you ever be embarrassed?"

A brief laugh escaped me. "I'd just met you and was sleeping in your bed."

"And?" He didn't get it. "It's not like you were the only one turned on. I just woke up first." Strong fingers skated down my back, then curved around my hip.

"You also left the bed," I pointed out.

The washcloth left my skin, and I glanced back to see Vareck washing his chest.

"I didn't think I was dreaming," he said quietly. "I tried to wake you up, but you insisted you were awake."

My mouth went dry. "I'm awake in all our dreams."

"But you've never said my name before." The vein in his

neck stood out, and he shook his head. "I got up because my control was fraying, and you were still asleep. Before I met you, I'd convinced myself I'd be fine if I could just meet you and get answers." Vareck snorted self-deprecatingly. "I'm a fucking liar. One look was all it took. We were a hundred feet apart, and you wore a mask, but the second I laid eyes on you, I wanted you."

My lips parted, and I shifted around so I was on my knees facing him. "I didn't think I was dreaming either." His eyes flashed, something savage peeking out. Something primal. "I remember you trying to wake me, but you were so warm and solid and *real*." I swallowed hard. "I felt how hard you were, and I couldn't help myself. When I woke up, you weren't there." I dropped my eyes to his chest, struggling to look him in the eye when I was being so honest. "I thought I woke you and after I laid down all those rules about not touching, I was embarrassed. It was pretty obvious from your body language you knew what I was dreaming about, but it didn't occur to me that we were having the same dream."

Vareck tipped my chin up, forcing me to meet his gaze. "I wondered if we were sharing the same one or simply dreaming of each other. That means all the other nights you've been at the castle . . ."

"Even when I was pissed at you, I couldn't stay away," I whispered.

His hand tunneled through my tangled hair, pulling me to him. Our lips met; our tongues instantly intertwined. It was a dance we'd done a thousand times, and yet it was all so brand new. I ran my hands up his chest, feeling the muscles contract beneath my touch.

Vareck groaned, pulling me toward him, but while the tub was large, it wasn't big enough for me to straddle his lap. Vareck wasn't a small man and my thighs were thick. When it became clear we weren't going to be able to make that position work in here, he released my mouth, forehead falling to mine. We both were breathing hard.

"You're going to turn back around and let me wash your hair. Then, when you're clean, you're going to take your sweet ass into the bedroom and wait for me."

"This is torture," I whined. One of my hands snaked down his chest to wrap around his cock. My fingertips didn't touch when I fisted him.

A violent jerk ran through Vareck's body before he cursed. "Godsdamnit, Meera. As much as I am dying to be inside you, one of us has to hold it together and get this fucking pixie dust off us." I opened my mouth to argue but paused as his eyes bled to black. When high fae used their powers, their eyes glowed. Confusion made me tilt my head, before it occurred to me what it meant.

Vareck wasn't just a high fae. He was a fury too.

Their kind didn't originate from Faerie. They came from one of the hell realms.

"Your eyes are black." Apprehension should have made me back away, but that was the furthest thing from my mind. "Does that happen often?"

"No. It's because I'm *this* fucking close to losing control." His voice was impossibly deeper. Darker. A week ago I might have been scared. Now? I knew he wouldn't hurt me, not in a way I wouldn't like. "Now turn the fuck around and hold still."

CHAPTER 28
VARECK

Anticipation hummed in my blood.

Meera waited in the bedroom while I finished washing myself. The distance between us was the only thing keeping me from losing my fucking mind. I needed a moment to think beyond the unbearable ache in my cock. My body reacted to every little sound she made, every breathy moan, every scrape of her nails against my chest.

I stepped out of the tub, water sluicing down every inch of my skin. I snagged the folded towel to dry myself off.

Meera thought I wasn't affected. If I wasn't so fucking desperate for her, I might have laughed. What the little vixen didn't realize, is that I had been on pixie dust before. Only a handful of times, but not once had I ever felt this level of burning need.

It spoke volumes that my eyes had changed, my fury this close to the surface when we hadn't done much more than kiss. Kaia was the only one alive that had seen the shift in me before. Ever since my father's demise, I worked hard to gain control of myself, and *it*.

Meera was systematically undoing that without even realizing.

My heart hadn't slowed, despite the minutes that passed. That concerned me. If I lost it and bit her . . . no. *No.* That wouldn't happen.

Neither me nor the fury that lived deep inside me would betray her trust like that. Even in the throes of passion I would keep my head. I had to.

I dropped the towel and stepped into the bedroom. Meera's wanton noises drew my attention. The light from the flickering fire cast a warm glow over her body. Without a stitch of clothing, she was an absolute vision, sprawled out on the large mattress, legs bent with the soles of her feet on the bed.

She was temptation incarnate, and I was starving.

Each step I took was more hurried than the last as I stalked toward her. Meera's face turned toward me, her wide eyes glowing emerald green.

"I want you inside me."

Her persuasion, even dulled by the Faerie dust, called to me, wrapping around my senses like a vice.

Thank the gods her magic was weakened.

"Shhh," I whispered, leaning down to kiss her softly. Her lips chased mine when I pulled away. "I'm going to take care of you."

The green of her eyes didn't fade in the slightest as she tracked my every movement. I stopped at the foot of the bed, taking in her waiting form. With her legs spread and nipples peaked, I couldn't imagine a better sight.

"Vareck," she ground out, back arching off the bed. "It *hurts.*"

I paused, schooling my reaction. While pixie dust was

an aphrodisiac, and it was clearly hitting her harder than most, it shouldn't be that bad.

Easing onto the bed, I settled between her thighs. My fingers pressed into her supple skin, stretching her further. I loved the way they dimpled under my touch. She was so soft, but not fragile. I didn't worry I would break her with my ardor.

She reached for me with both hands as she tried to sit up. I moved one hand to her stomach, holding her down. My breath ghosted over her glistening arousal. I traced the tip of my tongue around her clit and couldn't help the satisfaction that ran through me when she jerked.

Fingers laced through my hair then pulled taut.

"I'm going to make it feel better."

That was the only warning I gave her.

Meera writhed beneath me. Needy moans rent the air. Her scent—her taste—pushed me further to my edge.

I realized right then that I was in deep fucking trouble because I would do anything for this woman. Seeing her this way—in the flesh and begging for me—was everything I wanted.

Not the crown. Not the power.

Even my guilt about the curse faded away in her presence.

I don't know what the future held for us after this, but I knew one thing. I wasn't letting her go. She was it for me.

If Meera wasn't all in, then I'd just have to convince her.

Starting now.

Her back arched off the bed as I pushed my middle finger into her tight channel. "You're soaked for me," I rumbled.

Meera's thighs trembled, her telltale sign that she was

close. I blew on her clit, thrusting my finger in and out of her. She detonated.

Her lips opened and closed as she gasped. I added a second finger. Her muscles clamped down. The hands in my hair clenched tighter. Nails that were sharper than I recalled scraped across my scalp.

She was just starting to come down from her high when I pulled out of her. If she wasn't wet enough for me before, she was now. Normally I would be happy to eat her for hours. Bringing her pleasure gave me immense satisfaction, but it did nothing to soothe the restless monster in me.

I climbed up her body, moving my forearms to either side of her head so I didn't crush her beneath my weight. "You still with me, Meera?"

She hummed against my shoulder, pressing soft, open-mouthed kisses against my neck. Her teeth grazed my skin. I stilled. Fuck. I'd been so worried about myself losing control that it didn't even occur to me that she might.

I tried to pull back just a fraction so that she couldn't easily bite me. I underestimated the woman's ferocity and her fae instincts because she lunged.

Teeth pressed against my skin, locking down. I barely flinched, but my cock sure as hell did. Her fangs threatened to puncture my skin. I wanted that. There was no point in lying to myself when I'd made up my mind.

Meera didn't, though. Not yet and not under the influence of pixie dust. Which left me with no choice.

"Let go."

A sharp, desperate whine went through her, but she yielded to my persuasion. When her hold on my head didn't get me to move closer, she let out a frustrated sigh and moved her hands to my shoulders.

"Why won't you let me?" She groaned, moving her hips

against mine. My shaft slid against her wetness, applying pressure to her clit.

"Because I promised to take care of you," I said gruffly. "Which means *no biting*." I prayed to whatever gods were out there that my persuasion held. Meera's powers were dampened because of the dust, but so were mine. The only difference was she couldn't think beyond the lust at all. Her attempt to bite me—bind me—proved that.

She wrapped her legs around my waist, the thickness of her thighs holding tightly against me, her nails pressing into my shoulder. I could feel the growl that was building in her chest. Apparently she was a vicious little thing when she didn't get her way. I hadn't seen this side of her because I always let her do whatever she wanted in our dreams.

But this was reality, and her biting to claim would have very real consequences that I wasn't sure she was ready for yet.

"I'm burning," she moaned, the sharpness of her nails breaking the skin. Sweat glistened at the base of her throat.

She needed relief, and she needed it *now*.

"I wish I could be gentle," I rasped, angling my hips to notch the head of my cock at her entrance. "But you're not the only one that's too far gone. Tell me if it's too—"

"Fuck me."

I slammed inside her. My head dropped to where her neck met her shoulder as I groaned. Meera clenched around me.

I slid out, savoring the friction of skin on skin.

"Gods, you're perfect." The floral scent in her hair was nice, but it wasn't what I wanted. Something about that agitated my fury, making me thrust back into her harder.

Meera cried out, losing herself in the fervor.

I licked a path up the column of her throat, the taste of

her sweat and skin soothing me. I sucked on a patch of flesh. She jerked beneath me. Nails pierced my skin as she raked them down my back. The violence of it spurred me on. My hips set a brutal pace that made her gasp and moan.

"Yes," she hissed. "Right. There."

She spasmed around me, pushing me to the edge of my release. I gritted my teeth to hold it at bay while she strangled my cock.

The second her orgasm let up, I reached back to wrap my fingers around the back of her knee, forcing her to release me. Her body went lax as her eyes fluttered open.

An expression I'd never seen on her before crossed her features. Her hazel eyes opened wide, almost like she was in shock. Her parted lips trembled. I summoned the tiny bit of tenderness left in me to brush my thumb over the apple of her cheek. Meera shuddered.

"You . . ." she breathed. "We . . ."

I sat back on my haunches and fisted my shaft, squeezing my base to force the orgasm back. "Get on your knees. Press your face to the mattress."

She swallowed, not moving, as if stuck in a trance.

"Now, Meera."

Her body rolled fluidly to her stomach. I lifted her hips, bringing her to her knees. "Hands behind your back," I commanded. This time she obeyed without question.

I held her wrists in one hand and her hip in the other. In a single thrust, I entered her, sinking deep. I groaned, taking in the woman beneath me. Her cheek pressed against the duvet. Every inch of her beautiful form was on display. I started to pull back, only to pause.

Where there should have been nails, instead were claws. Soot blackened her fingertips to the first knuckle, then tapered off into her soft skin color.

Meera had questioned if she was part human. I'd doubted it based on her strength, but the proof of it was now undeniable.

I didn't know what she was, but it wasn't human . . . and it wasn't fae.

Smudges of red stained her lower back. I recalled the way she'd scratched my back. The sting was still there, dampened by the arousal that was steadily pulling me under. Whatever she was would have to wait.

"Vareck," Meera moaned.

My gaze snapped to hers. The strange look from before was gone, replaced with a feverish need. I slammed into her, reveling in the way she tightened around me. My heart rate kicked up. A haze descended over me.

I didn't want to hurt her, but you wouldn't know it from the way I fucked her. Meera's sweet sounds filled the room, mostly unintelligible, as I plunged in and out of her.

I couldn't stop, even if I wanted to. She felt so good. So right.

"It's like you were made for me," I rumbled.

The need to ruin her was instinctual. Primal. I had to take, and take, and take—until there was nothing left for her to give to anyone else. No piece of her that craved another. I would break us both apart to rebuild something precious. Our pieces would fuse together until she couldn't bear to leave me.

My cock jerked. The release slammed into me with the power of a god. Meera followed after me with a scream. I rocked my hips shallowly, needing to ride every last wave inside her.

I let go of her hands to wrap my arm around her waist. I rolled us to the side without separating. Bliss settled over me even though the pixie dust was far from done with us both.

I almost didn't notice.

"You're—" I broke off, trying to form the words, but what I was feeling, it was impossible. There was no way . . . and yet the magic couldn't be denied. It was like a blind man seeing the sun for the first time. It was the start of spring after an endless winter. I finally understood why Meera looked shocked. What she was trying to say before. "My mate."

I hadn't bitten her, but it didn't matter. Meera wasn't a chosen mate. We were fated, even if I hadn't claimed her.

So much made sense now.

The dreams. The way I hunted for her. My inability to let her go.

I tightened my hold, pressing a kiss to her temple. I didn't know how it was possible. I also didn't care. This beautiful, funny woman was mine.

Meera shifted, slowly rocking her hips against me. "I need you," she groaned. The husky lilt of her voice was all it took for me to harden once more.

I thrust into her slowly, reveling in the way we came together.

This was going to be a long fucking night.

And gods help me, I was going to give her everything.

CHAPTER 29
MEERA

I inhaled deeply, my chest rising as the crisp morning air filled my lungs. The first rays of dawn crept through the drapes, warming my bare back. Glowing embers replaced the fire in the hearth. Goosebumps lined my skin where the sheets had slipped down, the soft fabric twined around my body as my hair spilled in loose waves across a pillow.

The after-high of Faerie dust had finally burned out, leaving behind a heady, intoxicating afterglow. Even the deep winter chill that seeped into the room couldn't chase away the lingering heat. It was almost a sin to wake up, to pull myself from this dreamlike trance.

I sighed, rolling over—only to jolt upright as shredded bits of pillow and feathers clung to my hair.

My breath hitched.

The bedding. The mattress. The sheets. All torn to shreds.

My gaze darted to the headboard, tracing the deep claw-like notches along the horizontal post. Memories slammed into me—*the swirl of his tongue, the pressure as he filled me, the callouses on his hands as he caressed my skin, all the way to the moment—*

Oh shit. My eyes dropped to the arm loosely draped over my waist. I followed it to the sleeping man beside me. My fated mate.

No lie, a significant part of me was panicking. Fae didn't have fated mates anymore. That somehow we were? It was crazy. Utterly insane . . . but also made a strange sort of sense.

I didn't know much about fated bonds. My parents were chosen mates. I'd never heard of people dreaming about each other long before they ever met. I doubt Vareck had either, or he would have connected the dots sooner.

Maybe it was because of the curse?

I wasn't sure, but I knew what I felt. The truth of it went soul deep, as undeniable as the sun in the sky.

I slipped from the bed, stuffing a pillow under Vareck's arm where I had been. A pucker formed between his brows, as if he sensed that I'd moved.

"You're up early." I jumped at the voice.

Corvo lay across the fur rug in front of the fireplace, warming himself with what heat the embers still had left.

I turned quickly, scanning the room for something to wear. Faux golden leaves lined the walls, twisting into decorative vines along the ceiling. Other than the bed, the only other furniture was a low-dresser and two armchairs with a small table between them.

I opened the drawers, wincing when they let out a small squeak. Each one was empty as the last. My lips pressed together. I could dress in the clothes from yesterday . . . if I wanted a repeat performance of last night.

I did, but the ache in my muscles told me it wasn't the

greatest idea. It also didn't solve the clothes problem, because eventually we did have to leave.

"What are you looking for?"

I glanced over at Corvo and glared. "Clothes. Also, do you have to stare at me while I'm naked? It's weird."

He chuffed. "I'm a cat."

"I don't care if you're a blue alien or the hottest man alive, it's still weird."

He rolled his golden eyes. "You're so dramatic, but fine. I suppose I owe you for the whole pixie dust thing . . ." My duffle bag from the castle appeared, still unzipped with a bra hanging out.

I blinked. All right, then.

My choices were limited since none of the clothes Vareck bought me were in it. In the end I selected a pair of jeans with rolled up cuffs, a plain long-sleeved shirt, and a stylish sweater vest to go over it.

While cute, I was going to freeze my ass off if I stepped outside. "Can you get my cloak?"

"What am I? A pack mule?"

"Didn't you just say you owed me?"

Corvo groaned. "Fine. Don't say I never do anything nice for you."

I snorted as my cloak appeared. I finished tying it around my shoulders, then looked at my bare feet. "What are the odds you can get me some shoes and wool socks too?"

They appeared, but he looked displeased. "I really ought to start charging you for this. I take payment in pets and tuna."

I padded over the rug to kneel beside him, giving a scratch behind the ear. Corvo purred, leaning into my hand. "Ohhhh yes. That's the spot." When I stood back up, he let out a sound of protest. "Wait a minute, where are you going?"

He glanced between me and the sleeping king. If a cat could have lifted an eyebrow, he would have.

"Downstairs."

His eyes narrowed. "I would think after last night you wouldn't up and run away again. I mean, it was amusing the first time, but like, V will be *pissed* if he has to chase you down now that you both know you're mates."

I whirled on him, pointing an accusing finger. "How do you know that?"

"I believe I told you this before you fell out the window."

I lifted my hands to form air quotes as I repeated, "Fell."

Corvo rolled his eyes again. "Point is, I've known since you showed up."

I crossed my arms over my chest. "How?"

His head tilted. "I'm a god. Duh."

My lips pressed together. "I thought you were a cat, hm?"

His tail flicked. "Semantics. Point is, even in this form, I still have my magic. You and V have matching auras."

My brows scrunched together. "Matching auras? What, like spirits?"

"Did I say spirits?"

"Well, no, but—"

"Think of it as colorful smoke that swirls around you. Everyone has a different color—but soul mates are the same."

I twisted my lips, not sure if I believed him. I mean, he thought he was a god. Sure, he had magic, but that didn't prove much. Most everything has magic in Faerie. Plus he was Vareck's familiar. I couldn't see a god being a familiar, but what did I know?

I shook my head and bent over to put on my socks and shoes. "I'm not running," I grunted as I stood up. My legs protested, every muscle in my body begging for a warm bath and good massage. "I'm going to talk to the innkeeper about something to eat and the closest portal out of here."

"That sounds an awful lot like leaving."

I sighed. "I need a few minutes to myself, but I'm not going anywhere." My eyes strayed back to the bed, where the king of Faerie slept. My chest warmed at the sight. I lingered for a moment, unable to help it. A part of me wanted to undress and climb back into that bed.

But that bitch was the thirsty ho that got us into this mess.

Still, I couldn't bring myself to regret it. Any of it. This thing between Vareck and I . . . it was a lot to take in. There would definitely be an adjustment period. We had a crap ton to talk about given I'm technically a criminal and he's royalty. But I would be a damned idiot to walk away from this without giving it a shot.

"Keep an eye on him," I told Corvo.

"I'm not his keeper." At my glare he added, "What's in it for me?"

"I'll ask if they have tuna."

He perked up at the suggestion. "Sold."

Shaking my head, I let myself out of the room, taking great care to close the door as quietly as possible. The wood creaked beneath my feet as I made my way downstairs.

No one was at the front desk, but the scent of cooked meat beckoned me forward. I rounded the stairs and followed my nose. Down a short hallway and to the right was a small eating area with a bar. I took a seat on a tall wooden stool that wiggled whenever I shifted my weight.

"Good mornin', ta' ya," a fae with a kind smile and crow's feet said. I recognized the voice from last night. He must be Farris. "I'm surprised yer up already, given the dust n' all. Anywho, what can I do for ya?"

A blush rose to my cheeks. "You got anything to eat for breakfast?" I cleared my throat, and Farris quickly poured a glass of water from a bronze tap and slid it across the counter. I murmured my thanks, taking a long sip.

"I got pan-fried venison and roast potatoes."

My stomach rumbled. "That sounds great."

He nodded once, looking me over. "Should I be gettin' one plate or two?"

I hesitated. "Two would be good. Is it okay if I take them back to my room? My . . . boyfriend is still asleep." Boyfriend felt too casual a word for what we were, but mate was too intense, if true.

Farris quirked a smile and gave me a friendly wink. "Gimme a few." He disappeared behind a curtain to where the sizzling of a pan was coming from.

The stool beside me scraped against the hardwood. I jerked at the sudden noise. The small room was empty, save for me and Farris. Maybe Vareck had woken to—

The thought stopped in its tracks. Fury rose inside me, clouding out any other feeling beneath its heavy weight.

"What the fuck are you doing here?"

Lou tilted his head, a slight smirk playing on his lips. "Hello lass, good morning to you too." Rakish eyes moved from my face down the length of my body, not that he could see much given the cloak. "Rough night? I heard about the dust. Then again, you disappeared with the king and now you smell like winter." He crinkled his nose in distaste.

"Cut the shit, Lou. There's no way in the nine realms that you just happened to be in Warwick at the same inn that I'm staying in. So I'm only going to repeat it once. What. The. Fuck. Do. You. Want?"

The leprechaun sighed. "All business with you. Seems getting laid hasn't changed that."

My hands curled into fists. I eyed the counter looking for something to stab him with. Preferably something sharp, but I wasn't choosy. "You sent me on a job that resulted in my being held captive, then worked with my captor to put a magic binding necklace on me—one that I fucking found for you."

Lou chuckled, seemingly unfazed. "Now, now. You got the necklace off, and by the look of things you should be thanking me for—"

"Get to the point," I compelled without thinking.

Lou frowned, but didn't obey. "That's not very nice, Meera. It also won't work. But alas, I'm a busy man so I'll keep it short. I got a job for you."

I stared at him. A solid ten seconds went by before I threw my head back and laughed so hard my eyes watered. "You"—I gasped, struggling to catch my breath—"You think I would *ever* take a job from you again?"

He cocked his head to the side, not smirking anymore. "You'll wanna take this one."

I snorted. "Yeah, no. Pass. You could offer me a million bucks and I wouldn't take it."

Farris appeared from the back room, carrying two steaming plates of food. He set them on the table, eyeing Lou curiously. His gaze dropped the medallion on Lou's chest, his leprechaun relic. A slight edge entered the jovial man's expression. "What can I get ya'?"

"Whiskey neat," Lou said, nodding toward one of the

brown liquor bottles on the shelf behind Farris. "Two fingers. Actually, make it three."

I shouldn't judge. There had been a few days over the last few years that I'd partaken in bad choices like drinking at eight in the morning. Most of them had to do with the jobs he sent me on, but it wasn't something I was proud of.

That said, Lou was a prick and deserved to be judged.

"What?" the leprechaun said, lifting a black brow to provoke me. "Got something to say Meera the Mighty?"

I rolled my eyes and then glanced at Farris with a polite smile. "What do I owe you?"

The innkeeper patted the counter gently. "Yer boyfriend paid me triple the room rate. We're square."

I nodded, thanking him for breakfast. Without looking at Lou, I got up and started to walk away.

"Take the case, Meera." The way Lou's voice changed stopped me cold. There was no charm to it. It lost its playful luster. Worse? He almost never called me by my name unless it was with the stupid add-on. I was usually 'lass' or some cute pet name.

"Why?" I bit out the question.

"Because your sister's missing."

CHAPTER 30
SADIE
FIVE DAYS EARLIER . . .

I sighed and ran a hand through my ponytail, my fingers snagging partway through. Days had passed since I found Meera's crushed cellphone and her dagger lying on the floor of her apartment. I'd searched up and down the Arcane District. I even went so far as to cross over into Faerie and try to enter the palace. It was useless. The palace had been locked down after the disappearance of the crown prince.

My chest squeezed because I knew it wasn't a coincidence. Meera went to Faerie the same night he was taken. She was more apprehensive about that job than any other she'd ever taken from that fucking leprechaun. If I could have, I would have stopped her, but the contract she'd willingly agreed to stayed my hand.

I should have put a stop to these jobs years ago.

Now she was gone, and I was no closer to finding her than when I started my search.

Which is why I stood in front of The Witching Hour. The most notorious supernatural hub on this side of the coast. If I couldn't find Meera, maybe, just maybe, I could find her broker who sent her on the hunt that got her kidnapped to begin with.

Music thumped to a bass, breaking the quiet of night when I opened the door. Inside the dark lit club, blue and purple lights flashed over a crowd. Sweat and sex filled the air, something that might have called to me under different circumstances.

I pushed through the crowd, shoulder checking any asshole that wouldn't move. The bar was packed, but I squeezed between two girls who were giggling into hot pink drinks that glowed faintly with magic.

"Hey——" one of them started.

"Amelia!" I called, raising my voice to be heard over the crowd. The dark-haired witch whipped around, a Cheshire smile crossing her lips.

"Sadie! I was just telling Meera the other day that she needed to bring you by. It's been forever——"

"I'm sorry to cut this short, but I need to find Lou. I know he does business here."

Amelia slowed to a stop in front of me. "Everything all right?"

I shook my head. She was a load of fun, and a great lay, but I didn't have time for twenty questions. "I just need to find him. Is he here?"

Her crimson eyes flashed, wariness edging into her expression. Her cheek was indented as she bit the inside and pointed toward the back of the club. "He hangs out at the corner table."

I nodded. "Thank you," I called over my shoulder before the crowd swallowed me whole. If she responded, I didn't hear it.

My blood hummed with violence as I crossed the threshold quickly. It was late, but the shadiest things were often done in the dark of night. I'd come here several times already and missed him, but as luck would have it—not tonight.

"I've gotcha now," I muttered under my breath, stepping up to his table, and planting my hands on my hips. The leprechaun glanced up from the cards in his hand, entirely too good-looking for what kind of asshole he was. Despite the cigar hanging from his lips, he smirked.

"Well, well. What do we have here? Sadie Wylde in the flesh. You coming to be dealt in or—"

"Where the fuck is my sister?"

If he was afraid, he didn't show it. "I'm afraid I'm not available for business at the moment. Do me a solid favor and fuck off."

I gave him a deadpanned expression while crossing my arms. "You really want to play it this way?" I scrunched my nose, grabbing a metal rod hooked onto the side of my belt. Knocking my wrist bracers together, the items glowed as I swirled the rod in my hand. I slashed forward, pausing at Lou's neck just as the head of an axe materialized.

"Where is Meera?" I didn't enjoy wasting time on trivial matters. "You really don't want me to ask again."

The four other men sitting around the table froze. Technically, weapons were banned from being used in The Witching Hour.

But magic? Well, that was fair game.

One of the assholes to his left, lifted a hand. I moved before his fingers could, throwing the axe. The blade grazed the edge of his palm before planting in the wall behind him.

"I wouldn't try that if I were you." I lifted both brows, holding up my empty hand. The blade unstuck itself and flew back to my waiting grip. "The next one I throw will take your hand clean off. Good luck growing that back."

My eyes flicked back to Lou. He watched me with a sour expression. "Why in the nine realms does everyone want Meera? Do I look like your sister? Do I have pretty, red hair that flows down my damn back? No. I'm Lou, the business-man. I don't know where she is. With the damn king is my guess."

"The fae king?"

"Is there another king you know of?" Lou chided, lowering his cigar to flick ash into a tray.

I'd suspected as much, but his confirmation helped. While I hadn't found a trace of my sister, I didn't come looking for her with a half-cocked plan. If the king took her, I needed leverage to get her back.

"Where's the prince?"

Lou leaned back in his chair, flipping a coin in the air with his thumb and catching it. "Don't know what you're talking about."

"Damon Einar," I snapped. "Where is he? I know you had her take him. She may not be able to give you away, but I sure as fuck will if you don't answer. I bet the king would just *love* to get his hands on the sleazy fuck who hired my sister to kidnap the heir to fucking Faerie."

He cocked an eyebrow. "You think you can find the prince, and what? Barter with the king for her?" Lou tossed his head back and laughed, despite the weapon being held inches from his throat. "She and the king looked awfully cozy last I saw. You sure she didn't just run off to—" I cracked my neck to the side, grabbing for the gun holstered to my back as I pointed it toward the man on his other side who was discreetly reaching for something in his pocket.

"Move another inch. I dare you," I said in a low voice before turning back to Lou. "The prince. I want a location."

"Put the damn gun down, Sadie."

This man must have a death wish. Few people could be on the other end of a redcap's weapon and appear unaffected, if annoyed.

"Not a fat chance." I flicked off the safety of the pistol. The leprechaun closed his hand around the coin, shaking his head.

"You're a smart lass. I'm sure Meera told you how the contracts work. I can't tell you where the prince is—even if I knew." His head tilted, eyes glancing behind me before flicking back to my face.

Magic wrapped around me and my hands both lowered against my will. I knew without looking that it was Amelia's. She might be the bartender, but she also acted as an enforcer when people got out of hand.

"Sadie, what the hell are you thinking?" the witch asked, grabbing my bicep. "You know the rules—"

Before she could pull me away, I dropped my parting words. "You better sleep with one eye open, leprechaun." Amelia tugged me, but I only moved an inch. "Meera's a Wylde. You should have known not to fuck with us. When Cadoc gets ahold of you . . ." I smiled cruelly. My second eldest brother had a reputation, one Lou seemed to know of given the thinning of his lips.

Threat made, I let Amelia drag me away.

"I ought to kick you out," she said. While beautiful, her red eyes were also unnerving. People moved around, but not a single person touched us. Either Amelia's magic was repelling them, or the axe still gripped tight in my hand had.

I shrugged, unapologetic. "Meera's my sister and best friend. I know that arrogant prick had a hand in her being taken."

Amelia tsked, her mauve lips twisting to hide the grin I

AURELIA JANE & KEL CARPENTER

saw in her eyes. "So you thought you'd hold an axe to his neck and a gun to his bodyguard's head?" She shook her head. "Fucking redcaps."

"Lou knew who he was dealing with when he screwed Meera over. If he didn't want to deal with a family of blood-thirsty fae—he should have fucked off after my brothers warned him last time. Not give her an even more dangerous job."

Amelia sighed. "Put the weapons away, Sadie. I get where you're coming from. I do." She had a thousand-yard stare on her face despite facing me. "But sometimes you have to follow the rules and play the long game." She blinked, eyes sharpening once more. "Draw another weapon and I'll have to ban you from here."

I slipped the gun back in its holster. "Technically the rules say I can't use it on another person, doesn't say anything about threatening someone."

She couldn't hide her smile this time, as she tossed her head back and laughed. "This is why I like you. Not often you find a girl with a temper like yours but the level head-edness and brains to not be ruled by it." We came to a stop at the edge of her bar counter where the panel flipped up.

"If I didn't know better, I'd say you're coming on to me."

"Maybe I am."

I rolled my eyes. "You're such a flirt."

"Only with the pretty ones." She winked. I laughed despite the emotions wreaking havoc on me. I'd been searching for days. Raging for days. Hopeless and desperate and above all, worried.

The slight reprieve was nice, even if it didn't last. My smile faded, reality edging back in. Amelia must have sensed it because her expression softened. "You heading out?"

I nodded. "I'm running on fumes right now. I need to sleep if I'm going to stand a chance of finding my sister."

She rubbed a hand up and down my arm in sympathy. "You'll find her." I wish I could be as sure as she sounded.

Instead of trying to answer around the lump forming in my throat, I started to back away with a sad smile.

"Wait." She glanced between me and the rowdy counter where people were growing impatient. "I know you need to go but would you mind grabbing me a bottle of Grey Goose from the back? I'm almost out up here."

"Sure thing."

She released a sigh of relief, turning to the counter as I switched direction for the back door right behind the counter where it was still flipped up.

The metal handle was cold to the touch, and the door was heavier than I expected. I stepped inside, squinting in the darkness as I felt around for a light switch. The door slammed behind me. I flinched but sighed in relief when my fingers brushed over the switch. I flipped it on. Bright fluorescent light filled the space. Shelves lined the walls, curving to the left. I walked forward, eyes scanning the inventory.

I almost didn't notice it.

Not six inches in front of me, the cement floor gave way to a swirling black vortex.

The door opened, and I turned my head without taking my eyes off the floor. "Amelia . . ." I started. High heels clicked behind me. "Why is there a portal in your—"

"It's a shame. I really do like you, but sometimes we have to make sacrifices when playing the long game."

I tried to spin around, but it was too late. Hands shoved me from behind and I lost my footing. The floor gave out beneath me.

Then I was falling.

And falling.

And—*thud*. I winced, touching my head where it hurt. Dust drifted above me; sunlight illuminated it in the air. I squinted my eyes, trying to make out the red clay ceiling above me.

"The witch send you here too?" a figure asked. I pushed upward, flinching when my muscles protested. I don't think anything was broken, but it sure as fuck wasn't for the lack of trying.

"Where is here?" I croaked, rubbing my shoulder.

The most beautiful man I'd ever seen stepped into the trickling light. My heart stuttered in my chest as he bent down, offering his hand.

"Hell."

To be continued . . .

Vareck and Meera's epic love story continues in Beyond the Winter Kingdom. Order Now.

Need something else to read in the meantime?

"Markus Del Reyes, I reject you."

He left me no choice.

I refuse to spend the rest of my life with my childhood bully for a mate. I may be a cursed shifter, incapable of shifting—but I wasn't desperate.

Not till the Alpha Supreme cast me out of the House of Fire and Fluorite for rejecting his son.

Now I'm packless.

Homeless.

No longer under the protection of a House.

Until the dark vampire king of Blood and Beryl turns his sights on me.

In return for protection from my former House, I have to become his fake mate.

I'll be a queen and a fraud.

It's a treacherous lie to live—and I find myself forgetting what's real and what's not with every stolen touch and heated kiss we share.

What starts as a business arrangement turns complicated when my heat hits, and the king insists on being the one to help me through it.

I've lost everything for doing what I know is right, but the greatest danger I ever faced was never losing my life ... it was opening my cursed heart.

START READING REJECT ME NOW

Acknowledgments

We often tell the story of how we used to work together as author and editor. That's how our relationship began. It morphed into friendship, and later, it became something bigger. The trust that was formed between us was strong, and we found a way to overcome the obstacles of a complicated work/best friend relationship. What we don't often discuss is what we first wrote together. It wasn't Dark Horse. It was this story, though a very different version. We built a world and then wrote a quick draft about it, releasing it under a pen name so it was "safe." It was *not* our best work by any means. That wasn't the point. We wanted to know how we worked together as writers, and if we could sell our ideas together. Obviously it worked out for us.

We always said we wished we had written something else because we enjoyed the world we'd built, and we wanted to revisit it and make it better. Then we remembered—we could. It was already our story. We could do with it what we wanted. So here we are, but this time, we've made it better, and we're using our names. We earned it.

So many people have supported us on our journey, and we're thankful to all of them.

First, we couldn't do this without our behind-the-scenes team, and we especially want to give our personal assistant, Lauren Quinn, our deepest appreciation. Her hard work is the reason our store runs so smoothly, and because of that, we have more time to dedicate to writing. We would be lost without her.

To the women who have taught us and empowered us over the years: Annie Anderson, Heather Renee, Heather Hildenbrand, Skye Warren, Becca Syme, Elana Johnson, Renee Rose, Nana Malone, and Amanda Pillar.

A special thank you to Cody Sammons, whose Maine Coon—Lylith—provided the inspiration for Corvo's description. The chapter spreader for Corvo is the real Lylith, and we are grateful to have her as a part of this book.

To Matt and Jude, I love you both. Sometimes finding words at the end of a book is hard, but that's an easy one to remember.

To Mr. Jane, you're my favorite main character. I love you.

To Aurelia's kids, no, I still haven't written a book you can read or tell your friends about. One day you can read them, yes, and trust me, you're going to wish you didn't. Thanks for being proud of me and encouraging me. Love you both to the end of the universe and back.

Lastly, to each other. We make it work, even when times get hard. We're so glad we took a leap of faith six years ago.

Made in the USA
Middletown, DE
07 August 2025

11912299R00203